REM

D0847659

THE PHANTOM BANDIT

Other Five Star Titles
by Frank Bonham:

The Cañon of Maverick Brands
Stage Trails West: A Western Quartet
The Last Mustang: Western Stories
Outcasts of Rebel Creek

THE PHANTOM BANDIT

Western Stories

FRANK BONHAM

edited by
BILL PRONZINI

Five Star • Waterville, Maine

First Edition
First Printing: March 2005

Published in 2005 in conjunction with
Golden West Literary Agency.

Set in 11 pt. Plantin by Al Chase.

Printed in the United States on permanent paper.

Library of Congress Cataloging-in-Publication Data

Bonham, Frank.
   The phantom bandit : western stories / by Frank Bonham ;
edited by Bill Pronzini.—1st ed.
     p. cm.
   ISBN 1-59414-136-3 (hc : alk. paper)
   1. Western stories. I. Pronzini, Bill. II. Title.
PS3503.O4315P48 2005
813'.54—dc22   2004028108

THE PHANTOM BANDIT

Table of Contents

Foreword

Frank Bonham's talent for combining picturesque historical and geographical settings with swiftly paced narratives makes him one of the premier Western writers of all time. Such novels as *Lost Stage Valley* (Simon & Schuster, 1948), *Night Raid* (Ballantine, 1954), *Tough Country* (Dell, 1958), and *Cast a Long Shadow* (Simon & Schuster, 1964) are highly regarded among both casual readers and aficionados of traditional frontier fiction.

The eight stories in this volume, like the tales in his previous Five Star Western collections—*Cañon of Maverick Brands* (1997), *Stage Trails West* (2002), *The Last Mustang* (2003), *Outcasts of Rebel Creek* (2004)—were all published during the 1940s and 1950s, when Bonham was honing his craft by producing short fiction for a broad variety of Western and adventure pulps and such leading slick magazines of the period as *Esquire*, *McCall's*, and *Liberty*. Evidence of the wide spectrum of Bonham's interests is the fact that each carefully researched story is different in background, theme, and lead and secondary characters.

"A River Man Goes to War", for instance, concerns conflicting loyalties among river boaters and travelers on the Ohio River at the start of the Civil War. "The Phantom Bandit" is a fictionalized account of the activities of the legendary safe robber and would-be poet, Black Bart. The protagonist of "Hurry Call for Hangin' Gus", and of a handful of other pulp stories, is one of Bonham's most unusual creations—Marshal Gus Hobbs will hang any man in New Mexico for $25, but he takes great pains to make sure the man is guilty before putting a rope around his neck. The burning wastes of Death Valley provide the background of "Death Valley Silver", a tale of the discovery of a bonanza silver mine and the struggles for its control among opposing factions. Mexico, the Dakotas, and a modern California horse ranch and rodeo are the other settings realistically depicted in these pages.

Bill Pronzini
Petaluma, California

A River Man Goes to War

I

They'd had their differences, Todd Macon and Jasper Peacock, yet never before an argument they couldn't thresh out in a day's wrangling. But tonight, as darkness closed in upon the deserted Cincinnati wharves, they sat in glum silence at opposite sides of the lamp-lit wheelhouse. Neither man could give an inch and ever again look his conscience in the eye. They were in a deadlock, with time crowding them closely. Todd's lean face was hard as he twisted his black New Orleans cheroot above the lamp chimney until it began to smoke. All over the nation, he knew, partners like Jasper and him, families, even, were being pried apart by the bloody wedge that had been driven into the heart of the country.

Down in South Carolina a fort had been shelled. There was no longer the slimmest hope that the nation's differences could be fought on the floor of Congress. The smell of blood and powder smoke was in the air, and millions of men were leaving farm and office to rush to the front. From the windows of the wheelhouse, Todd Macon could see the cobblestone waterfront climbing to the city. In the deep dusk it was deserted, the stones, damp from an afternoon shower, stained a dull red by the setting sun. Only three other steamboats lay sawing at their spiles; two of them were already smoking up.

Along the wharves, peace—but up in the city bonfires crackled at street intersections and crowds formed and dissipated like dust whirls along a wind-whipped way. The Queen City had worn her neutrality like a crown. But Abe Lincoln had at last called upon her for loyalty to the Union. In a matter of hours, it would be known whether the Rebel element or the loyal would take the ascendancy in the sprawling Ohio River trade town. Her wharf boats were jammed with tons of pork consigned to Charleston, with tubs of butter and sacks of wheat the Confederacy was counting on to help feed her soldiers during the winter.

Upriver and down, churning paddles threshed the river to foam as packets sought safety in waters of known stripe. Southern boats raced south to beat the blockade at Cairo, Northern captains reaching for Pittsburgh, should Cincinnati go Rebel. But the *Natchez* still lay nuzzling her rope bumpers, undecided.

Julie, Jasper Peacock's eighteen-year-old daughter, angrily kicked the draft of the stove shut. "Are you two going to sit there all night, stickin' your jaws out at each other?" she demanded. "We're the last packet in town but three. You'll never settle this without getting up on your hind legs and caterwaulin' a little."

Todd spoke without turning from the window. "No more caterwaulin' to be done. Far as I can see, we'd as well get busy with saws and cut this tub in two. You and Jasper can take your half down to Memphis. I'll straighten up for Pittsburgh."

Against the red glow of the city he was sketched in long, straight strokes. Todd was tall and lean, with muscles that were close to the bone. His face was long, lanky-featured, and brown. His eyes were the sultry color of the river at flood.

"Bring on your saws," Jasper Peacock said. "The *Natchez* is South right down to the bull rails . . . and South she's a-goin' if she hoists a bucket."

The lamp put specks of gilt in Todd's eyes as he turned. "She's South like Boston baked beans! They laid her keel battens in Paducah. Paducah declared for Abe Lincoln last week. Besides, you ain't going to find a free crew to take a boat into slave territory in this town. Those gents are holdin' onto what they've got. If she pulls out of here at all, it'll be upriver. You might as well give up, Jasper. You're licked six ways from nothin'."

Jasper Peacock got up on his short, bowed legs, a squinty-eyed mastiff of a man, deep-chested, heavy, and hairy of limb. His ears were big, his scarred face full of crow's feet and deeper lines. He wore his leather-visored pilot's cap at a right angle to his face. As tough a man, for his size, as ever tromped a wheel, river men said of him. "I was hopin' you'd listen to reason and save me having to play my ace," he said. "But you're as pig-headed as all the rest of the damned Yankees. I've got my legal rights as captain of this boat, just like every state's got the right to govern herself. And no ex-mud clerk's going to stand in the way. Julie, ring up a head of steam!"

"Comin' up, Pop!" It was what Julie Peacock had been waiting for. She hurried forward and reached for a bell pull. On his long legs Todd Macon was there an instant sooner. He had her wrist in a hurting grip as he yanked her aside and faced Jasper.

"None of that, you broken-down old Reb! Not a paddle does she turn while I've got half the stock in this outfit."

Julie tried to break loose. She was long-legged and wiry, clad in a striped jersey and short skirt, and she had temper to match her strength. But Todd's big hand kept her from reaching the cord.

Across the threadbare carpet Jasper came like an ice-breaker attacking a head of mush ice. Todd's wide mouth broke into a grin and he thrust the girl away from him.

13

"Gonna tune my whistle, eh? Well, lower the heel and pitch in! It's as good a way as any of settling it!"

"Cut it out, now, you two!" Julie cried out. But she had the common sense to grab a chair out of the middle of the floor as they began to circle.

A distraction came, in the sound of a heavy and uneven stride crossing the hurricane deck to the pilot-house stairs. There was an arresting quality of strangeness in the sound—an eerie thump-and-drag that conjured a picture of a cripple dragging himself up the steep companionway—that caused both men to turn slowly to face the door.

They were standing like that when the door opened. It seemed at first as though two men must have been coming through at once. Then the stranger came into the light and Todd saw that it was only one man, although he filled the portal to bulging. He stood in the lamplight, a white-bearded, fanatical-eyed giant, leaning on a thick cherry-wood staff carved like a snake. The fires of hell lighted his eyes. His nose was like a scimitar, his beard a stringy, square-cut tangle of dirty gray hair. Todd stared at him, thinking that if ever there had been a zealot, a prophet, this was he. He thought of Brigham Young, and John Brown, and Moses.

"My sons, my sons!" His voice was the rumbling of boulders down a subterranean riverbed. "On this night of nights, with a thousand brothers at one another's throats, must honest boatmen like yourselves go mad with hatred?"

"Honest?" Jasper snorted. "He's a low-livin', cross-compound son-of. . . ."

"Peace!" The prophet raised his serpentine staff. "I did not come here to listen to profane ravings."

Jasper's eyes snapped. "There ain't nobody holdin' you back if the language gets too hair-chested for ye."

The stranger's eyes flashed, but his answer was restrained.

14

"Would you gentlemen be good enough to offer me a chair? My leg. . . ." He rapped his thigh with a knuckle, bringing forth a hollow sound. "A poor, dead thing of wood and steel. Tires a man to come far on it, and I've walked a weary way."

Todd spun the chair. "Sit down," he said quickly.

Lowering himself, the big man fought with his artificial limb and failed to make it bend. Savagely he attacked it with his staff, until a rusty joint creaked and he fell into the chair. Then he looked up at the partners, breathing hard.

"Now, then! My name is Hogg. Parson Hogg, late of Bentonville. I've rowed, walked, and ridden seventy-five miles to hire a boat. Now I find only four boats in town. The captains of three of them, being cowards, would not listen to my proposition. There remain you gentlemen. May I ask where your sentiments lie . . . with Lincoln or Jeff Davis?"

"We were just settling that," Todd said, "when you came in."

"Perhaps my proposition will help you to decide. Would you be interested in a trip of four hundred miles at four dollars a mile?"

Julie Peacock's tanned face lighted up. "Would we!"

"Politics permitting," Jasper qualified.

The black hairs of Hogg's brows, sticking up like pitchfork tines, pulled in toward the bridge of his nose. "Politics," he muttered. "The devil's bait to lead peace-loving men from the way of righteousness. Well, here is my problem. You know Father Amos?" Their blank looks caused him to rap the floor impatiently with his staff. "I see you do not! Father Amos is a true believer in the vineyard of the Almighty. At Cow Island, below Bentonville, he has a church and nearly a hundred followers. I say *has,* but, unfortunately, the town went Rebel yesterday and burned his church because he had preached Union. Father Amos and his band managed to escape, but their homes have been destroyed."

Resentment kindled on Jasper's red face. "Name your business, Hogg."

Hogg struggled to his feet. In his ragged brown coat and pants, with his shapeless boots that were big enough to bathe a dog in, he appeared a seedy-looking prophet indeed. But his head was flung back and his eyes burned down on this miserable sinner who was Jasper Peacock.

"I am saying," he intoned, "that Father Amos and his people have taken refuge on an island seventy-five miles below here, where they are hiding without food or shelter. I helped them to escape. Until I find a boat captain with the courage to help me take them off that island to the safety of a Northern town, I shall continue on up this river."

Jasper Peacock flung open the door and stood by it. "Proud to have made your acquaintance, Parson. But this here is a Confederate boat."

Todd Macon, clapping the purpling parson on the shoulder, grinned. "Only his half, Parson. I'm half owner of the *Natchez,* and me and the larboard side are dragging our smoke North in about two toots of the come-ahead whistle. You look like a husky 'un. Maybe the two of us can lash this river rat to a pile until we get where we're goin'."

With a backward reach, Jasper Peacock took a quart bottle of his favorite patent medicine from the shelf at his back. Brandishing it like a club, he matched the younger man's grin with a wicked flash of teeth under oakum mustaches.

"Have at 'er, gents! The second battle of the war is going to be fought right here!"

Julie was down the wall and beside her father, a fire-axe in her hands. In horror, Hogg raised his heavy staff. "Peace! Peace!" he said, not looking at Todd. "Young man, I believe I can reason with your partner, if you will leave us alone for five minutes."

Todd's brown eyes were on Jasper as he rolled his sleeves back from lean, hard forearms. "Man's got to have a brain 'fore you can reason with him."

Swinging his staff horizontally with some force, Parson Hogg stopped Todd's advance by thumping it heavily across his chest. This time the heat of those courage-shriveling, hell-lighted eyes was for Todd.

"I asked you to leave, pilot!"

Todd's anger melted as he looked into them, and he felt like a small boy being chastised. For a moment, resentment boiled through him. Then he touched the brim of his cap with two fingers. "Good luck, Parson," he said slowly.

Walking up and down the tarred hurricane deck, he rolled and reduced to ashes two cigarettes. It was early June, and the damp night air held a bone-penetrating chill. There was a finger of ice in Todd's heart, too, that made his long face seem even longer.

They'd tripped up and down this old river for six years, he and Jasper and Julie. Every hazard river folks can meet, they had worried through together. Black, blizzard-torn nights when the head of the *Natchez* was a solid chunk of ice and a man had to crawl on all fours to reach the texas. Flood times, when the river was mined with hidden snags. Fog, wind, and darkness—the three horsemen of the boatman's Apocalypse. For all his cantankerousness, Jasper was a man to stand a trick with. And Julie . . . ? They'd never talked about love, wouldn't have known how to start. She was too independent to invite such talk. To Todd's tongue the words didn't come anyhow. Well, maybe it wasn't actually love. He respected her judgment where river things were concerned. Had to admit, grudgingly, that she was almost as good a pilot as he was. That she could stow a trip of freight so the boat didn't haul her paddles out of water and spin them dry. Still, he had this same respect for Jasper. He guessed the difference was that he'd never wanted to kiss Jasper.

Julie had never known any mother but the river. An old Negress cook on one of Jasper's earlier boats had taken care of the girl after her mother died when Julie was still a baby. But it was to the river that she owed her real education. She learned not to trust a smiling face that hides treachery as the sun-rippled countenance of the river conceals its savage teeth. When the wind howled and the river was plowed by portentous cross-currents, Julie sat among the cotton bales, chewing a wad of cotton and laughing at the lies the water was telling, knowing the bottom was deep and smooth. Thus she learned that the most blustering of men aren't necessarily the most dangerous.

Some of the river's tawniness had gone into her smooth skin. She was red-haired and green-eyed, with a figure that took a man's mind off his work. Todd had had the picture of her before him on many a long night watch; he knew that, if they split up now, he'd see her on many lonely watches to come.

From time to time Todd thought he heard soft laughter from the wheelhouse. Puzzled, he would stop and cock an ear toward the glowing windows high above him. At length Parson Hogg was limned in the doorway. He clanked down the steps, his cranky artificial leg banging against the risers.

A yellow-toothed smile parted his dirty white whiskers. "If you'll speak to the engineer about some steam. . . ."

"The old hoss didn't agree?"

"Jasper Peacock has enlisted in the army of the right. He said to tell you to stand the first trick . . . and to show me to the best cabin."

After he had lighted a lamp for Hogg and brought him a pitcher of water, Todd stood outside the room and scratched his head. The tattered prophet of doom had done in five minutes what he had failed to achieve in a week. Still puzzled, Todd went down and stuck his head into the oily reek of the engine room.

"Touch 'em off, Big Sam!"

Big Sam, the engineer, jumped down off the wood rick, a lanky Negro the color of tanned cowhide. Eighteen pairs of eyes peered from under the boilers, where the roustabouts were keeping warm.

"Which way we goin', Cap?" Big Sam inquired. " 'Cause, if it's souf, I'm huntin' a new boat."

"We're goin' north . . . by way of Cow Island," Todd said. "We're on an errand for Mister Lincoln, you might say. We'll raise the island by dawn and loaf along so's we'll pass Cincinnati tomorrow night, on the up trip. Nobody knows how the town's going. You boys'll be all right. That's a guarantee."

When he went up again, Julie was shuttling coal into the stove. Jasper, cursing a headache, grubbed among the bottles on his medicine shelf.

"Damn a man that'll argify his pardner into a sickbed!" Peacock grumbled. "I won't be wu'th boiler scrapin's this trip. Got one of my scalp lifters comin' on."

He took a long pull at a favorite elixir, hiccupped, and replaced the bottle. No man on the Ohio had more rugged health than Jasper. But no man courted ill health as he did for the opportunity to grouse. Every patent medicine vendor had a sure sale in him, so long as the alcoholic content of his product was up to standard—ninety proof.

"What kind of a trick are you pulling on the damn' old gimp?" Todd demanded.

Jasper's glance was peremptory. "Keep your tongue civil when you speak of Parson Hogg. He convinced me I had my logbook made up all wrong. But I'll take no I-told-you-so talk from you."

"Don't worry," Todd said. "You won't get any. Because I've got a hunch there's a few rotten ones in this crate of eggs!"

That feeling still rode him, when Big Sam signaled that the *Natchez* had her 240 pounds of blue ruin creaking in the boilers. Todd rang up and the packet backed full head into the sweep of the current. Live steam hissed into cannon-like cylinders, stubborn pistons drove into motion, and the *Natchez* moved down the river with dense white heads of steam bursting from her escape pipes.

II

There is a saying on the river that you can tell how the pilot is feeling by the way he toots his whistle. Todd fetched up a single, mournful blast of farewell. At best, it was a treacherous plank they were venturing onto. Cow Island may have laid dynamite traps to intercept boats making north. Even if they took Father Amos and his pack safely off the island, they had still the risk of a blockade at Cincinnati to anticipate on the return trip. So Todd's heart was heavy and his eyes were keened to vigilance.

Running light, the packet's threshing wheels shoved her along in jig time. It was a dark night, the river like an oiled road plying between crowding, green-black banks. Todd had for a guide only his pilot's memory and an occasional streak of light across the river. They put a dozen little towns behind them, the lights growing fewer at each passing. Down in the texas, Todd could hear Hogg's full-lunged voice rolling out a hymn. Another voice was audible when the preacher paused for breath.

"Damn old hypocrite!" Todd's lips mouthed the words. Jasper Peacock was singing psalms as though he was at a camp meeting. He hadn't, Todd thought cynically, had a pious thought in his life.

Later, Jasper came up and stood a two-hour trick. It was four o'clock when Todd returned to the pilot's bench. They passed an old barn crumbling on the river's bank. By that he knew they were nearing the town of Cow Island.

As the town came indistinctly out of the sycamores and cottonwoods growing to the water's edge, Todd reached for the speaking tube. "Slow bell, Big Sam!" he called down. "Keep a head o' steam but let the wheels drag."

He went to the starboard bank and they drifted silently. The *Natchez* was just abreast of the wharf when, like lightning jagging through a black sky, gun flame smashed across the water. Todd's head and shoulders were showered with glass. He felt blood streaming from a cut on his cheek. As he heard the thunder of the rifles, other guns stippled the wharf darkness with scarlet blotches. Sweat was suddenly on his face and palms. He was no coward, but he knew real fear. These riflemen were gunning for the pilot. He had the sense to duck, yanking the bell pull as he sank.

Balled lead whined through the cabin, smashing through the glass and wood. Something *thunked* against his head and rolled across the floor. He saw that it was one of the wheel spokes. Before another salvo could come, he rose to the wheel. His bellow would have carried to the engine room without the use of the speaking tube he put to his lips. "Double gong on both sides! Throw in the fireman!"

The packet shook like a dog leaving the water. Her windows rattled and the fractious wheel tried to throw Todd across the room. He kicked the bench out of the way and stood, spread-eagled, on his long legs as the paddles geysered water higher than the jack staff.

On the companionway there was a sound as of old iron being dragged up the steps. Parson Hogg staggered inside. "Pilot! Pilot! Where in tarnation are you?"

There was enough light in the wheelhouse to paint Hogg's reflection on the window in front of Todd Macon. What the lanky pilot saw was Parson Hogg aiming an old Dragoon pistol at his back. Hogg knew well enough where he was. Instantly he was sprawling out of the way, grabbing at the Colt shoved under his belt.

Hogg either could not see the gun in his fist, or pretended not to. He lowered his own pistol and came forward. "The

22

Lord be praised!" he said. "I was afraid they'd shot you. To the wheel, man!"

He turned, with that, and emptied his gun in the direction of the wharf. The grip of doubt was still upon Todd. Julie came into the wheelhouse, then, and he turned back to the wheel.

Powder was still being burned back in the town, but distance was now between boat and rifles like a protective wall. Julie's fingers touched Todd's bloody cheek. "Todd! You . . . you're hit!"

Todd raised his shoulder and wiped at the blood. "Just a glass cut. Where's Jasper?"

"Coming up. He was down on the guard when it happened."

"Tell him to stay there," Macon said quickly. "We'll be at Cow Island in ten minutes. Have the landing booms swung out."

Cow Island came at them out of the grayness of early dawn, a low, tree-jumbled piece of land cut off from the mainland by a channel hardly wider than the steamboat itself. There was a natural landing spot at the lower end of the island. Todd ran below it, shipped up to starboard, and held her steady while the roustabouts choked a stump with heavy lines.

Landing stages were run out to span the strip of water between boat and bank. Out of the leaden mist of dawn a swarm of men rushed from the trees to secure the gangplanks. Laden with boxes and bundles, they poured onto the *Natchez*. It was as Todd Macon turned to go below that Parson Hogg loomed out of the shadows to put a gun barrel in his stomach.

"Now, then, my fine young Union fool!" Hogg bored the gun deeply, his mouth smiling savagely. "Your part of the job is over. Just take a deep breath, raise your hands, and don't get funny."

23

Tension ran down through Todd's lean muscles. "Hogg, you psalm-singin' river scum, what's your game?"

"Questions and answers will come later," Hogg rapped. "You'll find out all you want to know before we trip out at New Orleans. For the present, you'll do as you're told."

It was vividly etched on Todd's mind how he had been duped. Hogg had played him for a fool—made him a party to the theft of his own boat! And Jasper and Julie had been part of the game, laughing behind his back all the way down the river. They had known from the start that they were not bound for Pittsburgh. Hogg was a Rebel! With that stab of despair came a twist of fury that jarred Todd into action. His left hand knocked the gun aside; his right he drove heavily for the Rebel's head. With Hogg stumbling back, cursing in his beard, Todd dragged his gun. But the gun sight hung on his belt, and, before he could free it, that adaptable cherry-wood staff of the parson's smashed against the side of his head. The lamps were snuffed out in Todd's brain. He fell to the floor beneath his wheel like a shot beef.

The pilothouse was filled with another light when he came to. Gentle fingers were stroking his brow. His eyes opened and he saw Julie sitting on the floor beside him, rubbing ointment on his forehead. Two little pinches of concern were between her eyes. She smiled when she saw he was awake.

"Better?" the girl asked. "Pop said this Wahoo Root Extract would fix you up."

Todd sat up with a snarl. His open palm smashed the bottle of medicine from her hand. Staggering to his feet, he went forward. What he saw down on the boiler deck made his lips crease hard.

Father Amos and his pathetic little band didn't look so pathetic in daylight. They were bringing the last of the boxes aboard. A lank-haired, mongrel litter of unwashed renegades, most of them were in greasy buckskins and coonskin caps or battered old felts askew on their heads. Others wore the remnants of fine clothing stolen from steamer passengers. All were daubed from head to foot with black mud. They cursed and shouted and drank potato whiskey from earthen jugs as they worked. Father Amos, mounted on a barrel, bellowed orders. He was a stunted, gorilla-limbed man with an abused stovepipe hat on his head, a long rifle in his hands, and knee-length tassel boots caked with mud. The pirates' luggage was boxed in long, flat cases and stubby kegs. The contents of these boxes were not hard to guess.

Todd could hear the howling and moaning of the roustabouts. They had been cooped up under the boilers, where a dozen guards were seeing that they stayed. The white members of the crew stood back at the fringe of trees on the island.

Todd confronted Julie with eyes as hard as brown crockery. "Who are they . . . Hogg and his whiskey-logged Father Amos?"

Julie's features showed resentment. "They're from the Big Muddy . . . packet men like us. Father Amos is really Amos Bullard. When they heard the war had started, they jumped a supply boat going to Fort Benton, in Montana, and took off all the powder and guns. But their boat ran through herself just above Saint Louis and they had to carry their cargo overland, in hopes of finding a friendly boat owner."

"And they found me!" Macon rapped. "A man who jumped at the chance to sell his pardner down the river. You know where I'm bound, don't you? To some prison where I'll rot till the war's over!"

Julie shook her red head. "Hogg promised to let you off at Cairo. He'd let you go now, only you'd pass the word and we'd be intercepted." Suddenly she took his hands. "Todd, why not come over to our side? You're only making it hard for yourself . . . and for me."

"I'll throw in with finks when the river starts running uphill. Amos Bullard . . . I know that name. The job don't come that's too dirty for him. He'll pirate a cargo if he can't get it otherwise. You've turned the *Natchez* into a pirate ship as sure as though there was a black flag on the jack staff."

Julie made no answer, for just then Hogg, Bullard, and Jasper Peacock came up the steps and into the wheelhouse. Winking, Bullard touched his fingers to the brim of his stovepipe in Julie's direction. Julie's cheeks reddened. Bullard threw the window open and bawled down at the sweating men on the foredeck.

"Haul in that gangway! Let go them lines!"

Jasper's grin was sheepish, but he was not unmindful of his superior position. "Sorry we had to hang one on you," he said to Todd. "Just remember we don't tolerate mutiny, and you'll get along all right. We're givin' you the run of the boat, but don't abuse the privilege by hidin' a wrench or slucin' bar down your pants leg."

The packet backed into the tug of the river, with Bullard at the wheel. Todd headed for the door, but paused to ask Parson Hogg a question. "Where are we bound?"

Hogg, letting himself onto a bench, had to bludgeon his artificial leg into submission. "We meet the *Red River* about halfway to Cairo. Heard of her? I don't reckon you have! Nor seen the likes. Boilerplate walls to her wheelhouse. Cannon mounted fore and aft. Built heavy for ramming. The *Red River* is the first of a fleet that's a-buildin'. We'll transfer our cargo to her late this afternoon. At Cairo she goes south while we 'scape up the Missouri to the Dakotas. There's gold boats comin' down from Salmon Creek, in Montana." His crooked grin showed. "I figger we'll pay for our fuel."

Parson Hogg's wild crew took over the packet from bull rails to texas. All the white members had been marooned on Cow Island. The Negro roustabouts would be auctioned off in New Orleans, but for the time being they were kept penned up under the boilers. Big Sam, being the only man aboard who understood a cross-compound engine, was still at his post. Hogg tapped a keg of whiskey and set it on the boiler deck, with a dipper beside it with which the renegades helped themselves whenever they chanced to pass—which was often.

After his initial fury passed, Todd Macon became conscious of one thing. That Amos Bullard was the wildest-eyed pilot who ever mistook a sandbar for a wind reef. Sitting on a packing box before the forecastle, Todd watched him bear down to within fifty feet of dangerous stumps and snags before pulling her over and gliding by them. There was no slow bell with Bullard; it was double gong from the time he took over.

Hurrying down the sun-shot river, the *Natchez* foamed across the shoals where Todd knew the lead would not have drawn more than quarter-less-one. The dense stands of green trees on the banks went by with the speed of a revolving wheel's rim. Every few minutes heard the hills toss back the jangle of a bell as Amos Bullard demanded more steam from the laboring firemen and engineer.

Then there came a time when the groaning steam drums had all they could hold. Bullard's demands for steam were unavailing. Todd saw him stick his head through the window and shout: "Hogg! Git up here and take over. I'll show that double-riveted engineer I ain't foolin' when I ask for steam."

Todd was on the main deck guard when the squat, gorilla-like pilot came down the stairs into the hot fumes of the engine room. He stood there, watching Big Sam and a striker shovel coal into an already cherry-red furnace. One hair-padded hand swung a knotted rope against his tasseled boot. His stovepipe was on the back of his head.

"You, boy! You the engineer on this scow?"

Big Sam's pigskin-colored face was muddy with coal dust and sweat. He leaned on the sluicing bar. "That's me!"

"Heard me ringing for steam, ain't you?"

"Givin' you all I got, boss. We carryin' forty pounds over what we 'lowed right now."

Bullard began to swing the hempen cudgel in a circle at his side. "You ain't by any chance trying to hold us back till it's too late to git past Cairo?" His big mouth was ugly.

"No, suh!" Big Sam pointed at the arm of the escape valve. "I got that weight right out to the blue ruin notch."

Without warning, the rope broke its smooth orbit to slam into the side of the Negro's head. Big Sam threw up an arm, a blue bruise showing where the big, water-soaked knot had struck his cheek bone.

Bullard was shouting: "You lyin' son-of-a-bitch! You ain't never heard of hookin' a keg of whiskey onto the escape arm, have you? You'd 'a' had 'er on there two hours ago if we were headin' upstream instead of down. Maybe you'll remember some of them little tricks . . . after . . . this!"

The final words were punctuated with savage swings of the rope. Big Sam was knocked off his feet by the staggering force of the knot. He cowered there while Bullard laid stripe after stripe across his bare back.

Todd stood it as long as he could. Then he vaulted the guardrail and went toward the pilot. Bullard sensed his presence and halted in mid-swing to confront him. He dropped the rope, eyes narrowing, and pulled a cap-and-ball Navy pistol from the holster at his thigh. His words seemed to pry through his teeth.

"All right, Yank! I got another kind of medicine for you!"

Todd stopped, because it was either that or suicide. Bullard snorted. Picking up the rope, he fashioned a slipknot in the end of it. His eyes still on Todd, he made a loop about a small barrel of resin and hung it on the arm of the hissing safety valve. Immediately the jet of steam was cut off, and the steam drum began to creak.

"Where we're goin', we're goin' fast," was his final warning. "Leave your throttles wide open and she'll burn up that steam. Try to cut down on me and you'll be the first to get scalded to death."

When he had gone, Todd helped Big Sam to his feet and threw a bucket of water over him. "I could cuss myself for gettin' you into this, Big Sam," he told him. "But they've tricked me as much as you. You're headed for that cotton field again. I'm on my way to the bastion at N'Orleans. At least . . ."—he lowered his voice, glancing around—"at least that's what they think. We've got till we pass Cairo to show 'em different. You boys keep on your toes. I've got a plan comin' up."

There was hope in the Negro's eyes, but as he went forward Todd hadn't the faintest idea what he intended to do.

III

At noon Jasper Peacock sought Todd where he stood on the boiler deck, watching the blunt prow of the *Natchez* pry the brown water apart. Todd looked at the thing he held in his hand. It was a tin rouster pan filled with food. His eyes raised questioningly to his former partner's face.

Jasper's stubbled cheeks reddened. "Hogg sent me down with it. He says no . . . no Yankees will eat in the saloon after this."

Todd took the tin pan and spun it into the river. Leaning on his elbows, he watched the tumbling bow waves plow over it.

Jasper stiffened. "You'll wish you'd et that by tonight!" His tone lacked sincerity, for he knew as well as Todd that Hogg's insult could not have been more degrading. When the younger man still said nothing, Jasper fumbled: "See here, Todd, they ain't as bad as all that. They . . . they're rough-livin' men, all right. I don't quite understand Hogg myself yet. But him and me see eye to eye on this State's Rights business."

"Do you see eye to eye with Bullard on how to handle your crew?"

Jasper scratched the back of his neck. "That was a leetle raw. But the feller's been drinkin' all morning. Give him an inch."

"Makes a lightnin' pilot, don't he?" Todd was pounding a wedge into that tiny crack of doubt that showed on Jasper's face. "We lost five paddles back there at Brewster Shoal when he let her smell the bar. It's just a question of time until the boat either runs through herself or blows a boiler."

30

"I reckon," Jasper Peacock ventured, "I'll be takin' over before. . . ."

Both men sprang back as a bottle crashed onto the deck and shivered into a mess of glass and liquid. The label lay in plain sight:

Dr. Franklin's Wahoo Root Extract

Jasper's eyes bugged as though on stems. Before he could utter a word, two more bottles smashed themselves to pieces on the deck. One gaudy label was visible like a sodden epitaph:

Plunkett's Famous Anti-Colic Formula

Todd was suddenly grinning. Plunkett's was Jasper's favorite of favorites. He waited for the old pilot's response, and it came in the voice of a bull buffalo.

"Hogg! What in the name of hell do you think you're doin'?"

Parson Hogg's massive head and shoulders showed in the glassless window. "Cleaning out some of this corruption!" he called down. "This shelf's got to come out before we can line the cabin with boiler plate."

Again the sky was raining elixir. Jasper, taking shelter against the wall of the texas, stuck his head out and bawled: "Keep your hands off them bottles!"

A whole armful of vials soared toward the deck now, and the old pilot, his eyes like holes burned in a blanket, watched them smash and slither across the planks and through the bull rails. When it was finished, he wiped sweat from his forehead with the back of his hand.

"Damn him! I'll be dead o' the miseries before mornin'!"

The sun caught up with the boat and passed it, sliding down the river to glare into the pilot's eyes. Jasper never got his chance at the wheel. Hogg took over after Bullard went off, and, as sunset brought a cool breeze down the valley, it was obvious that Jasper Peacock's station was not much higher than that of Todd.

There was a vibrancy in the atmosphere now. Parson Hogg had passed word that he expected to make connections with the *Red River* any hour. Some of his men stationed themselves on the foredeck, ready to swing out the landing booms and be ready to transfer the munitions on a moment's notice.

Todd had eaten a bait of dinner in the cook shack and was heading forward when he heard the muffled cry aft. Apprehension ran a stiffness down his spine. *Julie!* Turning, he sprinted along the deck. In the shadowy corner formed by the fantail and the wall of the deckhouse he picked out the struggling shape of two figures. In the gloom, Amos Bullard looked more than ever like a gorilla in man's clothing, his long arms trying to lock Julie against him, one hand over her mouth.

Todd's left hand pivoted him, while his right traveled a long two feet to smash on Bullard's nose. The renegade staggered back until the fantail banged against his head. Closing in, Todd drove again for his face. But Bullard's brain was protected by a thick skull; the stunning effect of the first blow sloughed away with one shake of his bullet head. He ducked Todd's fists and closed with him. Only the wooden rail kept them from falling fifteen feet to the main deck as they went down in a threshing tangle. Fists chopped, thumbs gouged, knees jackknifed into groins. It was a boatman's fight—no holds barred, and the devil take the hindmost.

Julie was in it, too, kicking at Bullard and hitting Todd just as often. The renegade's fists bludgeoned into Todd's chest and stomach with staggering force. One of his eyes was closing, where Bullard's head had butted him. Bullard was after his throat now, with hands that seemed to have steel claws for fingers. And he made the hold good. Twice he banged Todd's head on the planking, thumbs searching for his windpipe, before the pilot could roll over on top of him. The pain caused by those spatulate fingers wedging into his throat would have brought a scream, but not a breath of air could go into his lungs or out. He felt his face choking with blood. His tongue flopped up and down spasmodically.

Bullard's face was close to his. The fleshy lips were drawn back from set teeth; the flat nose was wrinkled. His eyes were like hot cinders. Todd knew, with a wrench of desperation, that he had only a few seconds to break loose. After that it would be Bullard's to strangle or release him. With all the force his body possessed, he hurled himself to the left, bringing his right hand up under Bullard's tucked-in chin. The force of the punch was not great enough to hurt Bullard, but Todd jammed his thumb up into the soft skin close to the windpipe. His fingernail tore the flesh as the finger probed deeply into the nerve cluster. Bullard grunted with pain and his hands came away from Todd's throat.

Todd reeled against the wall, and got to his feet. Bullard was slower in rising, and he left his chin unguarded as he came up. Into that unprotected spot Todd Macon slung a blow that had all his back and shoulder muscles behind it. There was a sound like a butcher cracking a joint with a cleaver. Amos Bullard was thrown back. The railing caught him at the waist. One full-lunged scream left his throat as his stubby body jackknifed over. A cold hand was in Todd's vitals as he watched him fall, twisting, to crash onto the guard fifteen feet below and sprawl into the dark river.

From far back, Bullard came up and yelled again, through

a throat choked with water. Hogg's voice answered him from the wheelhouse. "Bullard! Where are you?"

The drowning man's voice was fading, as though borne away on the tide of the river. ". . . water! Macon . . . shoved . . . !"

Todd felt, rather than heard, the thud of something striking the paddle wheels. It was a whisper of sound that traveled forward through bulkheads and planking, chilling the blood of every man who had heard a man's back broken by a steamboat's paddles. Afterward there were no more cries from Amos Bullard.

It kept Todd standing there with a stomach tightly bunched like a fist. Above, Hogg could be heard yelling for a man to take the wheel. Suddenly Todd heard Julie's voice, a small scared voice.

"Oh, Todd! Todd! What have we got in for?"

"You mean what have *I* got in for! Hogg knows I killed Bullard. He'll be fixin' to swing me from a loading boom when he finds me."

"We're all in this together, you and I and Pop." Julie's eyes filmed with quick tears. "Pop and I were fools. We were so wrapped up in this State's Rights business we couldn't see the end of it. Good men like Big Sam being overlorded by curs like Bullard. None of us has ever owned a slave in his life, and we wouldn't want to. But we forgot that we were taking all those poor free men back to slavery. And besides . . . I don't think Hogg ever intended to give the boat back to us. I think he's commandeered it for his own selfish purposes. He's thinking about what he can sell those guns for, not just the good of the Confederacy. I think even Pop realizes it now."

Todd could hear Parson Hogg clattering along the hurricane deck toward the companionway that came out within twenty feet of them. Bitterness darkened his eyes. "It's something to hear you say that, anyway. But it's too late to think of changing things now. We'll raise the *Red River* in a few minutes. After that, you and Jasper are bound up in Missouri . . . until Hogg tears out the bottom of the boat on a bar somewhere. And me. . . ." He glanced sharply through the gloom, as Hogg's staff thumped on the top step. "That's my cue to go to the bank *pronto!*"

Julie gripped his arm. "What will you do?"

"Maybe swim ashore. Anyway, I'm getting out of here." He had swung over the rail and was poised by the toes of his boots on the edge of the decking. "Remember me to Jasper, the old hoss, if I don't see him again. So long, Julie!"

He dropped out of her sight into the gloom. She stifled a scream. An instant later the *Natchez* heard him strike the guard of the main deck, yell, and thresh briefly in the water. Then no more was heard of Todd Macon.

IV

The chill of the river went into Todd's marrow. Clinging to the slippery guard planks near the stern, he shivered as he dragged himself back aboard. The twelve-foot drop to the guard had numbed his legs to the hips. He had been lucky to get a hand hold on the carlings after he deliberately let himself splash into the river. Up above, he heard them shouting back and forth.

"He's rivered!" That was Hogg's cannon-like voice. "Lay me a light at the bull rail! I'll pump him so full of lead. . . ."

"Yonder he goes!" a man shouted. "He's makin' for shore."

A gun crashed three times, and across the water a log rocked like a sluggish alligator. Other guns came into the fracas, so that the water from the bull rails to a point fifty feet away boiled with lead plunking harmlessly into sand shadows and bits of flotsam. The heavy dusk turned every mark on the river into a possible fugitive.

Renegades swarmed aft, to keen the darkness for the swimmer. But Todd was scuttling up the deck and ducking hastily into the engine room. Big Sam stood blank-faced, ash hoe in his hands, as Todd came inside and leaned back against the wall by the door.

"Where can a man hide in here, Big Sam, if they take a notion to search the boat?"

Big Sam's brown face cracked into a grin. "Y'all rivered that Mist' Bullard?"

"For good. But you can have the satisfaction of knowing that it was your engines that turned the paddles that broke his back. I reckon he had enough steam this time."

"I don't heah 'im ringin' for more!"

Haste prodded Todd from the door. "You won't hear me, either, if you don't hide me some place. They'll be down here directly."

Sam's eyes rocked up. He was peering among the pipes and carlings of the ceiling, above clanking, sweating, black machinery. "If a man was right spry, and didn't set on no steam pipes"—he frowned—"he could tuck hisself in yonder. There's a big hole in the bulkhead that the pipes go th'ough."

Todd was already swinging up by a cool pipe. His hands sought gingerly among the network of big and little pipes for the ones that carried live and escape steam to and from the drums. Finding two he could safely crawl on, he backed into the small space Big Sam had indicated. In there, the darkness was complete. The engineer chuckled.

"You done disappeared all right!" Abruptly he grabbed up the hoe again and began raking his fire. "Somebody comin'!"

Todd could see Parson Hogg and the three other men as they came through the door and stood with bared guns in the red glow of the open furnace. Hogg's eyes caught the flames and his teeth flashed.

"Boy, you see him crawl aboard?"

Big Sam's head shook. "I heered you shootin' at him. He nevah crawled back on this boat."

One of the men said: "He's lyin'. Look at him shake."

"No, suh! Look around. Don' see him, do you?"

Walking back, Hogg glanced into the coal bin and resin barrel. Then his eyes traveled up and along the carlings. "Garth," he said, "look at that. Ain't that a man's hand on that damn pipe there?"

In Todd's veins, needle ice formed. It was too late, now, to pull his hand back into the shadow. He saw the parson's gun come up. His mind worked like a trapped rat frantically seeking a hole through which to escape. But there was no way out. He was on the point of diving headlong onto the renegade when the boat's whistle blasted. A bell rang and Big Sam jumped for the reverse cam. Hogg glanced about. Todd's hand yanked into the darkness.

"The *Red River!*" Hogg snapped. Peering again toward Todd, he cocked his head on the side. "Don't see it now. I reckon I was wrong. Time enough to make sure later."

The boat's sudden slowing threw him onto his bad leg, so that for a moment he was wrestling with it and cursing. He finished by pouching his gun and gripping his upright staff with both hands. The others were impatient to be out.

"Not so fast!" Hogg said. "You know what you're to do now?"

"Run out the heel and make fast. Then transfer the guns and ammunition."

"After you collect for them, fool! Remember that, if you forget everything else. If the South can't pay, we'll ransom them back to the North. I'll be at the wheel with a rifle in my hands, in case they try to outfox us."

As they went out, one of the renegades remarked: "That'll be a lot of help ag'in' two cannons on the head!"

With the sound of their footfalls on the boiler deck, Todd swung down. "That was narrow," he said slowly. "Listen, Sam. You wanted a chance to go back to Pittsburgh. Are you willing to fight for it? Wrenches and crowbars against guns?"

Big Sam raised the ash hoe with both hands. "I sooner go down chippin' on Hogg's head with this, as live to chop cotton with it."

"All right," the pilot said. "Soon as you make connections with the war boat, run back and bring the rest of your boys forward. They won't likely set a guard on 'em. If they do, you've still got your hoe. I'll need you right here, but tell the rest of them this. . . ."

Big Sam listened, and his mouth widened into a grin. "I'll tell 'em!" he finally said.

Todd took a sluicing bar from the engine room. He made it safely to the boiler deck. There he watched the renegades lower the gangplank from the now stationary *Natchez* to the head of the *Red River*, whose paddles were turning just enough to keep her bow to bow with the other boat. The war boat was a squat stern-wheeler with boiler-plate-lined decks to shelter riflemen. Behind the shields, Todd made out lines of armed men. A couple of small brass cannon were bolted to the foredecks.

One of Parson Hogg's lieutenants crossed to the *Red River* and spoke with the captain. There seemed to be heated words, but in the end the pirate returned to the packet with a small iron box under his arm. Soon thereafter, the transfer of cargo commenced.

The realization of how great were the odds he was bucking bore suddenly upon Todd Macon. His army was a little handful of free Negroes; the other side, heavily armed, outnumbered them four to one. Courage and desperation might outbalance the number odds. But what would balance the cannon?

Through the shadowy deserted upper decks he made his way to the texas. Inside, he ran to the companionway and mounted to the hurricane deck. Coming out on the bare stretch of tarred roof, he was wary. Hogg was in a position to see him if he should glance around. But Todd reached the wall of the lofty wheelhouse unobserved.

He was just rounding the corner of it when he saw another form sliding toward the steps that were Todd's own goal. In the same instant, the man saw him. It was too late to backtrack. Although the man had a gun, Todd hurled himself upon him, iron bar upraised.

Jasper Peacock's voice, hoarse with alarm, barked: "Todd, you damned fool!"

Todd stopped with a jerk, but the bar remained aloft. "I don't know where you stand now, Jasper," he panted, "but I ain't taking chances. Put that gun down or I'll part your scalp."

The old pilot lowered his revolver. "Two against forty, and you've got to make war with your own pardner," he remarked. "I'm going up there and take over. I've got my belly full of things as they stand."

"That's straight?" Todd asked him.

"Watch me!"

Jasper started up the steps. With a little lift of satisfaction, Todd followed. At the top, Jasper turned the knob—and found it locked. Hogg's voice came through the panels: "Who is it?"

Todd essayed a nasal imitation of Hogg's lieutenant: "Garth! I've got the money here."

The answer was double-barreled. "Garth, hell!" the parson shouted. "That's Macon talking!" A bullet came through the door, passing with a snarl between Todd and Jasper.

With a shove, Todd put Jasper aside and lunged for the lock with a swing of the bar. It splintered, the door banged wide open, and Todd went through asprawl. Parson Hogg stood with his back to the wheel, his whiskered face distorted, the gun in his hand spewing flame. His first shot passed three feet above the falling man; his second whipped at Todd's hair.

But Jasper Peacock's first bullet, aimed from the darkness, caved through the parson's stout chest to tear at his heart. He went back against the wheel. Once more he fired, this time through the floor between his feet. His good leg failed him, but that cantankerous artificial limb of his, even in death, refused to bend. It kept him erect as a plank until he toppled forward on his face.

Todd Macon vaulted over to take the wheel. In a swift glance, he saw how things stood on the foredeck. All of the parson's men were back-and-bellying the gun cases across the gangplanks. But some of them were staring up at the pilothouse, surprised by the sound of gunfire.

Todd blew two long blasts of the whistle. There was, for a moment, no result. Then the darkness gave up the forms of eighteen roustabouts. At the same instant, the *Natchez* gave a forward thrust that caused both gangways to bow upward and snap in the middle. Men and boxes were flung high. Some, falling between the two boats, were crushed as the bows jammed heavily together.

The tumult was complete when the roustabouts, swinging every weapon the engine rooms afforded, rushed the renegades. Big Sam now had his wheels in reverse. The widening strip of water between the boats was filled with threshing men. So sudden and so vicious was the attack that the Negroes had swept the deck almost clean of pirates in ten seconds, caving in skulls and crowding their enemies into the water before more than a dozen guns had barked.

Steam was roaring from the *Natchez*'s escape pipes. Full head she backed for a hundred feet, then shipped up to larboard. The fight on deck was over. Todd watched the men hunt shelter as the *Red River*'s decks ran bright with gun flame. He put the wheel hard over. Big Sam anticipated his every order. The packet trembled and moved upstream even as Todd reached for the come-ahead bell.

Jasper was looking back. "Hold down your hair!" he gasped. "They're fixin' to fire the cannons!"

Todd groaned. "What's holdin' those men below! I told them. . . ."

A great lurch of the floor stopped his tongue. Simultaneously there was a splintering crash to starboard. The roar of a cannon mixed with the noise of a smokestack tearing free of its guys to crash on the hurricane deck and tumble into the water in a geyser of steam.

Flame spouted from the stub of the iron stack, close beside the wheelhouse. The short hairs of Todd's neck lifted stiffly. The next shot would be true. They were gunning for the wheelhouse. Then Jasper, standing at the rear windows, grunted in surprise.

"What in tarnation! One of them roustabouts is driftin' back to the *Red River* in a dinghy! What in hell is this all about?"

Todd dropped the tie-down over a spoke and went back. He looked down at the small rowboat drifting under the very bull rails of the pursuer. "That's no roustabout," he said. "It's a boat full of powder kegs. We didn't have any cannon, so I took a chance that Big Sam could figger his fuse just about right. . . ."

It was evident that the engineer had. Drifting close to the Southern boat, the dinghy attracted the attention of a Rebel who tried to capsize it with a boat hook. As though his touching the boat had been a signal, three kegs of powder went off with a terrific explosion.

The force of it caved in the remaining windows of the pilothouse. It seemed to Todd that hell itself had erupted. A vast fountain of fire mounted to the black night sky. On the crest of it rode a great chunk of the *Red River*'s forecastle. A round, bowl-like depression appeared in the river where the dinghy had been. It must have measured fifty feet across, and the bottom of it touched the sandy bed of the river. Into this bowl, huge fragments of the steamboat tumbled like scantlings dumped from a wagon into a hole. There were six more rapid explosions as the war boat's boilers exploded.

Starkly illuminated for a moment by the fire, the bodies of two-score men could be seen to soar upward. Twisting, sprawling, they disappeared into the darkness. A moment later the flames died out, save for the burning hulk of the *Red River*—a boat badly damaged. Todd Macon, with a sick feeling in his stomach, went back to the wheel and picked up the speaking tube.

"All right, Big Sam. Let's have some steam!" he shouted. "We're homeward bound!"

The *Natchez* limped into New Albany shortly after dawn. Here they would spend a week or two seeing the packet put back in shape. After that—Todd and Julie stood on the hurricane deck as Jasper warped her in, thinking a lot about the future and not talking much.

"Did Pop have anything to say to you?" Julie asked.

"He ain't opened his mouth since we got away from the *Red River*, except to grouse about having the miseries in his back."

Julie smiled. "You know what I think really turned him against Hogg? Seeing his medicine shelf broken up! Even Bullard, trying to get fresh with me, might not have turned the trick. But he had to have his booze."

Todd's eyes were speculative as he frowned down at the brown water. "Jasper's going to have the miseries proper when he finds out what I aim to do today."

"What's that?" There was a lot of tension in the girl's voice.

"I'm putting in a salvage claim for his half of the boat. I was more or less responsible for bringing her back in as good shape as she is. And he's not getting off scotfree after trying to do me out of my half."

Julie's eyes, sober but puzzled, searched his face. "I . . . I don't blame you, Todd. But I can't believe you'd really do a thing like that."

"Then you're in for a surprise. Unless Jasper is willing to make a deal with me, I'll insist on a transfer of title into my name. I'll teach that old rounder to make a fool out of me!"

"What kind of a deal?" Julie asked guardedly. Her eyes were wide in her beautiful face.

Todd's arm went around her and he pulled her back from the old pilot's view. "Another transfer of title. Julie Peacock's coming over to the Macon line for good. Will you talk up the idea to your old man?"

Julie's arms slipped up to pull his face down to hers. "I guess I'll have to, Todd. You're still first officer, and I've been on the river too long to think of mutiny. Especially when I like the kind of orders I'm getting! Let's go and see what Pop has to say."

Freeze-Out

When Bob Gaines settled Antelope Valley, he possessed 150 cows, a wagonload of furniture, and a warning from the sheriff of Tecolote.

"You're going to be a neighbor to a bobcat and a grizzly bear. Ira Stagg's the grizzly and Sam Nolan's the cat. They've never been able to get along with each other, and how do you think they'll get along with you? They'll chew you to pieces in six months."

Gaines was thirty years old and tired of working for other people. He was a lean, thoughtful man. He made friends easily; hardly a man in New Mexico could say he was actually his enemy. He figured a mild-mannered fellow like he was, yet not easily frightened, should make out.

Antelope Valley curled lazily down between the Black Mountains on the west, and the Red Hills on the east. It was about two miles wide and six long, and, lying coiled there like a snake in the sun, it was beautiful. The timber was light and the grass golden; the stream ran nine months of the year and two windmills pulled the water up during the other months. But the man who sold the valley to Gaines had seemed glad enough to leave.

In a matter of weeks, however, Gaines was acting as go-between to Sam Nolan and Ira Stagg. From his Black Mountain range, Nolan, a gaunt red-headed man who looked like Abraham Lincoln, would come down to say: "Will you tell that chuckle-headed Texan two of his steers are in my Marble Cañon pasture? He's got forty-eight hours to claim 'em before they run headfirst into a barbecue pit."

Stagg, a robust, savage-tempered, yet rather shy man, with brows like a blacksmith's thumb smudges, would receive a watered-down version of the report. He would usually be able to cap it. "Don't go out of your way, but if you see that hound dog in chaps, you might mention that his Black Angus bull is bogged in Frijole Creek. I reckon his head won't go under for another twelve hours, though."

So the titans of Pinal County were able to call each other, by proxy, names they would not have used in person, and, besides, they were saved a certain amount of labor by having Gaines there. Once in a while Stagg would chase a couple of bull calves over Bob's way. "Them critters have got too big to dehorn. If you can handle 'em, they're yours."

Not to be outdone, Sam Nolan would descend from the mountain with a cold-blooded bronco. "This jughead and his brothers are eating a lot of grass that'd make good beef. You can make a third-rate cow horse out of him or sell him to a packing house for seven bucks."

Gaines had no pride about accepting these gratuities, for it took all the tact in the world and a considerable amount of extra riding to keep the peace for them. But he would not have moved away for anything, now. In about a year, he figured, he would be able to send railroad money to a certain girl in Albuquerque.

Then one day a bounty hunter named Colorado Wolfert stopped by the stone corral at the north end of Bob's range, where he had just penned some calves for weaning. Wolfert was paid jointly by Stagg and Nolan to kill mountain lions.

"Been hearing some shooting over here," Colorado said curiously. "Kinda got to wondering if anything was doin'." A young fellow, he had thin red skin and bleached hair and brows, with a lacing of fine lines about his eyes.

"I've been hearing it, too," Gaines admitted. "I figured it was you up at the head of the cañon."

"If it was me"—Colorado smiled—"there wouldn't have been but one shot. This was about six, and it wasn't nobody popping jack rabbits. A rifle, and it went on for quite a while."

Bob said: "I'll ride up with you."

Near the head of the valley, it narrowed down until it was merely wilderness cañon in which outlaw cattle might hide. Many feeder cañons entered and the cañon sides were steep, with cedar and pine standing against the lean. They were riding along when they came upon three calves standing aimlessly in the middle of the wash. None of the animals wore a brand, but they were bawling strenuously and Colorado and Bob shot each other glances of apprehension. They had not been weaned, but someone had been on the point of weaning them when he was interrupted. Their eyes had been filled with sand so that they could not find their way back to the point from which they had been run. It was an old rustler's trick.

They rode on. Tales of rustling, half-believed charges of brand blotting and night raids, recurred to Bob, the profane accusations Sam Nolan and Ira Stagg made against each other. But he had always discounted them as being in the tradition of feud talk.

Suddenly they reined up. The horses minced. Just ahead, against a bank of the wash, lay a man in checkered shirt, chaps, and Levi's. Gaines's eyes flinched. A drum roll seemed to sound in his head, warning him back, warning him away from what had happened and from what would happen. For this was the body of one of Ira Stagg's cowpunchers. . . .

"It's Lynn Cordiner," Colorado said.

One side of the cowpuncher's shirt was caked with blood and dirt. There was black blood in his mouth and nose and his elbows hugged his sides, as he lay face down on the sand.

They rode by. Both men carried their carbines across the swells of their saddles. Farther up, they found the man's pony, near a live oak beneath which lay his saddle gun. There were two empty shells near the trunk of the tree; a bullet had gouged bark from it and exposed the white meat beneath.

"You and me," said Colorado thoughtfully, "had best recollect what we were doing about the time this happened. 'Pears we may be asked."

But Bob was shaken with recalling that, while Lynn had been having his hour of terror and death, he had been hazing calves along and listening unconcernedly to the shooting. It seemed to him that there should have been some final ring in the death shot, some tragic undertone, to tell him a man had just gone across the Divide.

It was late afternoon, with a shimmer of frost in the sunlight, when they brought the dead man down from Antelope Valley in Bob's spring wagon. The road split—left to Stagg's Cross Anchor range and, beyond, to Tecolote, the county seat; right to Sam Nolan's broken kingdom of timbered ridges and sunless cañons. Bob Gaines said: "There'll be an inquest. Nolan ought to be there rather than hear about it later. Ride up and get him, Colorado. But don't start before tomorrow. I don't want him overtaking us. I don't want that inquest held on the road."

The bounty hunter wheeled his horse, an eager, loose figure in the deep mountain saddle.

Ira Stagg's ranch buildings lay on the shore of the Red Hills. The last light of the summer ran fluidly on the windows as Bob approached. Men went about the evening chores and the voice of Stagg's wife came from the chicken yard.

Stagg's foreman, McDaniel, a tall, erect, humorless man, approached the wagon. Bob did not speak, and McDaniel frowned and looked into the back of the wagon. If a nude woman had been lying there on a panther skin, Gaines thought, McDaniel would have thought it beneath him to react, as he seemed to feel it unworthy of him now. He stared a while and merely said: "I'll get Stagg."

Cowpunchers helped unload the body. It was beginning to stiffen and lay in a tortured attitude on the ground. Ira Stagg came breathlessly, his short, thick legs moving quickly. He knelt by the dead cowpuncher. Then he stood up, frowning, not seeming particularly upset. But Bob wished he would curse and shake his fist and make his gigantic threats instead of bottling what must have been an explosive rage.

Finally he said: "I always like to promise a 'puncher of mine that being shot at ain't part of his job. Until I can make that promise again, I reckon I'll have to double wages and furnish free ammunition."

They reached Tecolote at noon the following day. With Stagg, McDaniel, and Bob came three other cowpunchers. The town lay on the west bank of the Río Grande, in a wide loop with crumbling cliffs on the far side. The main street ran down to a drab wintry *bosque,* while at the head of the town, gray and austere in a square of dead grass, stood the courthouse. There was some time to kill while the coroner made his examination and a jury was convened. They went into a bar and heard San Nolan's rumbling bass. Immediately Nolan saw them and left the bar. His long, hungry features were grave, and there was something approaching sympathy in them.

"Ira . . . ," he began, "this . . . this is. . . ." The words would not come, but suddenly he put out his hand.

Stagg inspected it. "Am I getting near-sighted," he said,

"or is there blood on that?"

He walked out, leaving a morgue-like silence. Bob strode after him. "My God, Ira!" he said.

Stagg did not acknowledge him. He and McDaniel crossed the street to another bar.

Bob walked slowly down the street. Sheriff Henderson's warning rang in his head: *You'll be betwixt the bobcat and the grizzly bear.* Right now the pressure was all between Stagg and Nolan, but when they squared off, he would be right in their line of fire. Beyond that, he did not like the look of things, should they ever come down to examining the situation. A dead man and three stolen calves on his range. It could look to some people as though Lynn had caught Bob Gaines with the sanded calves.

In the afternoon, after depositions from Colorado Wolfert and Bob, the coroner's jury brought its finding into the small musty room in the courthouse. Sam Nolan was there in his black town suit, sitting in a back row with his flat black Stetson on his lap, solemnly listening to the foreman.

"In the matter of the death of Lynn Cordiner, a human being, we find death to have been caused by a Forty-Four or similar caliber rifle in the hands of a person unknown. And if they ever catch the. . . ."

"That'll be all," the coroner said.

The evidence lay on a table: one large-caliber slug, considerably mashed, obviously a rifle bullet of about 500 grains. Sheriff Henderson permitted Gaines to inspect it. Behind Ira Stagg, the Cross Anchor cowpunchers had departed in a body with a hard jingling of spur rowels. A moment later Nolan left.

Bob put the bullet down. "No rifling marks. A paper patch."

Henderson made a quizzical sound and looked at it himself. He shrugged. "Don't prove anything. I use patches myself. Rifling scratches make a bullet carry uneven."

Bob smiled. "Matter of opinion." He did not mention that he himself owned an old Sharps that took paper-patch shells.

The sheriff put the bullet in an envelope and licked the flap. "Here we go!" he said. "Don't say I didn't warn you."

Bob's temper surged up. "This doesn't have to be a beginning," he snapped. "Find out who did it, and I'll lay ten to one it wasn't any local cowboy!"

"Suppose you find out. I'll be going up there to look around one of these days, but I never was much good at sifting needles out of haystacks."

Gaines waited at the wagon for the Cross Anchor men. They had ridden down to a saloon in the cold dusk. Colorado had already started back. When the five men came back up the steep road, it was nearly dark and Bob was moving up and down the walk to keep warm. He called and raised his arm, but they rode past with heads dipped against the wind, and not a man looked his way, not Ira Stagg or McDaniel, or any of the cowpunchers. He stood there a moment, his arm slowly descending.

As he was about to climb into the wagon, lanky Sam Nolan jogged up the road and reined over. He dismounted and nodded greeting. He set his boot sole against a spoke of a wheel and frowned a moment. In the early night, the austerity of his face was emphasized, the deep ruts in his cheeks, the dark eyes in their deep caves, standing out as bold strokes of a charcoal pencil.

"Bob," he said, "do you want to sell that land of yours?"

Bob scrutinized him. "Why, no. I'm just getting dug in."

"It might be a good idea, then," Nolan rumbled, "if you were to sign on with me as a 'puncher for a while."

Bob swore. "Sam, you can't declare war on a man just because you figure you've been insulted."

"Wasn't I?" Nolan rapped out.

"He was upset. After all," Bob pointed out, "a man of his was killed."

Nolan did not comment. "What was the talk today? That Cordiner caught one of my men stealing beeves?"

Bob nodded.

"Fine! Did anybody happen to mention that the calves were mine?"

Bob stared. "How do you know that? They weren't branded."

"I found three cows without their calves on the ridge between our places! And I hadn't started weaning."

Bob spoke earnestly. "That only bears out what I've thought all along. That somebody without a stake in either spread pulled it. Maybe a gang of cow thieves."

Nolan's hollow glance rested on Bob. "Or a bounty hunter. Or a shoestring cowman up thataway."

Anger boiled up in Bob, but Nolan turned away to remount with the long motions of a crane. He held the reins lightly in his gaunt hand. "I'm telling you to sell to me or get out, Gaines. I may not tell you again."

He touched the pony's flanks with the spurs and left town at a rack.

Bob slept under the wagon a mile out of town. He could not curb his imagination from making little excursions into what would happen to a man trying to raise cattle in that lonely strip between the firing lines. At the same time, he was a man who became more unco-operative the more he was pushed around, and he was taking a pushing from both sides just now.

Toward sundown the following day he reached the fork, cut north a mile, and swung through the oaks into his yard. As soon as he entered, he saw Stagg, McDaniel, and some other cowpunchers waiting.

It was evident that they had been there for some time. Stagg was tilted back in a chair beside the door; McDaniel, somber and grim-lipped in a striped jersey, pony-skin vest, and black chaps, sat on the ground at the other side of the door, smoking. The others were grouped near the corral.

Stagg and his ramrod arose. Bob looked at each man carefully. Stagg said tersely: "Bob, I'm buying you out. I'll give you two thousand for the land and you can take your cattle with you."

"I'm not selling!" Bob snapped. "Nolan wanted me to sell last night. I told him what I'm telling you."

McDaniel interrupted: "You got any paper-patch shells?"

"A few. Not Forty-Fours."

"How can you say what caliber a slug was after it's mashed through a man's ribs?" McDaniel reached down to pick up a Sharps outside-hammer rifle that had lain at the angle of the wall and the ground. He leaned it against the wall and looked at Bob.

Bob lurched past Stagg, who held him roughly. "We're five to your one," he said, "I wouldn't try it. I make no accusations, Gaines, but I don't want to have to look at you while there's any doubt in my mind. We'll help you move your stuff out."

A man near the corral approached and Stagg turned to enter the cabin. Bob seized his shoulder and pulled him back, but at that instant he saw McDaniel closing in to slug at his head. Shattering pain exploded behind his ear, and he went to his knees. He held onto the doorjamb and was pulling himself up when the foreman hit him again. He fell once more, but pushed himself to his hands and knees. Then there was an ebbing of strength and a feeling of the warmth in him draining through his fingers, and, despite the effort he made, he sagged to the floor.

It was chilly, the mountain day dying, when Bob managed to work his way outside. He sat on the ground against the wall with his head in his hands. After a while he gazed about him. They had thrown his bedding, table, and chair out the windows. A sad jetsam of china and spilled food lay outside the door. As he stared at it, he suddenly swore and kicked at the coffee grinder lying near him, but it was for him the face of the ramrod, McDaniel. *They know damn' well I didn't kill Lynn! But they needed a whipping boy.*

He sat in thought for some time, smoking three cigarettes and trying to find knowledge in their smoke. Then he got up stiffly and found an undamaged lantern. He lighted it and hung it in the cabin and began to move his possessions inside. He bolted the door and pulled the flour-sack curtains. *Now, by God!* he thought grimly.

But there was no satisfaction in him, nothing but a feeling of being on a train rushing to catastrophe, and unable to get off it. . . .

In the morning he saw clearly that he could not make his boast good by talk. There would be no normal activity while the menace of conflict hung over the range, and he had no confidence that Henderson would do anything to resolve it. He lacked both the intelligence and the guts. Because of this, Bob decided on an investigation of his own.

He had climbed to the ridge between the ranch buildings and the upper valley when he heard riders below. Looking back, he saw six miniature figures of horsemen lope into the yard. He pulled up to watch them challenge the cabin, and then he saw one man stride inside. A moment later two others swung to the corral and started slashing the rawhide thongs that supported the poles. They fell, and from the cabin hurtled the same battered furniture he had salvaged the night before.

Bob yanked his saddle gun and swung down in fury. He leaned against a rocky shoulder of the trail and pressed his cheek against the walnut. Then, with one of the horses in his sights, he slowly lowered the gun and let his emotions escape in profanity. The thought of what could have happened if he had hit one of Nolan's men brought sweat out on his face. He jammed the gun back in the boot and stood there until he saw someone dump kerosene on his furniture and bedclothes and toss a match onto the pile.

The men mounted again. There was a discussion that ended in Sam Nolan's riding alone down the cañon, into the Antelope Valley wash. The rest headed back.

Bob spurred the bay along the trail above Nolan. A mile ahead, he could cut down from this wooded peninsula that angled into the valley and intercept him. What that cowman needed, he thought, was a whipping.

But there was something in the almost furtive manner of the rider that caused him to keep a puzzled watch on him. He remained on the trail above and behind Nolan as he rode upcañon. Nolan came to the place where they had found Lynn Cordiner's body. He did not dismount, but rode all about the spot, studying sign, and finally headed up the cañon.

Bob puzzled over it. There was nothing above this point but a fastness of timber, stone, and jagged slashes of cañon. Then suddenly he recalled that Colorado Wolfert's camp was up there. It came to him that Colorado was about to get the treatment, too. He was smiling tightly as he jogged on along the hillside.

Once he stopped and gazed, long and thoughtfully, at the oak tree beneath which he had found the symbols of the death fight. He let these things turn over in his mind, examining them from every angle. The bullet that had slashed the tree trunk had come from this general direction. Suddenly it struck him that the gunman must have left behind him something to denote exactly where he had stood—paper patches from his shells—and, if he could discover the spot, there might be tracks to follow.

He put his horse down the rough slope through the buckbrush tangles and began searching for the kind of solid ambuscade a sniper would have selected. He inspected a dozen manzanita tangles, a few rocky cairns with natural embrasures. He had about given it up when he saw a glint of paper on the ground beneath a cleft boulder.

Lighting down, he retrieved the paper. It was a regular, slightly frayed strip two inches long, badly powder-smudged on one side. Apparently it was a patch from a rifle. Properly attached to the slug, a patch would leave it as it burst from the gun muzzle; a patch that stuck caused the slug to waver, so that most marksmen scorned special pastes and employed saliva.

There was no way of telling how many shots had been fired, or how many had come from this spot. At least two must have been fired, since one had hit the tree and one had struck Cordiner. In ten minutes of searching, Bob found three patches. He began hunting tracks, but the loose, gravelly earth had not held them. As he went over the ground, he discovered a fourth patch. This one was quite ragged, and, as he examined it, he saw that it was not a regular patch, but one that had been torn from a piece of paper. Probably the gunman had fumbled in inserting the shell and torn the original patch off; he had had to improvise one from a page of a tally book.

He squinted closer. This was not from a tally book; it bore smudged relics of printing. The characters were indistinguishable, for both sides of the slip were badly powder-burned, but in his fingers the paper had a familiar, tough feel.

"By God!" he said aloud. When he rode on, he went at a stiff trot toward Colorado's camp.

He smelled the camp before he saw it. There were always a dozen pelts of mountain lion or cougar drying, and sometimes a spoiled lion carcass lay under a mantle of bluebottle flies not far from camp. Bob rode in and saw immediately that he had arrived in the middle of something.

The camp was a careless sprawl: stained gray tent, scattered cooking utensils, a rock fireplace, a heap of odds and ends under a tarp. A fire was going and a coffee pot hung on a crosspiece above the flames. Beyond, four men squatted on their heels: Colorado, Sam Nolan—and Ira Stagg and his ramrod.

Colorado stood up, looking tense and uncomfortable. Nolan stared at Bob from those gaunt eye sockets. "You, too!" he said.

Bob dismounted. "Not breaking anything up, am I?"

"Oh, no," Stagg said ironically. "I'm out cutting sign and stopped here for a powwow with Colorado, so of course this dragged-out hank of cowman drops in to accuse me of bein' out hunting his strays again. What's on *your* mind?"

"A lot," Gaines said. "When things look right, I'm going to take a fall out of your right-hand man. But I won't try it with four men to back him up, next time. And when I get down with him, I'll clean Sam Nolan's plow. That was nice, Sam. I saw it all from the ridge."

Nolan's face colored, but he said staunchly: "I warned you. I only came up here to warn Colorado. I want no more mavericks on my range. After today, I'm burning them all with Colonel Colt's Circle Dot brand."

Bob grubbed a cup from a pan of unwashed dishes. "I saw you stop by the tree where Lynn was killed," he said, as he poured the coffee. "Lose something?"

Nolan started. "None of your damned business!"

Stagg gave him a sharp look. McDaniel sat on his haunches with his feet splayed to avoid the spurs. There was caution in his hard, dark features, but there were shrewdness and boldness, too.

Bob grinned, and sipped the coffee. He let his eyes move about the half circle of watchful men, and it was a certainty in him that the man who had crouched in the rocks that day was here at this campfire. The taut silence was like that of a poker game, when the last raise was made and a man had to risk everything or back out.

He spoke quietly, then, glancing between Stagg and Nolan. "You boys have been telling it pretty *bravo*. You're going to run all the little fellows out on a rail. Did it ever occur to you that some of the little fellows might be handy with a rail, too?" Their eyes mocked him. He went on. "I've got too much tied up here to leave. And if you offered me anything like a fair price, I still wouldn't, because they aren't shoving decent ranches at you these days. So if you begin to crowd me, I'm going to have to do some crowding of my own."

"All by yourself?" Stagg inquired.

"Did I say that? I've got enough cash that I can buy myself some friends. Though you probably wouldn't get along with them at all. I doubt that a night would go by that you didn't have a tank dynamited or a line shack burned."

58

Nolan, regarding him steadily, growled: "There's men plaiting hair bridles in Santa Fé for just those things, Gaines."

"Well, if they lock them up for raiding, I suppose I ought to be swearing out complaints against you two."

For a moment they were stopped. Before anyone could top his bluff, he played his big card.

"I'll tell you what I will do, though. I'll play you a game of poker. If either of you can freeze me out, I'll sell out to him for what I paid, and get out tomorrow."

The others exchanged glances. Stagg seemed pleased. "That's all right," he said, "but I haven't got over twenty bucks with me."

"I couldn't stay with you if you were heeled, anyway. We'll go into this even. Ten bucks apiece. When a man's out, he's out for good. If I take you both, you make up a kitty of five hundred dollars to pay for wrecking my cabin."

There was an awkward instant of Stagg and Nolan, looking sheepishly at each other, forced for once into agreement. Nolan cleared his throat. He dug a slim wad of bills from his pocket and peeled off a pair of fives.

Stagg dug in his pocket for a five and some ones. Bob had only a twenty. "Anybody break this?" he asked. Neither of the cattlemen could change it, but McDaniel produced a couple of tens. "Dollar limit," Bob said. "Colorado, how about a deck?"

The bounty hunter brought a dog-eared pack from his tent. They cut for deal and Stagg won. He threw out the cards, opened with a dollar, and Bob stayed with him while Sam Nolan dropped out. Colorado, his thin-skinned red face intent, loomed over them. McDaniel leaned back against a rock, smoke drifting from his lips.

Bob lost the hand, after two raises. He gave Stagg his ten and received a five and two singles. On Nolan's deal, he lost the two. Both ranchers were smiling; there occurred what approached camaraderie, as they found themselves bucking a common adversary. But in Bob, tension was mounting, for he had sunk everything in this stratagem, and, if it failed, he was through.

He dealt, but threw in his cards. Nolan added three dollars to his pile in the betting, and the cards went back to Stagg. The pot was opened. Everyone stayed in, but on the draw Bob dropped out. Nolan and Stagg battled it out for two raises before Ira Stagg took it with a full house on jacks and treys. Stagg gave a low, rumbling laugh.

"Sonny," he told Bob, "I was sending men home in their underwear when you were licking striped candy."

There was some trouble over making change. Bob had a five but owed Stagg one out of it. Nolan owed three. On the ground before Stagg there were three ones, whereas he needed six to make change. It could be done by a little juggling, but Bob spoke up hurriedly, turning to Colorado.

"Break this for me, will you? Five ones in the game aren't going to be enough."

Colorado was not displeased at having to bring a roll of bills as thick as a man's wrist from his hip pocket. Nolan stared at it; the hunter laughed.

"You boys are in the wrong business. I collect wages from you and the territory pays bounty on my kills. A fellow in Albuquerque buys the pelts when they're cured."

A little ostentatiously, he peeled off several tens before he got down to any ones. He was about to hand the bills to Bob when he started a little and pulled them back, looking in shock at one of them. But Bob was reaching for them.

Colorado sounded alarmed. "This one's torn. I'll turn it in at the bank."

Bob snapped the banknotes from his hand. He spread

60

them on the ground. There was a roughly rectangular portion about two inches by a half ripped from a corner of one bill. "How'd that happen?" he asked.

They were all staring at the note. Bob heard Colorado breathing heavily. Colorado reached for it. "It was that way when I took it in. Didn't notice until later."

Bob fitted into the torn place the burned patch he had picked up down the cañon. Except for a few burned edges, the fit was perfect. "Did you get that one for a pelt or for a calf you stole from Stagg or Nolan?" he wanted to know.

Colorado's face was blank, but his eyes were alive, tawny, darting, angry. "You're crazy!" he said. "The patch was mine, sure. I don't carry a whole box of shells when I go out, and the patch came off one of the shells I had with me when I got a shot the other day. I tore that piece off and made a new one."

"What kind of game would let you load and fire four times? I found the rest of these patches in the same spot. The only game I know that will let you take that much time runs on two legs. I'm guessing that Lynn caught you with the stolen beeves and you shot it out with him."

Colorado looked at the other men; Stagg was rising to his feet. Nolan's hand slipped across his thigh to his holstered Colt. Suddenly the hunter's foot moved and dirt rose in a gritty screen that blinded the others for an instant. He stepped back, getting behind the boulder against which McDaniel sat, and Bob saw the gun.

He went rolling aside. He heard Colorado's revolver crash and something struck the earth near his leg. He had his thumb on the hammer of his Colt. Through the pale gauze of smoke and dust he sought Colorado behind the rock. McDaniel had gone scuttling across the ground. Stagg was huddled against the rock, and Nolan still sat where he had, but with a gun in his hand.

Bob pointed his Colt at the head-and-shoulders target the yellow-headed man made above the rock. He let the hammer fall and his hand leaped high. When he brought the gun down again, he saw that Colorado had lurched back, that he was going to his knees. But Colorado was still in it, firing across fifteen feet of ground at the man who had trapped him.

The shot came, but it was a wild one. Bob had made his second one count, and a trickle of smoke hung from the barrel of Sam Nolan's .45 as he watched Colorado fall.

They sat around for an hour, talking, their backs to the camp, and finally Stagg said to his ramrod: "Go look at him again."

McDaniel came back. "I told you he was dead before. He's colder'n any man *you* ever saw! Let's git it done."

They got it done, wrapping Colorado Wolfert in his own blankets before they buried him, and afterward making a pile of his possessions and burning them in the campfire.

"No use bringing Henderson up here," Nolan said. "He'd just fuss around and get himself exercised for nothing. If you want a thing done in this country, do it yourself."

Stagg agreed, which was a remarkable thing in itself, and the first time any such remark had passed between them.

When they reached the turn-off, Nolan told Bob: "I'll ride up and help you get squared away. You got a wagonload of furniture coming whenever you're ready to go to town."

And Ira Stagg, who had never been outdone in a thing like this, scratched his head. "Want you to figure on repping for yourself at my roundup next week, Bob. Some of your calves have been tagging around after some of my cows."

"Thanks," Bob said. "I'll make it." *And without any sheepishness,* he added to himself. He figured that any little favors they wanted to drop he had coming.

62

Wanted!

I

Outside the railroad restaurant a Mexican pony rubbed off winter hair on a telegraph pole. Swain Barker laid a hand on its mane as he passed. Entering the café, he heard the whistle of the westbound passenger train in the stony hills east of Cabrito. Two Mexicans, lying in the shade of a wood rick, scrambled up.

Barker mounted a green-plush stool at a far end of the U-shaped counter. Heaps of sandwiches lay on the counter and steam rose from the beak of a brass eagle atop the coffee boiler. A shirt-sleeved counterman brought him two sandwiches and a cup of coffee and said: "She comes."

Barker stirred gritty sugar into his coffee. "Yeah." He was a sturdy, dark-eyed man with a close beard the color of a strong cigar. He wore his hair hogged like a mule's mane and the line of his mouth was tight.

As he began to eat, he saw a girl opposite him at the counter. She smiled and nodded, and Barker froze up inside, but murmured: "Good morning."

She was the daughter of Alva Cosbee. He had learned this in the course of learning everything he could about Cosbee. Cosbee owned a herd of horses being shod for a trip into Sonora. Tomorrow or the next day he would be across the line in Mexico and Barker saw his time shortening.

In a drifting cloud of smoke, steam, and dust, the train pulled in. Passengers took all the seats and stood about to eat sandwiches; a conductor came into the doorway, watch in hand. "Ten minutes!" he called.

Barker made it a habit to keep his eyes down. But now he let them drift slowly down the line of faces. It was a long way to Arizona from Louisiana, but Army people traveled long distances. His glance passed a ruddy, lean-featured countenance and at once his eyes snapped back to it. The man was watching him acutely. His eyes were pallid in the florid, slick skin; he began to smile and gave Swain Barker a nod.

Barker drank his coffee without taking his eyes off the man. He did not acknowledge the nod, although he knew he couldn't keep up a pretense of not recognizing him. He knew how Tom King's mind would be going: *Is he wearing a gun? Had I better take him right now, or wait?* He waited until the Army man—who wore civilian clothing—had his mouth full of sandwich, then he placed a coin by his cup, swung off the stool, and moved toward the door. The place was cluttered with weary passengers stretching their legs. He bumped someone, murmured—"Beg your pardon."—and was knifing toward the door again when a person turned a smiling face up to him. It was the Cosbee girl.

"I'd think you were trying to make that train if I didn't know better," she said.

Talk was the thing he wanted least at this moment. He knew by the friendliness of her manner that she had been hoping for such an encounter. It was a small and lonesome town on the border, and the few Americans in it were bound to single one another out. But Swain Barker had sought no one out—least of all the daughter of a man he was hunting.

"I wish I were, miss," he said.

"Don't tell me you're tiring of our little town, Mister Finch?"

"The town's tiring of me," Barker, alias Finch, said. "There's none of my kind of work here, apparently."

"What is your kind of work?"

"Easy work," said Barker.

"That's everyone's. As a matter of fact, we're leaving at sunup ourselves."

"You're going with the herd? Into Mexico?"

"Why not? We've got a Dearborn wagon. I've always wanted to see Mexico." Her deep blue eyes were animated. Her features were tidy and delicate, and he liked the neatness of her. He saw she was prepared to talk as long as he was. He smiled apologetically and said: "I'm trying to catch someone out here before the train leaves, Miss Cosbee. If you'll excuse me. . . ."

Her eyes cooled a little. "Certainly."

"I'll take the liberty of bumping into you again soon, Miss Cosbee. It's been a pleasure." He smiled, as if to make amends, although God knew why.

He went out, stopping on the doorstep. Tom King had slipped out ahead of him. King waited with his hand deep in his trouser pocket. He said, without the smile this time: "I don't know where you're carrying your hardware, Barker, but I've got my hand on mine."

Barker sighed. "Would you believe it, King? I haven't even got a pistol. You can't buy so much as a second-hand cap-and-ball out here for less than thirty dollars."

"The price shouldn't hold you back. You had ten thousand dollars the last I knew about you. The beard almost fooled me, you know. If you hadn't stared, I'd have passed you over."

Barker hesitated. "Will you do me one favor? Put the manacles on at my hotel. The girl in there . . . you know how it is. A man talks himself up. The eastbound's tonight. We could get on it after dark."

King studied him. "All right. I'll only be taking you back

65

to El Paso, myself. I'm just out here on personal business. And who should I run into but you! I'll have to get some irons made up."

The hotel room looked out on the railroad tracks. Its walls were lined with fly-specked muslin. There was a china chamber pot, a cheap Mexican chiffonier, and a scarred commode. At the foot of the bed lay Barker's small cowhide trunk, bought for four dollars in New Orleans with money he had made on a wharf-side bull gang. Barker lay back on the bed with a sigh, linking his fingers under his head.

"Well, it's too bad," he stated. "I only caught up with Cosbee a week ago. Another week and I might have got somewhere with him."

"Cosbee's in town?" King asked. King had served as executive officer under Captain Cosbee before his retirement last fall. Thereafter, he had served briefly under Captain Swain Barker, until Barker's trial for embezzlement of battalion funds.

"He's going into the export business, the best I can tell." Barker yawned. "He's got himself three hundred horses. He'll trail them into Sonora to sell."

"Mexicans don't buy horses. They catch burros."

"Rebel armies buy them. A cavalry outfit under General Villalobos is holed up in the mountains."

King frowned at the tiny cloverleaf Colt on his palm. "Villalobos? Never heard of him."

"Lieutenant! Lieutenant!" Barker scolded. "I told you you'd never amount to a damn as a cavalryman. In fact, I've often wondered if that's why all the records that could have helped me disappeared. Villalobos . . . if you'd ever read your *Tactics* . . . was the Mexican sprout who almost whipped Scott in the Mexican war."

"That'd make him pretty old for an uprising."

"Fifty? If Villalobos can put together some cavalry, he'll take northern Mexico in six months."

"Maybe you should have gone to Mexico and sold yourself as an expert," King said. "Of course, your record might have traveled ahead of you. . . ."

Barker lifted the lid from the chamber pot and spat. "If I'd got away with the money the judge-advocate said I did, I'd have had enough cash to buy a pistol, and, if I'd had a pistol, you'd be lying on the floor in there with ladies brushing flies off your face."

"What did you expect to get by escaping?" King asked. "You knew we'd get you, sooner or later."

"I expected to come back, after I'd found Cosbee and got the truth out of him. That he'd paid off six thousand in gambling debts with money stolen from the battalion fund. Money raised by selling rifles and equipment in back alleys!"

King said doggedly: "You signed for every item you claimed he stole."

"Is that unusual? What officer hasn't stuck his successor for a few things he'd lost? Only it's unusual for the gun cases an officer counts to be found empty, later on. That's where he stuck me. And he'd juggled his books so they never did unscramble them."

King smiled and didn't bother disputing it. He was pleased with things as they were. He had liked Cosbee, had felt inferior with Barker, and hated him. His red, shiny skin creased about the eyes. He told Barker suddenly: "Take your belt off and put it on the bed. We'll see what we can do about keeping you on ice, this time."

Barker stood up. Then he found himself still holding the white, rose-patterned cover of the chamber pot. He leaned over to replace it, and at that instant his wrist snapped and the china cover flashed toward King's head. King raised a hand to ward it off.

Barker went into him. A big, dark, angry-eyed man, he smothered King with his bulk. The chair went over backward. Barker had King's gun and threw it aside. He heard the wind go out of King as they landed. Groaning, King tried to roll aside. With a chopping blow, the fugitive smashed at his jaw. His fist continued to move with the hurried motions of a man splitting kindling. In an instant the lieutenant was a sodden shape on the floor. His eyes were unfocused, his jaw hung loosely, and his tongue showed between his teeth. Blood spattered his face. It was hard for Swain Barker to realize a man could be wrecked so completely in so short a time. But men were not like armies, he reflected.

With a bandanna, he made a gag. With King's belt, he trussed him. He loaded him into the bed and under the covers. There was a quantity of money in the lieutenant's wallet and a few letters. One of the letters had been written a month ago by Alva Cosbee, from El Paso.

Barker looked at the letter a long time, and wondered just what part coincidence had played in King's happening into this little border village at this particular moment . . . ?

At sundown Barker left the hotel room. He told the desk clerk, with sheepish good humor: "My friend's drunk himself under every table in town. Let him sleep it off. I'm checking out. This is for the extra night. Get a boy to take him a cup of coffee about eleven tomorrow morning."

He carried his cowhide trunk on his shoulder. Standing in the windy evening street, he heard the bawling of a cow wanting to be milked, the distant *roop-roop* of a hound; two Mexicans passed him, chattering in Spanish. He saw a tattered rag of smoke from the supper fire at the horse camp, a quarter mile south of the railroad tracks, and set out for it.

The horses moved lazily under chain hobbles, tailed up to the streaming wind. A couple dozen Mexicans in dirty white shirts and pants squatted to windward of the fire, eating tortillas and beans. Another Mexican and the white men—two of them, and the girl—ate at a sort of officer's mess in the shelter of the leather-curtained wagon. As he trod across the wind-stripped gravel, they stopped eating to watch him. Barker was nervous, although it was unlikely Cosbee would know him. They had met only once, on the parade ground, when Cosbee surrendered his command, an hour before he left Fort Borden. Barker had grown the beard since then. He suspected that his eyes and mouth were a trifle harder than they had been; lean eating had fleshed him down.

Setting down his trunk, he stood in a half-slouching attitude. "I was told you're going into Mexico with the horses," he said.

"What's your name?" Cosbee snapped. He was a thick-featured man of fifty, heavy-limbed and powerful, with a big belly and a fist of a nose. He had been a drinker, a man's man; the marks were on him: grossness, a lazy amiability.

"Finch," Barker said. "I'm trying to get to Alamos. I can make a hand with the horses, for board and protection."

"What do you want protection from?" said the other American, a strapping, self-confident man with sandy hair, thick arms, and aggressive good looks. Barker knew something of him. His name was Guinn Sanders, a horse trader from El Paso. Barker had decided he must be Villalobos's liaison man.

"From the same things you will . . . Yaquis and soldiers."

"Got a horse?" Cosbee asked.

"No. I thought I could break one of yours as we went."

He let his eyes go to the girl, and there he saw a depth of

curiosity that disturbed him. She must have observed his sudden meeting with Tom King. She must have wondered thoroughly about it, being a woman and bored.

"You don't look like a horse breaker." Gay Cosbee smiled frankly at him.

"Don't I? Put me on one."

Cosbee reached a pottery cup from a box, poured it half full of whiskey, and raised a canvas water bag. "Use water, Finch?"

"No, nor in my coffee," Barker said. He took half of it in a long, savoring sip, sighed, and said: "That's not Mexican liquor, sir."

Cosbee liked the sir. He liked the compliment to his whiskey. He liked a man who could drink with him. All these reactions surfaced briefly in his eyes while he chuckled. "No, my friend, it's not Mexican. Came all the way from old Kaintuck'. It'll take the bottom out of an iron spoon, but it will leave velvet on a man's belly."

"Father," the girl murmured.

Cosbee arose. "Rudy, take care of the lady a while. Sanders and I are going to show Mister Finch some horses."

They walked toward the horse herd. Cosbee spoke vaguely of where they were going. "There's a big *hacendado* east of Hermosillo. He'll pay fifty *pesos* gold for every plug we bring him. But this isn't Arizona we're going into. What would you do if we were attacked?"

"Fight, I suppose."

"Ever serve in the Army?"

"No, sir. I'm a peaceable man."

"Well, if you're not too peaceable, I can use you. When do you want to leave?"

"No hurry."

"But you wouldn't mind leaving in a hurry? Say to-morrow?"

"Suits me." Barker shrugged.

They started back, a looseness in him, a kind of nervous fag. So he was going with his quarry. He was going to ride knee to knee with him!

"Of course," Sanders pointed out to Cosbee, "we can't pay him anything. Not for deadwood."

Their glances touched, and Barker saw Cosbee wink. "Maybe he isn't deadwood. Want to make a hundred *pesos*, Finch? For one night's work?"

Barker slowly shook his head. "I've never murdered a man before. I won't start now."

"I'm not asking you to. I'm going to ask you to raise a little hell in La Mojada, across the line. Sanders will go along. I'd like to be sure that the Federals are out chasing somebody instead of laying for me in a dry cañon. They headquarter in La Mojada. All I want is to have them tolled away about six hours' ride. I'll take care of the rest."

Suspicion flagged Barker. He looked into Cosbee's full, florid face. He saw its grossness and intemperance, but he did not observe craft. "If Sanders is willing to take the risk, I won't balk," he declared.

Cosbee offered his hand. Barker gripped it firmly. *The warm hand of friendship,* he thought. *Given by a thief and accepted by a liar.*

Barker was given a tin plate of boiled goat meat, beans, and papery tortillas. Cosbee went off to post night guards, swinging a lantern as he walked in the cold dusk, whistling "The Girl I Left Behind Me". Sanders departed to rustle saddle gear. Standing by the wagon, Barker heard the voice at his back.

"What happened to your friend?"

71

His head came around. A curtain had been rolled to half height and tied; Gay Cosbee sat on a cot. She was a faintly smiling shadow less than a yard from him. He saw the gleam of a brush moving through her hair.

"The man at the station? He's staying to prospect for business openings."

"Didn't you tell him there aren't any prospects here?"

"You can't tell some people anything. I knew him in Big Spring. As if he didn't have enough trouble, he wants to import some Mexican cattle."

"He looked familiar to me." Her voice was quietly speculative.

Barker's glance was long and steady. Alva Cosbee's daughter must have known King well. She would have recognized him at once.

"Someone Father and I knew in the Army," she went on. "Were you ever in the Army?"

"No, ma'am. I'm a confirmed and confounded civilian."

He could see a glint of white teeth. "You could fool anyone, the way you carry yourself."

Barker made a long grab for a change of subject. "You know, I wish you'd think over going to Mexico. A woman might not mind the cities, but the villages. . . ."

"I've been an Army girl for eighteen years. I can't see anything much worse than I've seen. We were being transferred to North Dakota, but about that time my father decided to retire."

"Dakota? That would be a pretty dismal spot, wouldn't it?"

". . . It *was* a dismal spot, Mister Finch. We spent four years there, once. The worst four years anyone ever spent. The worst part of the Dakotas. Then after two years in Louisiana, they decided to send him back."

"Well, if you're going to be stubborn, all I can do is wish you luck. You're blonde, and that will help. The men will trail you around like dogs. Good night, Miss Cosbee."

"Will you call me Gay? And will you be careful?"

"Why, Sanders and I are just going down the line for a beer. We'll meet you somewhere in a day or so, I think."

She held the ties of the curtain, her features sober. "I hope so, Mister Finch. But unless you're careful, you won't."

II

Sanders was a sober, careful companion, pushing steadily through the sagebrush toward a range of mountains visible in the gray-blue moonlight. The village of La Mojada lay off the toe of the Santa Marías. The trail to Villalobos's refuge passed, Sanders explained, a few miles west of La Mojada. The idea was to toll Captain Mendival's Federal detachment east of town.

"What do we do?" Barker asked. "Carry off the women?"

"Just the strategic ones. We'll find them in La Armida. Cosbee's making for El Refugio, in the mountains."

"He makes contact with Villalobos there?"

"What do you care?"

"Natural curiosity, friend."

Sanders turned his face forward. "No, he meets a liaison man there. They make a deal and he takes the horses on to Villalobos."

"He's a damned fool if he's going into rebel country without a deal already made."

"He is a damned fool," Sanders said, his voice easing. "Just put it like that . . . he's a damned fool. He's a good scout, probably a good soldier, but a kid of four could rob him blind. It'll be rough if he ever falls in with a sharper."

It sounded to Barker as though Sanders had given the proposition some thought. "This looks tight enough." He shrugged.

"Then you're a babe in the woods yourself. The general's buying horses, not Cosbee. If a rep of Cosbee's brought the horses, he'd pay off, and no questions asked."

Barker said: "Would he? Or would he take the horses and kiss the rep good bye?"

74

"Not if the rep had already made arrangements with him. I'm just speculating," Sanders said.

"So am I," said Barker, and they glanced at each other, and Sanders smiled faintly, and then asked carelessly: "Where you from, Finch?"

"Big Spring. I had a feed business that folded. A fellow was telling me there's money in bringing up Mexican *panocha* from the Yaqui River Valley and having it milled in Tucson. I thought I'd try it."

They came to a dim glow of lights. "La Mojada," said Sanders.

The town lay flatly on the desert. A few frazzled palm trees broke the flat-roofed silhouette. They came into the main street, a crooked avenue of mud-plastered fronts, the shops mean and dark, the windows of the homes barred slots in thick walls. A handful of men with serapes folded across their mouths lounged on the streets. *Furtive-looking shapes,* thought Barker, *but more than likely merely hungry, half-sick peasants.*

A cluster of two dozen horses was tied at racks at a corner intersection. There was a large *cantina* here with green-slotted doors. The windows were soaped, but through the doors they glimpsed a large saloon crowd and heard a brass horn and a thumping guitar.

"La Armida," said Sanders. "Mendival's unofficial head-quarters. We'll leave the horses in back."

Sanders led the way back. "Watch me," he said. "Just kind of follow along."

"What's the signal to get out?"

"You'll know. They'll give it."

La Armida had a fragrance of dust, beer, and perfume. It was more of a dance hall than a saloon, Barker observed. There was a small and filthy bar dispensing chiefly beer, a

75

number of cheap tables, and a small area where men and girls danced to the two-piece band. Most of the men were in uniform—gray, sleazy pants and shirts, and sandals. The girls' costumes ran to greens and purples, but to women-hungry men there would be little to complain of in garishness.

Sanders moved to a table, speaking right and left, as if he were known, but Barker noticed that only the girls responded. He saw them looking at him, and a pretty, thin girl at a table with six officers smiled at him. Instinct told him to ignore her; special orders caused him to remove his hat and bow slightly in her direction.

Sanders, taking a table, said: "Good start, Finch. That's Mendival with the sideburns."

Captain Mendival sat at the girl's right. He was a tidily built man of fifty, with coppery skin and gray sideburns and hair, an intelligent-looking Mexican with careful eyes. His right hand lay on the table; the girl continued to stroke it abstractedly with her hand while she smiled at Barker. Barker rubbed his beard with his knuckles and grinned as he slung into a chair.

A girl walked up and put a hand on Barker's shoulder. *"¿Bailamos?"* She was full-faced with nice eyes just touched with lines and a bosom loose under a magenta gown.

"Not yet," Barker said. "Who is the girl with Mendival?"

The girl glanced. "Delia," she said. "Maybe you would like Delia, eh?"

"Maybe. Tell her I'm the best dancer in El Paso."

"Tell her yourself."

A waiter came with beer. "Got whiskey?" Barker asked. "Take a shot to the lady, yonder."

The waiter carefully set the beer down. *"Señor,* our customs. . . ."

"I don't give a damn about your customs!" Barker said

sharply. "Take a whiskey to the lady." He thumped a silver dollar onto the tray.

The waiter went back to the bar, stony-faced, and then crossed to stop at the officers' table. They watched him set the whiskey before the girl, with a murmured word. Sanders grunted as she glanced up, surprised, her eyes sparkling. She touched the glass to her lips.

"She's a troublemaker, Finch," Sanders said. "If we weren't looking for trouble, she'd have brought it anyhow. I don't know whether she likes you, or just wants to see you killed. It'd come to the same thing."

Barker went to Mendival's table. Mendival rose, holding politeness like a glove, his dark Indian eyes puzzled. He looked into the face of the big, bearded American.

"What is it you want, *señor?* The girl is with me, you understand?"

"The dancers are for hire, aren't they?"

"Yes," Mendival said. "The girl is hired."

Barker looked down at her. She was smiling up, her eyes full of small, dark gleams, her features fine and cocoa-toned. She wore small gold crosses in her ears. Barker had never seen a woman so ready to make trouble as this one.

"Will you dance with me?" Barker asked.

She rose. She put a finger on Captain Mendival's lips, pouting. "Only five minutes, Papacito. *¿'Sta 'ueno?*"

Barker took her to the dance floor. The music was blatant, bright with Latin rhythms; it brought the girl, Delia, close to him; it slid her hand up between his shoulder blades to the back of his neck.

"You are brave, *señor,*" she said. "Do you know how brave you seem to be?"

"I'm lonesome." Barker sighed. "I know how lonesome."

He had the feeling, as they danced, that you could not

have slid a sheet of paper between them.

The room was smoky and full of people who minded their own business but still watched a certain insane member of a race known to be mad. Guinn Sanders was sitting with a girl now. She was trying to pull a ring off his finger and he was smilingly shaking his head.

The music stopped. The horn player shook spittle out of his horn. Drawing away, Delia let her palms measure his chest for a moment. *"¡Qué hombre!"* she breathed.

Barker laughed and, picking her up in his arms, carried her to his table. He set her down and shouted for a waiter. From the small, untidy bar, another girl drifted, leaving a rumpled and angry-eyed soldier. She sat beside Sanders and laid her arm across his shoulders.

Sanders grinned at Barker. "Show a five-dollar bill and we'd have to fight them off."

Barker watched the deserted soldier take a mouthful of *pulque*. He saw his lips gather like the mouth of a purse, and spoke sharply to Sanders: "Look out!"

The sour-smelling *pulque* left the soldier's lips and struck the back of the horse-buyer's head. Into his face came a swift and wild fury. The square face reddened. Sanders threw his chair aside and walked to the bar. The soldier, a lanky Indian youth with dusty black hair, made a groping motion at the top of his boot. Sanders's fist smashed into his face. The Mexican started to sag, with a hurt, puzzled look. Sanders's hand sustained him and he chopped down into his face with three slugging blows before he let him fall.

There was a dead instant, and then a beehive hum in the room. A voice shouted in broken English: "Damn' *yanqui* sons-of. . . ."

Mendival's voice snapped sharply: *"¡Silencio!"* He came to the Americans' table, where Barker sat, leaning back with an

78

arm around Delia, and Guinn Sanders stood rubbing his fist.

Mendival was pasty with anger. "*Señores,* leave this place! I am patient with you. I do not want trouble with Americans, when I have enough trouble with rebels. But I am not responsible for what happens if you do not leave this moment."

Regarding him in slow humor, Barker finally stood up. "Sure, we'll leave." He took the girl's hand. "But I'll take my little friend here."

"I think not."

As Barker shoved the whiskey bottle into his shirt and pulled the girl up, the captain threw off the flap of his holster. Barker swerved into him with a vicious overhand blow. The captain fell back into another Mexican. An apology rang in Barker's head: *Sorry,* compadre! *You're just a decent little Mexican on the wrong side of the fight.*

A revolver roared and a wheel of smoking lamps rocked against the ceiling. Barker overturned the table into the oncoming gang of officers and sprinted for the door. The first shot crashed as he went through the slotted portal after Sanders. It smashed plaster from the lintel and left a brown hole against the stained white.

They were outside in the street. At the rack, horses were stirring. They mounted. Sanders leveled his revolver and fired three shots into the Federals. Then he rode on. Angered, Barker followed him.

They took a side street west, doubled south, and slashed toward the foothills. As they left the crowded town blocks, the first signs of pursuit showed. A pair of horses ran on the white moonlight road, and guns flashed. They heard the slugs burn the air above their heads.

"That Mendival will make soldiers out of those farmers yet," Sanders said. He reined his horse into thick chaparral and Barker had to ride hard to keep within sound of him.

The night burned out. On a desolate ridge of the mountains, they rested their horses in a thicket of thorn brush. The foothills ranged away, beautiful in the clear amber dawn, and from a hillside they saw a thin rope of smoke rising. Mendival's horses had played out.

For the first time in eight hours, Swain Barker relaxed. "Now where?"

"El Refugio. It'll take us three days. Watch for game. We'll be eating bootlaces before we haul in."

On the third day they glimpsed the Yaqui River, winding gray-green down a distant valley. They descended into a rough side cañon. The earth was red, clothed in gray brush. The trees were small and leafless, with tufts of cotton bursting from pods. They came around a turn and heard faintly the sounds of children, dogs, a mule bell tinkling, and roosters crowing. The village was small, following the turns of the cañon. Huts clung to the hillsides and lay beside the stream.

Sanders indicated a cleared area. "Old Cosbee's beat us in."

Barker thought: *This is a hell of a long haul back with a prisoner.*

He saw the huge cactus-wand corral filled with horses, and the small white huts nearby. A few riding horses were tethered to the low branch of a tree; in the saddle Barker discerned the Cosbee girl's Dearborn. He was at once elated and troubled.

At a broken building of adobe, Guinn Sanders said: "We can get beer here before we go up."

There was warm foamy beer from a barrel, a pool table on the dirt floor.

"Cosbee pay you before we left?" Sanders asked.

80

"I was to collect here."

"See that you do. He'll have you in debt for more than he owes you before you catch your breath. Like as not, he's figgered a way to beat me out by now," he added grimly.

"Why did you go in with him then?" Barker casually chalked a cue.

"It was a quick turnover of these horses. But before we left, he was crying about wranglers' pay and smithing costs. I'm the one that has the in with Villalobos, anyhow. If I wanted to, I could push him out cold. If I had help, that is. . . ." The remark lay like a coin on the green cloth.

Barker watched him across his beer. The tough, blond man seemed so ruggedly simple, and he was so complex. He was straightforward in his conversation and circuitous in his thinking. He was too slippery for Barker to gamble on.

"All I want," Barker said plainly, "is a hundred *pesos,* and out of this."

Sanders spat on the dirt floor. "Don't blame you. But if you needed a thousand *pesos* the quick way, I could probably tell you where to get them. Well, we'd best get up yonder."

Outside the house, there were only Cosbee, his daughter, and the Mexican work boss, Arvizu. Cosbee was sunburned and hot, but greeted them jovially and called inside the house for drinks. Gay wore a cotton dress for coolness, and smilingly watched the men come from the hitch rack. Swain Barker sank down in the shade with his back against the house, smiling at the girl.

"You don's seem to be suffering."

"I told you it could be no worse than a frontier fort."

"What's the word from Villalobos?" Sanders asked.

Cosbee lit a cigar. "He's waiting for us. We'll bring him down to the village this afternoon."

"What's he coming down for?"

"To look at the horses. If he likes them, he'll tell us where to leave them and how we'll be paid."

"Will it be quick?" Gay asked.

"He wouldn't say. Maybe he'll take the horses tomorrow. Maybe next week. . . . Guinn, when you're through with that drink, we'll get going."

He went into the hut, coming back with his revolver belted on and a straw sombrero on his head. Gay reached her hand to him.

"When will you be back?"

"Tonight. What time, I don't know. It may be dawn."

Sanders sighed. "And I thought I'd sleep in a bed to-night."

He went to saddle a new mount. Apprehension entered Barker. He found himself in the position of wanting to warn a man he would as soon have killed that he might be in danger. He hesitated an instant before he told Cosbee: "I had a fall with your horse. I don't think he's hurt, but if you've got a pocket knife, we'll look at his hoof."

Cosbee went with him. Barker gripped the pony's foreleg between his knees. Cosbee squatted, grunting and red-faced. His features were swollen with heat and blood.

"Looks all right to me," Cosbee said curtly. "The frog's been bruised a little, but it's not bothering him."

"Something's bothering me, though."

The captain scowled. "This is a roundabout way of getting your money, Finch!"

"I just wanted to say, without naming any names, that Mexico is a great place to watch yourself."

Cosbee straightened. "I trust my partners. Is that the name you aren't naming?"

Barker shrugged. "Just be sure you're necessary to a deal before you go too far into it. Make yourself needed. You need

Sanders because he knows the country. I don't know why he needs you, if he does. If there's a pay-off, try to be the one who knows where it's going to be. They're your horses, aren't they?"

"For a man who just wanted to go along for the protection, you're doing a lot of worrying. You can ride on if you like."

Barker laughed softly and straightened. "I always was a worrier. Excuse me. I'll stick around a day or two to rest up."

"All right. While you're at it, keep an eye on my daughter tonight, without going to too much trouble about it."

Darkness came slowly, with supper smokes and a lessening of village noises. Strings of burros came in with bristling loads of firewood. Cosbee and Sanders departed. After dinner, Barker told Gay: "I'll throw myself on your hospitality for another couple of days before I leave."

"I wish you'd do something for me before you go. Shave off your beard."

"Why is it every woman wants to know what a bearded man would look like shaven, and a shaven man would look like with a beard?" Chuckling, he started away, but she called his name softly. The dusky light nearly obscured her features, but he saw she was serious, and he heard a warning in his mind: *Look out! She's the kind who can trap a man before he knows it.*

"You'd have to be much more lonesome than you are to seek my company, wouldn't you?" she said.

He was caught off balance.

She went on. "I wouldn't chase a man for the world. But I don't understand why you should dodge every time you see me. I thought you'd run, that day in the railroad restaurant. It was a small enough town that the plainest of women could expect to have a man's arm offered her now and then. And this one is smaller still. What's wrong with me?"

"Nothing is wrong with you." He smiled. "In Cabrito, I didn't have the money to court a girl. Here . . . well, I'm in a gamble, Gay. I don't know how I'll come out. Maybe I'll be a lot better off than I am. Maybe worse. It's something I can't talk about without spoiling."

She regarded him quietly. "I didn't mean to embarrass you, but I wanted to know. In the future," she said, "we'll just assume that we're business acquaintances."

On a sudden impulse he moved toward her. "I wouldn't want to go that far," he said. He put a finger under her chin and bent to kiss her, and a sudden tightness gripped his throat. He started to put his arms about her, but stopped with his hands gripping her shoulders. They were small in his grasp, shrinking from him, and he held her and pressed his mouth hard upon hers. Then he let her go, abashed. His hands hung, weighted.

She left the chair, seeming uncertain whether to be angry or not. "If that was impulse," she said, "it was poorly timed. If it was pity . . . you'll be the first man I ever really hated."

Barker shook his head. "If I wanted to pity someone, I'd pity myself. . . ."

Darkness filled the cañon. Coyotes yapped on the ridges; a jaguar screamed. Everything predatory was hunting tonight, and Barker came to a decision. Things were bad enough without falling in love. Cosbee would not escape by virtue of having a pretty daughter. He might plan to lie around here for weeks, whereas Barker must move quickly.

The women finished in the kitchen and trudged up the road. There was no light in the Dearborn, no lamp in the hut. Barker found matches and entered Cosbee's room. He struck a match. The room was like a cell. Patches of whitewash clung to the walls. There was a crucifix over a broken wooden

cot, and a straw rug on the floor. Cosbee's large suitcase lay
on the cot.

Barker lighted a candle and opened the bag, which was
stuffed with soiled linen. He turned up a crusted shaving
mug, cans of leather dressing, and five quart bottles of liquor.
There was a canvas-covered company funds book. The first
date in it was only a month old. **Purchase of fifty saddle
horses. . . .** He threw it aside. Cosbee had merely brought
the book along from the fort for his own use. There was no
correspondence, no other ledgers.

As a last resort, he raised the straw pallet and felt under it.
He discovered rawhide springs and nothing else. He was
straightening when Gay's voice said quietly: "If there's anything you can't find, perhaps I can help you."

They faced each other across the dim room—the bearded,
staring man, and the haughty girl in night sacque and robe.

Barker made a blind plunge. "I'm sorry, Gay. But I'm not
a thief. I was looking for the money your father owes me. I
heard that he planned to hold me up on it."

Gay walked straight to him, gazing into his eyes. "You
looked so much better in uniform, Captain Barker, and
without a beard . . . and the look of a thief in your eyes. Why
have you followed us?"

III

Barker sat on the bed. The girl stood looking down at him. *She knows everything about me,* he thought. *But how much does she know about her father?*

"The beard would never have fooled anyone who'd really looked at you," Gay told him. "I suspected from the first. Why did you follow us?" she repeated.

"Well, I had to follow someone. I'm an escaped criminal, Miss Cosbee. I was getting on the train for prison when I broke loose. I holed up until I could grow the beard, made a few dollars, and moved west. Then I ran into your father. I . . . I don't know why I thought he might be able to help me."

"You're still lying."

"I'm trying to tell a story that will please you. What do you know about me?"

"Just what Lieutenant King wrote us. That you'd stolen government funds. You got twenty-five years, didn't you?"

"Fifty. That was doubled when I escaped."

She appeared genuinely troubled, almost angry. "I can't understand the things men do! You were making good money. You had respect and position. Why should you do it?"

"Would you believe me if I told you I didn't?"

"I'd like to. But who else could have?"

"I'm trying to find out," he told her. "That's why I followed your father. He knows the Army. He might be able to give me something to work on."

She bit her lip. "Swain, if you were telling the truth, you'd have talked to my father before he led you two hundred miles from the States."

86

He shook his head. "In the States, he'd have been bound to turn me over. Here, he couldn't turn me over if he wanted to."

Horses came suddenly from a cañon trail into hearing. Barker strode to the door but Gay shook her head. "You don't have to run. If you aren't ready to talk to him, I'll give you until tomorrow night. Because I have an old-fashioned idea that I know the truth when I hear it. . . ."

When Cosbee pulled in with six other horsemen, Barker was standing before the hut. Gay had hurried back to the wagon. Cosbee's face, in the vague light, was tired and sweat-streaked. Barker scanned the wooden features of Guinn Sanders, the stolid faces of the Mexicans.

One of the Mexicans spoke in a low, hard tone. Cosbee said wearily: "He's all right. Just a herder of mine. You've got this village posted anyway, haven't you?"

The Mexican said: "In this business, you eat suspicion with your meat. Where are the horses?"

Two riders held the mounts while lanterns were lighted. Cosbee introduced Barker gruffly. "Finch, I think you know who this is," he told Barker.

Villalobos was tall, heavy in the shoulders, a sauntering, easy-moving man in a big straw sombrero and a black suit that was too tight for him. He wore a thick iron-gray mustache. He looked critically at Barker with his dark eyes, then surprised him by shaking his hand.

"I take pleasure to know you," he said. It was like an assayer's report, and Swain was pleased.

They walked up to the corral with six lanterns. Sanders took charge, pointing out this horse and that in the beam of a bull's-eye lantern. "Half-blood thoroughbred, General. That gray, now. . . ."

Cosbee interrupted. "You may be able to tell him something about women, Sanders, but not about horses. He knows they're all Army trained. The rest he can see for himself."

Barker's eyes sharpened. Army trained? But certainly not of an age to be Army discarded. So what were they doing here?

The same thought was in Villalobos's mind. "I want no trouble with your government, *amigos,*" he said. "You have bills on these horses?"

Sanders said easily: "Every last one. The Army's choosy in peacetime. Look at the brand under the US. I&C . . . inspected and condemned. Condemned for a scar here, a gall there. But sound."

"At night," one of the Mexicans said, "all horses are sound."

"You'll see them in your own corral," said Cosbee. "You don't pay until they're delivered."

Villalobos moved around the cactus-wand corral, inspecting the nervous animals. He came back. "*Bueno.* Bring them day after tomorrow. I tell you then where is the money."

Cosbee passed a bottle around. Finally Villalobos said briskly: "*Pasado mañana.* My friend, I would like to buy something else from you," he added.

"Guns? Too risky."

"Yourself. I could pay you little now. But a year from now I could give you a ranch, a plantation, a mine. I have the men, *capitán,* but not the officers. You could train for me twenty officers a month."

Cosbee's eyes were hungry for it. But then he seemed to look into himself bitterly and see that, while he had the knowledge, he no longer had the strength of a line officer. "I'd like it, but . . . there's my daughter, you know. I wish I could."

Villalobos smiled. "If you change your mind, *capitán,* you can always find me." He gave them a hand salute and went to his horse.

Cosbee spent the morning tending the horses. Barker assisted him. He had got into a new tack and his mind wouldn't leave it. "Know anything about cavalry fighting, Finch? That man Villalobos will take Mexico if he gets half a chance. And here he's been half his life . . . buried. A farmer. A ranch foreman. And finally a tortilla revolutionist." Barker saw his face stirring with sour memories. "Not that he'd have fared any differently in the States. Me, a captain! I was a brevet colonel in the war. I schemed some of the tactics they fight by now. But they stick me away . . . hand me that dandy brush," he said tartly.

He told Barker how shrewd he'd been. He said the Army was the best job in the world. He said it was the worst. He frowned at his daughter, hanging clothes on a line, and said if he didn't have responsibilities. . . .

They were waiting, now, for the following dawn, when the horses would be trailed out. And this was Barker's last chance.

While the others slept in the hot afternoon, he came to his decision. He reckoned how much food he must secure in the village; where he could get mounts. He had no plan beyond this: to kidnap Cosbee tonight and get as far north as possible before he was missed.

He thought of Gay, and began to weaken. Then his mind swerved back to his last hours in Cabrito—to the suffocating pressure of knowing he might be taken at any time. He recalled the grim hour with Tom King in the hotel room, when he had been ready to risk his life to avoid going back. And he would not go back now, not without Cosbee.

He made an excuse to go into the village. He found a windowless shack on the steep, rutted street where groceries were sold. A horse went by and the proprietor glanced out curiously, and went back to packing Barker's purchases in rawhide sacks. Barker inquired the road to the first large town. The town was Sahuaripa, big enough to absorb them while any possible search burned out. He paid for the food and procured three burros. He left them near the fork of the Sahuaripa road, with a Mexican boy to tend them.

At sundown he walked back to the horse camp. The herd was quiet, pulling at trusses of hay in the corral; herders carried wooden buckets of water to the troughs.

A horse with a strange brand and an American saddle stood behind the shack. He stared at it. Cosbee's voice came from the interior. "Finch? Come in here."

Barker stepped in and saw the captain propped by one elbow on the cot. Gay was watching with tight, frightened features. He saw her mouth open suddenly and heard her cry out, but it was too late to dodge the blow that slashed at him from behind. He stumbled forward. . . .

He came to consciousness sitting in a chair with his arms tied behind him. He brought his head up groggily and saw Sanders sitting on the bed with a cigarette in his mouth, not looking at him. Chewing a black cigar, Alva Cosbee stood at the door, gazing out. The man who had struck him, Tom King, was coming from the bed with a pitcher of water. He was unshaven, dirty, and looked half crazy. The scars of the beating Barker had given him in Cabrito were still scabbed. One eye was discolored, and a gap showed in his teeth as he grinned at Barker. He threw the water in his face.

"You never thought you'd see me again, did you?"

Barker started to say something, but King slapped him

90

with the back of his hand. Cosbee was pushing King back with one hand, the red-faced, horsy lieutenant resisting.

"That's conduct unbecoming an officer, Lieutenant," said Cosbee. "You had your shot at him."

Someone in gray came forward. It was Gay. She looked at him without expression. She said nothing, but began to cut the rawhide cord. King came forward angrily but Gay said: "There are three of you, Lieutenant. You should be able to handle him."

King ill-temperedly stood back. Barker felt the dry humor of Cosbee's glance on him. Cosbee grinned. "You know, you're a damn' good liar. All this time I thought you were down here on business. What did you mean to do to me?"

"Whatever I had to, to get a written confession."

King's eyes were quick and uneasy. "Gay, you don't have to listen to this. You'd better go along, if I know this man's filthy mouth."

Cosbee wearily waved his hand. "Relax, Tom. This is Mexico. I think she's suspected for weeks who the real renegades were."

King had the girl's arm in his grasp and was taking her to the door. "Gay, I want you to go on. Wait in your wagon until we decide what to do with him."

Cosbee chuckled. "Maybe I'll have to decide what to do with you. I still don't know why you hightailed after me as soon as he'd escaped."

"To recover him, of course. I got leave to do it. Good Lord, the trouble I've been to following him, and now. . . ."

Sanders drew on his cigarette, watched, and said nothing.

King was still trying to edge the girl to the door. She suddenly struck his hand off her arm. "Will you please leave me alone, Lieutenant? Father, I want to know all about this."

Cosbee poured himself a drink. He said: "Prepare yourself

for something, then. The truth sometimes stings. It's the old story of a man getting sore at the Army, drinking too much and losing so much to the cardsharps . . . all at once. I owed six thousand dollars in New Orleans when I got wind that I was to be transferred to North Dakota. I'd be damned if I'd fight Indians in the snow for anybody, not a second time. And I couldn't leave without paying my gambling debts."

"So you took the money, sold rifles, and stuck me for the bill." There was a feeling of ease in Barker, a sudden clarification.

"That's right, Captain. I stuck you for the bill."

King's face was sallow. He was staring at the captain with rising fury.

"*We* stuck you, I should say," Cosbee added. "I couldn't have done it alone. Somebody had to check my books and attest to them. That was Lieutenant King. Somebody had to keep you from looking into the empty rifle cases. That was him, too. He only got a third, though, because the idea was mine."

King's words were slow and deep-pitched. "This is the grandest piece of madman's strategy I've ever witnessed. What is it, conscience or insanity, Captain?"

"Conscience. It's been there all the time . . . dormant. I planned from the start to write a confession . . . not mentioning your part in it, of course . . . and send it to the War Department. But not until I was out of reach and set up with some cash. That's now."

"Unfortunately," King said thinly, "I want to stay on the right side of the border. Do you think I can trust this man to protect me, with his ideas of persecution?"

"They weren't exactly ideas," Gay said. "They look pretty real to me."

Her father stopped her at the door. "Listen, girl. Don't

pass judgment until you've been in the same spot. I was always going to bail Barker out of it. I was even going to return the money, sooner or later."

She let him finish speaking. Then she went outside. Guinn Sanders arose, dropping his cigarette, and rubbing it out with his boot. "Where does this put me?"

"Why should it put you anywhere? We collect tomorrow and split. King gets the hell back. Or stays here. I don't care what he does. His deal and my part in it were finished a long time ago."

"What about me?" Barker said.

Cosbee winked. "You don't think I'm going to have you around putting bullets in my back! I'm giving you the confession and a couple of hundred dollars. You'll have your freedom back. But you're leaving tomorrow."

"All right." Barker stood up. "You've forgotten somebody, haven't you?"

"Gay? No. Will you do something for me, Captain? Take her to the coast with you. Put her on a boat for Frisco. We've got relatives there. I'm staying, you see."

Sanders chuckled. "Going to be a tortilla general, eh? Well, good luck. But you'll find the chili hot, the beer warm, and the *señoritas* cold."

He went out, and Tom King suddenly strode after him. He was at the door when Barker's hand caught him. Barker swung him against the wall and smashed his fist into King's mouth. King staggered, and he struck him again, caught him, and loaded him out the door.

Guinn Sanders was waiting. He laughed. "You've got it in for lieutenants, haven't you?"

"Just his kind of lieutenant." Barker observed Sanders give the man a hand to his own tent in the trees.

He stood there several moments, emotions swirling in

93

him. It had been too suddenly resolved to be believable. Until he had Cosbee's written confession in his hand it still would not be believable. With a sudden shrug, Barker pulled himself together and went back to check on Cosbee.

Cosbee lay in his room in the hut and drank whiskey. He would be stupidly drunk by bedtime. Someone left the camp and walked up the road. Barker watched a moment, belted on his Colt, and followed.

He caught up with the girl. Her features were tight, as if locking back her emotions. "You aren't proud," she said, "to be following the daughter of a man who betrayed you."

"I'm too proud to have you on my conscience. I don't hold it against him, Gay. A week ago, I'd have killed him to clear myself. Now I've filled in the rest of the picture. He didn't have to say what he did. He could have helped King take me back. Men stay quiet in Leavenworth."

They walked on. Candles burned behind wedge-like windows; children fussed in stuffy sleeping rooms; a dog yapped at them behind a hedge of cactus. She stopped and faced him.

"I'm ashamed," she said. "Ashamed of him and myself."

"Liquor and gambling are a man's own business," Barker said gently. "He asked me to take you back, Gay. To put you on a boat for San Francisco. We'll take a guide along as a chaperone until we can get a coach."

"When?"

"Tomorrow, sometime. He'll have to get the money first, I suppose."

"A sorry kind of money to go home on," she said.

Barker's hands took hers; they slipped up her arms to her shoulders and gripped them. "Would you go back on my money?"

She searched his face; she bit her lip and shook her head.

94

"All this time you've known about us . . . and you can ask me that!"

"I have asked you," he said, "but you haven't answered."

"And I can't, Swain. I haven't even got used to my father being an embezzler. I need to sleep for three days and not think at all, and then think straight."

They started back. "Three days is a long time. We'll be at the coast, by then."

"Then will you wait until we're at the coast?"

IV

Someone was still in the yard when he moved back to his lean-to. The man slouched against a tree, a cigarette in his mouth. Barker stopped, his hand was on the brass back strap of his Colt. Sanders spoke softly from the shadow pool of the tree.

"Walk easy, Barker. Live long."

"I'm walking easy."

"Good. Keep on walking that way."

Barker's dislike for the man was gathering; his conviction was that his amiability was a cloak for ruthlessness.

"I got this far without advice," he said.

"That's why I was figuring tonight. You came a long way against a stacked deck."

"Shall I sleep on that?"

"Sleep on how many people would be ahead if you died in your blankets?"

"I'd sleep better on how many men would profit by seeing you dead. Cosbee, for instance."

Sanders chuckled. "That's chancy figuring. Look where he'd be if you were out of it. He could go back clean. So could King. I've been thinking he might get around to that, with King to crowd him into it. I'm trying to make up my mind what to do about him. I thought I might take you in as a partner, Barker."

"A silent one?"

"Not so silent. I took a fancy to you in La Mojada that night. I'm down here every few weeks, you know, on some deal or other. Why not tie up with me for a while? A year with me and you'd never do another lick of work. It would have to start tomorrow, though. Talking Cosbee out of his share . . . one way or another."

"You talk plainer all the time," Barker said.

"Suppose you talk plain for a minute, then."

Barker snapped: "I'll talk plain. If there's an honest idea in your head, it'd be snubbed by the others. And just to see that Cosbee gets a square shake, I'll go along in the morning."

Sanders spat on the ground. He looked at Barker steadily. "You talk more like a preacher all the time." He turned and started away.

An instant later he pivoted. Barker had misfigured the man. He had not realized that Sanders was making his last offer. Sanders's Colt glinted in the darkness.

"Keep your mouth shut," he said. "Pull off your gun belt."

Barker looked at him. "You're a pig, Sanders. A damned pig." He pulled the belt off.

Sanders took it and backed away. "Your horse is saddled. We're pulling out."

Barker measured him, but Sanders kept his distance. They left camp, cutting from the village toward the Yaqui River. The cañon bottom sprawled out as they approached the river. There was a musty smell of dead river growth. The sky was black, punctured with stars. The horses made small, scuffing sounds on the rocky trail, and Barker looked for a thicket, a tree, a boulder to give him shelter. Sanders's pony crowded his own.

Then they were in a deep chaparral sloughing off into the Yaqui, silent beneath low cliffs. Now Swain knew where they were heading. Rivers were traditional for this kind of work.

The trail was an ox road winding toward a village down the river. It was hedged deeply by thorn bushes chopped back with machetes. In the air was a scent of blossoms and moisture. Suddenly Barker halted, staring to the right.

"Listen," he said.

Sanders was fooled for an instant; an instant was all Swain wanted.

When Sanders's head jerked back, Barker's saddle was empty. Sanders began firing into the brush, viciously shouting after him. He crowded his pony into the thicket, but it backed out. He swung down, yanking a rifle from its scabbard.

Barker, twenty feet in the thicket, blood running from a scratch on his forehead, stopped. Insects clicked and rattled in the brush. He heard the horses and Sanders's low, cursing voice. He remained still until the horse buyer fired into the thicket once more. With the rocking thunder of the shot about him, he piled toward the river. He made another thirty feet before he halted.

Now he heard Sanders telling him what he would do to him. He thought of waiting until Sanders got close enough to jump, but Sanders was a savage adversary, and he was armed. Barker moved ahead. Again the gun roared, the bullet slashing through dry branches above Barker's head.

Suddenly Barker stumbled; something had struck his feet. He heard an angry grunting, and saw the flash of a tusk. He lay ready for battle, but the wild pig lunged away. The crashing was a mighty and a blessed thing, and Barker listened to the banging of the gun and was happy. The crashing continued, the shooting went on; he could hear Guinn Sanders struggling after the *jabalí*.

Barker put one arm across his face and began to run. He twisted, shoved, crawled. He moved until the brush thinned. Then he halted. A shot came distantly, striking through the thicket fifty yards to his left. He reached the bank of the river and slid down the red sand to the stream. He pulled off his trousers and boots, left them on the sand, and entered the water. Lying on his back, he floated downstream. He wondered whether the stories he had heard about man-eating cat-fish in the Yaqui were true.

The stars rocked above him. The water was kind to his cuts, which numbered something under a thousand, he thought. As he writhed himself gently across a sandbar, he saw a silhouette on the riverbank. Then it was gone. He let himself drift ashore and lay there, listening to the croaking of frogs.

It was noon when he returned to the horse camp. He walked in from the north, after swinging wide, in case Sanders had the road under watch. His hands and face were slashed by thorns; his clothes were thick with dried red mud, and he felt the watchful eyes of the villagers as he moved on to the camp.

He came up through the trees, and halted. Where the Dearborn wagon had stood, there was a rectangular weedy space in the trampled ground. The horses were gone. Barker felt a wrench of terror.

He turned and ran back to the tiny store. The proprietor came sleepily from a back room, his hair rumpled. *"¿Mande?"*

Barker tried to talk with his hands. *"Los . . . los hombres de caballo . . .* the mustangers . . . where are they?"

"Se fueron, señor. They are leaving at break of day. *Por los . . .* by the mountains, *sí."*

"The girl?"

"By herself, in the wagon, on the road to Sahuaripa. With a driver, *sí."*

Barker turned and stared out the door. Suddenly he drove his fist against his palm. "Is there a gun . . . *una pistola* . . . for sale?"

The man smiled. "Alfredo, the blacksmith, has a musket

he made when the *bandidos* were here."

Barker stepped into the road and hurried to the Sahuaripa fork, where he had left his burros. The boy was still with them, asleep in the shade. Barker paid him off, mounted one, and turned the rest loose. He had a moment of being drawn toward the lonely tire ruts toward Sahuaripa. But when he rode, it was northeast, up the trampled horse trail into the mountains.

In about two hours he heard horsemen approaching. He pulled into the brush. But they were all Mexicans, gossiping loudly as they came. Barker rode into the trail. They were the wranglers of Cosbee's herd.

"The *capitán*," he said. "Where is he?"

"At the corral. Four, five kilometer, *señor. Mas atrás.*"

"And Sanders and King?"

"With him."

"Cosbee was all right . . . not sick or hurt?"

The Mexicans hoarded a private joke. "*Borracho, señor.* Big dronk."

They rode on.

The trail pierced rugged hill country tangled with brush. There seemed nothing living in this dry jungle but himself and a million birds—buzzards and dipping horse sparrows, and hard-shelled insects that glittered in the air. The trail turned up a dry cañon toward a notch, and abruptly he was on the edge of a bowl almost cleared of brush, with a stone wall to form a giant corral. It looked like a forgotten cornfield. There were a few tall trees at the far end, where the clearing ran into a high pass. He saw a flash of white cloth. He sat perfectly still on his burro. Then he rode ahead.

The white was a man's shirt. It was Alva Cosbee, lying in the shade with one hand on his belly and the other arm sprawled out. Cosbee had been shot twice. His left shoulder was sodden with blood; his jaw was nearly shot away. He was dying. Barker squatted beside him and brushed flies from his face.

"Captain," he said. "It's Barker."

Cosbee looked at him, breathing heavily. His lips moved. "Barker," he said, trying to fit it into his mind. Then he grunted. "Get them for me, Barker! Kick their damn'. . . ." His head rolled, and Barker got a palm under it to hold it steady. With his free hand, he commenced unbuckling Cosbee's gun belt.

"Was it Sanders or Villalobos?"

"Sanders and King. The Mexican paid off. It was buried in the corral. We sent the men back." He touched his mouth. "Whiskey."

Barker found a bottle in a saddlebag on Cosbee's horse, grazing not far off. But Cosbee drank only a little, letting most of it run out of his mouth. "Hell of a place to die," he said. "I was in every battle worth a damn in the war. But I had to be bushwhacked by a couple of cowardly Judases."

"Which way would they go?"

Cosbee roused suddenly. He was trying to get up, but Barker eased him back. "The dirty swine!" he panted. "Go after them, mister. Kill them. Spit in their faces! They've gone after Gay. Think they could leave her running around loose, after this?"

Barker left him again and brought the water bag from his horse. He placed it beside his hand. "This will get you through. I'll send some men up to bring you back."

Cosbee, eyes closed, nodded. "Listen, Barker. I was a combat soldier. A line officer. If you're the same kind, get out. You'll rot away in a peacetime Army. And when you get a chance to get back into it . . . then your damned brain's gone and you know you'd never be able to cut it. That confession . . . I didn't get it written. Gay will tell them. Maybe King's got papers."

When Barker had finished saddling the horse, the captain was still talking, but it was in a strong, authoritative voice, and he was saying: "No! Bring up the artillery first! Then we'll go in on the flank. . . ."

For two hours the trail was easy to follow. They had gone over the hump into the valley of the Yaqui. There were a hundred small trails, a dozen tiny villages, and he went as hastily as he dared. The villagers were Indians, peaceable but suspicious. He would ask for a cup of water, inquire by signs after Sanders and Tom King, and ride on. He reached the wide, lonely bottoms of the river. He passed the El Refugio crossing, where he had eluded Sanders. The sun was sagging above the hills. Barker's impulse was to whip the horse on until it dropped, to reach Sanders or the wagon before dark, because it was after dark that Sanders's kind of strategy came to flower. Yet he watered the horse meagerly and let it rest a few moments before he rode ahead. He was convinced now that the Sahuaripa road would strike the river and follow it, that this had been part of Sanders's strategy from the moment he put Gay's wagon onto it. The whole thing made a straight line for him after the act of murdering Cosbee.

A moment later he saw a curl of smoke twisting up through the windless amber air. Someone was camped under the bluffs beside the river. He got the horse off the road and onto the sand and let it single-foot. He held Cosbee's snub cavalry carbine ready. Below him the river swerved behind a tawny cliff. Small islands of trees stood in the *bosque;* deltas of grass patterned the water. On one of these he discerned a man standing with two grazing horses.

He knew the lean shape of Tom King.

Barker dismounted and left the pony behind a motte of brush. He hung his hat on the saddle horn and went down the stream, the carbine balanced in his hands. The smoke rose from the right, fifty yards from King. King's head turned and he discovered Barker. He reached for his revolver and shouted toward the camp.

"Sanders! Someone coming." Then he faced Barker and bawled: "Who is it? *¿Quién es?*"

Barker paced on, and did not answer. He was in the shadow of the bluff; apparently King wasn't sure whether it was he or not. Now he could see the leather-curtained wagon in the brush. Gay hurried from it. Then she stood very still. "Father?" she called. "Swain?"

King exclaimed something and raised the revolver. He was a crack pistol shot; Barker recalled that from Army days. He sprawled forward. The Colt flashed and the bullet ripped a trough in the sand beyond him. The report was like a blow in the face. He heard Gay's scream and saw Sanders lunge from the camp with a rifle, working the bolt as he ran.

Barker perched King's lean silhouette on the bead of the carbine. King was standing sidewise to make a smaller target; he was squeezing a pistol-range bead on the man lying on the sand. Barker saw his face, filled with hurry but with satisfaction that this moment had come.

It seemed to Barker that the hammer would never drop. The instant was frozen: King, string straight on the sights, taking careful aim, Sanders on one knee, rifle butt to shoulder. The carbine bucked. King was obscured by a dirty fog of powder smoke. Levering up another shell, Barker saw him stumbling back. He saw him drop his revolver and go into a twisting fall.

Sanders's gun roared and there was an explosion beside

Barker's head. He heard the smashing of the wet sand and was struck savagely in the neck. For an instant he was paralyzed. His head sagged into the breech of the rifle.

He came to his knees, his neck and shoulder bloody, sand crusting his face. Seeing him rise, Sanders halted and snapped the gun up. There was too little time for Barker to raise his rifle. He fired the carbine like a pistol. It slammed his arm back, but Sanders stopped cold. He went back and lunged forward again, trying to fire the gun. He cursed Barker and rammed a shot over his head. He tried to operate the bolt of the gun; the hot shell flashed out, but he could not force a new one in. He went heavily to his knees and reached a hand forward to break his fall. Then he was down with his face crushed against the sand. . . .

An Army girl, Gay did not flinch from blood and dirt. She had bluestone in a medicine kit, and used it to cauterize the bloody trough across Barker's neck. She smiled at his complaining and fixed a bandage, and afterward they sat in the back of the wagon while the Mexican driver took them on to a village. After a while he put his arm around her.

"They say Mexico is hard on women and burros," he said. "I guess it's so."

"It's been hard," she admitted. "It won't be any longer. Everything that could happen has happened."

He had told her about her father, but it had been less than the shock of knowing how he had left the Army. It was all a dark picture in her mind she would never look at.

He brought her closer to him. "No," he said. "Not everything. There'll be a judge at one of these towns. That's the last thing that's going to happen. That's what we'll remember, when we want to remember something."

The Phantom Bandit

Greer always brought a man from the stage station with him to carry the sacks back to the office. He would come to Boles's wicket and ask bluntly: "Ready?"

Boles would admit the men through a door in the rear and bring the money from the vault. That Saturday in July there was an extra sack. Greer's mine holdings at Sonora were growing; every month a little more gold went up the hill to pay the men for digging it out.

Boles remembered how he had transferred the bags from the cart to the guard's arms that morning. "Two thousand, three thousand, and four thousand, Mister Greer!"

Greer's mouth was stern. "Keep your voice down." He glanced around. He was a self-important man with a torso like a pear, his vest tracing the rise of his stomach, his frock coat open. "It's enough to have to carry this through the streets, without shouting our wares."

Boles, practiced in servility, said: "Sorry, sir. We grow so accustomed to handling money. . . ."

"That you don't care whether the depositor loses it or not. Well, be careful, or you may not be handling much more of mine."

After the men left, Boles carefully recorded the transaction and returned to his wicket. Greer was laughable, with his clumsy, sophomoric secretiveness. You had only to observe him a few Saturdays and you knew whether the money was going out that afternoon or the following. He was always in a rush when it was going the same day. Otherwise, he stopped for a cigar with Mr. Pangborn, the manager.

The money, therefore, would be in the Wells Fargo box this afternoon when the stagecoach rolled out of San Francisco. That fact, however, did not particularly interest Boles. At least, not ir˞ ˞ediately. . . .

Saturday afternoons followed a pattern. The possibilities of variety were small for a forty-year-old bachelor making $16 a week. Boles took home a pail of steam beer, a quarter pound of Swiss cheese, and a loaf of Italian bread. In his small room overlooking the ferry slips he took off his coat, shirt, and shoes. He made his sandwiches. He sliced them diagonally and laid them on a plate, and with his first sudsy glass of beer he carried the sandwiches to an armchair by the window, where the curtains stirred gently in the breeze. On the way, he saw himself in the mirror.

God! he thought. He was beginning to look like the creatures you saw sitting on their porches along Sansome Street Sunday afternoons. He was not a figure to inspire romance in any maiden's heart, or respect in his own. He was getting a belly, although his chest looked like a birdcage. His arms, coming out of the short sleeves of his undershirt, were scrawny. His hair was departing, and his eyes were gloomy, defeated.

I'm rotting, he thought. *Gangrene of the soul.*

It was a disease that came from handling too much money for too long—other people's money. Ten years of standing behind a wicket and giving other men gold for paper, and writing figures in their passbooks in return for gold left in the trust of the bank. Now he was assistant teller, taking home each Saturday afternoon about what Charles Greer spent on cigars in two weeks.

For $16 in San Francisco in 1878 you could live in a decent boarding house like Mrs. Barker's and buy a dignified black suit every year. Decency and dignity, the earmark and brand of his trade. Boles, beyond a liking for steam beer, had no vices, unless you would call poetry a vice. He read Villon, the Brownings, Dante, and, as he read, his pale, confined soul sought to burst out of its cell. Sometimes he would seize pencil and paper and write poetry, which revealed, like cracks in a furnace, his hidden fire of longings. But it was very bad poetry, and Boles had the good sense to destroy it.

Yet, some quality in him, unused, rankled unbearably. Each man inherited a certain amount of combustible material, he thought. He could burn it, warm himself at the glow, or he could let it lie like wet kindling within him. Boles doubted that he could get even a good spark out of his.

But the same afternoon it began to smolder. All afternoon he sat at the window, watching the ferryboats turn white shavings from the blue surface of the bay. The salt air went into his lungs, the free ocean air, and it was good. The smells of a busy harbor, the noise and rush of traffic, came to him, and he digested them. When dusk came, he wore the shining armor of resolution.

He was thinking of Charles Greer and his $4,000. He kept thinking about it all week. By the end of the week he had a plan. He also had a second-hand shotgun that he kept hidden in a corner of his closet. The story of Charles E. Boles from then on can be followed from the San Francisco newspapers of the day. Boles was as able a little man as he was determined, and his story was written in headlines. By the next Saturday, his blueprint was ready for the carpenter.

Greer was as tense as usual when he came for the payroll money. He scowled as Boles counted it out, but this time the teller anticipated the complaint.

"I don't know why you worry so, Mister Greer. You've never lost a gold shipment, have you?"

"No, but. . . ."

Boles smiled and raised his shoulders. "Well, then!"

Greer left the gold with the guard. "Wait for me," he directed. He went into the manager's glassed-in office and sat down.

That night Boles told Mrs. Barker, his landlady: "Don't look for me before tomorrow night, Missus Barker. I'm visiting some friends at Petaluma."

Mrs. Barker smiled at the mild, be-spectacled bachelor. "So late in life do we change our ways!"

"I thought I should get out more. Exercise keeps a man young. My friends have an old boat. I'm taking some oars up so we can go out on the river." So he was, but on the San Joaquin River, with the gun wrapped in the brown paper with the oars, and a linen duster and flour sack folded about them.

East of Stockton, the terrain was mostly wheat land with hardly a tree to an acre, but viewed up the long sweep to the foothills the effect was that of a forest of gray-green oaks. More distantly, the red soil of the Sierras began to build into mountains, lightly timbered with piñons and oak. Here the stage road toiled up through many turns, to the gold town of Sonora. At one of these turns Boles stationed himself. He was tired, after walking all night. He had not dared rent a horse for fear of being traced.

During those last few moments he was jubilant. He had no doubt that he could do it. For a man of intelligence, it was simple. The road agents who came to grief were the ones who bounded from the brush, waving a gun, and demanding that the driver stop. Like as not, the stage did not stop, and the highwayman got shot or had to shoot. Boles had the answer to that. He was so sure of himself that there was not even a load in his gun. Beyond that, his idea of adventure did not embrace murder. He rather relished the thought of the danger it meant to go into such an undertaking unarmed.

Time went slowly. He took a pencil and a waybill from his pocket and composed a bit of doggerel. He chewed the pencil, deciding how to sign it. Alliteration won. He wrote, "Black Bart, the POS." On a sudden inspiration, he cut several manzanita branches and fixed them in the brush, like barely exposed rifle barrels.

When he heard the distant fall of horses' hoofs, the ringing grind of iron tires, he donned the white duster and pulled the flour-sack mask over his head. He waited behind a boulder. Just as the stagecoach clattered around the turn, he leaped into the middle of the road. This was the moment of death or success. Boles's brain worked. The shotgun messenger's gun was across his knees; the driver was relaxed, his foot on the brake.

Their faces were just beginning to register surprise when Boles jumped upon the double-tree between the two lead mules. The tree supported him. He let his feet drag, bringing the running animals to a stop. Down the narrow alley of frightened mules he directed the double barrel of the shotgun at the pair on the box.

"Keep your eye on that guard, boys!" he said sharply. "Cover the windows!"

The guard's gun slipped from his knees. The driver raised his hands. Their eyes had not missed the guns directed on them from the roadside.

Carefully Boles walked around the team and stood beneath the guard.

"The box," he said. The Wells Fargo box crashed at his feet. "Let's have the other one, too," he said. Greer's payroll money followed. Boles handed up a folded paper. "Your receipt," he said. "Good morning, gentlemen. I wouldn't stop immediately."

The stage rolled on. The shortest and most efficient stagecoach robbery in California history was over.

With gratification, Boles read of himself in the papers the next day. It seemed he was burly, hard-eyed, with the air of an experienced highwayman. He was accompanied by four cohorts who did not venture into the road. The poem was the only thing that seemed out of character. There was a statement from Charles Greer that demanded the culprit be apprehended and hanged. Greer felt the robbery keenly. He had been too thrifty to pay Wells Fargo to carry his payroll. Every one of the $4,000 was out of his own pocket. All but $500 of the money was buried; Boles had brought home only what he could conveniently carry.

Out of that brief hour of danger was born a deep tranquility in Charles Boles. He found a patronizing attitude toward his work, like a wealthy man who holds a job merely to keep from being bored. He smiled when he took his pay each week. He became, in fact, a little drunk on complacency.

The next time Charles Greer came for his payroll money he had a Wells Fargo man with him. He had decided it was good business to pay for the protection. Yet it seemed to make him no less nervous. He breathed noisily through his nose while the money was counted into the box.

"Stop dawdling!" he snapped. "You'll fool round with it until we go off the gold standard."

"Mister Greer," Boles stated, "no man as clever as this Black Bart would show his cards by hanging around a bank."

"Know all about it, do you?" Under his gaze, the teller's eyes moved back to the strong box. "But doesn't it seem logical that he would be more careful than that? Besides, if I had just stolen four thousand dollars, I'd lie low for a while and spend it."

Greer said: "Yes, I suppose you would. But we're dealing with a different kind of man. He'll come back soon. And he'll get a little lead with his gold this time."

It was a moment for silence, Boles knew, but it was Black Bart who stirred his tongue. "I daresay that, when he needs money again, sir, he'll get it. He struck me as rather capable."

Greer's reaction was not to dispute the statement, but to stare. His hands opened a cigar case, and then with a grunted word to the Wells Fargo man he proceeded to Mr. Pangborn's cage. At his wicket, Boles had difficulty with his fingers as he handled checks and passbooks. He had said too much!

That night he packed his small valise and told Mrs. Barker he would be back too late for Sunday dinner. His friends at Petaluma were expecting him. But after he had secured his shotgun from the creek-bottom cave where he had left it and the money, he started off along the Roseville road, following the valley instead of seeking the foothills. He was about to prove that Black Bart did not play favorites. . . .

Monday morning, at breakfast, there was a new face among those of the half dozen regulars at Mrs. Barker's.

Mrs. Barker paused behind his chair as she brought in the coffee pot. "Folks, this is Mister Price, our new boarder."

John Price was a pleasant enough young fellow who told Boles, as they walked uptown, that he had a job in a lumber yard, accounting. He was down from Marysville, and a little lonesome, full of small talk.

"Read about this bandit, Black Bart?" he asked Boles. "He did it again! Got five hundred dollars off the Auburn stage yesterday morning. Steps right out and says . . . 'Hand it over, boys. Here's your receipt.' "

Boles's smile was tolerant. "A good bandit, perhaps, but a very bad poet."

They walked on, talking of this and that, and finally Price asked him: "What do you do with your week-ends? I thought we might get together, go over to Mission Beach or something."

Boles had reached his corner. His eyes were cool. "I have some friends . . . some very old friends . . . with whom I usually spend Sundays. Perhaps sometime, when I don't go up to see them. . . ."

"Sure," Price said. "Well, I'll see you tonight, Mister Boles."

This young man would not bear encouraging, Charles Boles thought. He would be a definite menace to a man who spent his Sundays the way he occasionally did. And yet, even at this point, he might have let Black Bart sink back into limbo. He had some money; he had proved to himself that he could do it. Future hold-ups might not be quite so easy, since rewards already totaled nearly $1,000. But everything was suddenly changed by the appearance of Jenny Rogers.

Only two weeks after Price came to stay, Jenny took a room at Mrs. Barker's. She was one of those blue-eyed, black-haired Irish girls whose strength is in their seeming fragility. She hardly raised her eyes during the first few meals. But one evening she looked up to meet Boles's gaze, and a shy smile touched her lips—and with Boles it was all over. From now on, it would not be his fault if he remained a bachelor.

He bought himself a new suit. He took to sprinkling cologne on his handkerchief and spending too much time brushing his hair and mustache. Romance was beginning to blossom in his bachelor heart.

He met her turning into their street one afternoon. She

was carrying some parcels, and Boles, with perhaps too much of a flourish, took them under his own arm. "This is a mighty great pleasure, Miss Jenny," he declared. "I had hoped for an opportunity to become better acquainted with you."

"It's surprising," Jenny said, "how close you can live to people in a boarding house without knowing anything about them."

Boles took that as an invitation to talk about himself, which has been the opening shot of swains since the Stone Age.

"And what do you do, Miss Jenny?" he asked finally.

"I work in a laundry," Jenny told him. "Oh, not over an ironing board, heaven forbid! I have charge of the girls who do iron, though."

Boles cleared his throat. "You . . . you enjoy your work, Miss Jenny?"

Jenny's voice was curiously defiant. "Yes, I enjoy my independence very much."

They were at the steep, gray wooden steps of the boarding house when Boles said: "I understand the vaudeville at the Golden State is very good this week. Would you care to go with me tomorrow night?"

"It's most awfully kind of you, Mister Boles. But, you see . . . well, not tomorrow night. Perhaps another night. . . ."

"Saturday?"

"I'd love it."

Boles was at his window when Jenny Rogers and John Price left together the following night. After they were out of sight, he discovered his fists were clenched hard; he was sick inside, with the disease called jealousy. He went to the mirror and stared at himself. He saw a man ten years older than John Price, and four inches shorter. A bank clerk. A man with only one talent, and that a thing he could not brag about.

But on Saturday night he found Jenny a charming companion who seemed not to realize, or to mind, the difference in their ages. During the next few weeks there were other Saturday nights. Boles was spending three times what the bank paid him on shows and dinners, on ferry rides and excursions to Mission Beach.

"I'll bet you love that laundry so much," he said one night, "that no man will ever take you away from it."

"I don't know," said Jenny. "Maybe I do. I do know I don't ever want a marriage like my mother had. She worked in a laundry, too . . . a laundry on our back porch. Father brought home so little that she had to do washing for half the neighborhood. I promised myself I would never do without things as Mother did. I can support myself very nicely. If I ever do marry . . ."—she shook her head—"oh, I know I must sound mercenary . . . but the man I marry will have to be at least in easy circumstances. Is that so unreasonable?"

"Quite reasonable!" Boles declared, and he was delighted with the sudden perception of an advantage over John Price. Price, obviously, did not fall into Jenny Rogers's category of a man in easy circumstances. Whereas, in a small cave on Arcade Creek. . . .

From that night, Black Bart, the road agent with the soul of a poet, became a figure in California. Black Bart had something to work toward. He became, as the papers of the time testify, a busy man. Various stage lines reported their passenger traffic off as much as twenty percent because of his activity. Wells Fargo and the United States Post Office kept the reward money piling up like poker chips. Offers totaled $18,000. The words **Dead or Alive** headed every poster.

He had imitators. Bill Smith, in the Sierras; Dick Fellows, on the Coast roads. But by one sign a Black Bart job could always be told. There would be no horse tracks near the scene. The poet of the highways was an incredible walker.

Charles Boles now had a system. He would strike the same section twice in a month, or he would turn his back on it for six months. His system was an apparent lack of one. From initial plan right down to the instant of stepping boldly into the path of the stagecoach, surprise was the key. After each robbery, he would leave gun and money in the cave. The gun by now was so rusted from exposure that he could hardly ear back the hammers. There was $11,000 in his cache. He thought: *Fifteen thousand will be enough. It will be plenty to take us East, or South, to Canada or Mexico.*

But no man's luck can run indefinitely. It was on his twenty-eighth hold-up that Boles first encountered grief. Having his hat shot off one time by the famous shotgun messenger, George Hackett, had not especially frightened him. But it was a deer hunter, appearing unexpectedly during the Auburn hold-up, who came close to costing him his life. He had seen him just in time to dive for the brush. He had thought, as he started to run: *It's all over!* But his legs saved him, carried him over mountain trails no horse could follow, and at dark he was at Arcade Creek. He had gained nothing by the robbery, but on the other hand he had lost nothing but his handkerchief mask.

Worn out, Boles pulled away the brush that hid his cache and dragged forth the old Wells Fargo box he used for a safe. That is, he reached for it. He groped deeper. He struck a match, and in the brief glow he stared into the shallow cave. It was empty.

The match fell. With the darkness, terror wrapped itself about Boles's throat. For the moment, he could not think of the money—only that the cave had been found, that they might be watching him at this instant!

Slowly he straightened, faced about, staring into the dark tangles of brush, waiting for the voice. *All right, Boles, we've got you*. His nerves were like a bundle of firecrackers; the squeak of a bat would have exploded them. But nothing violated the silence except his own breathing.

Loss—the full shock of it—made him weak and sick. Out of his wealth there remained only what he had cached in his room, $1,000, no more. Six months ago he could have lost it all and shrugged. But what he had lost tonight was Jenny. He had been lucky so far, but he knew tonight that even his luck could not endure another year.

He left the gun in the crotch of a tree not far from the road.

At breakfast, John Price said: "They almost got him this time, folks!"

He showed them the headlines: **Farm Boy Finds Black Bart's Cache**. Boles listened as he read the story. According to the sheriff at Oak Grove, he had missed the bandit by less than an hour, after hurrying out to the cave following the discovery of the fortune.

Wells Fargo officials believe, the story went on, **that Black Bart is an entirely different type of man from the sort they have been hunting. Since only a few hundred dollars of the stolen money was spent, he is apparently a man of quiet habits, not given to drinking or gambling or some of the other habits we customarily associate with criminals. . . .**

There was interested discussion, in which Boles did not take part. But it had its effect on him. If he robbed any more stages, it must not be for many months. He had come so close to being captured that he was still shaken.

On the way uptown, Price asked: "By the way, what was the name of that family you were visiting in Petaluma yesterday?"

Boles glanced at him. "Martin."

"That's funny," Price said. "I didn't have anything better to do, so I ran up there yesterday. I inquired around, but nobody in town had ever heard of the Martins."

"There's no reason why they should," Boles said. "The Martins live fifteen miles above town, on a farm. I take the Petaluma boat to get there. Better ask me next time."

The effect of it did not strike him until later. Then he felt as if he were choking. He had come so close—*so close!* The deer hunter, the stolen cache, Price's following him—for the first time in ten years he enjoyed the tight security of his teller's cage.

On Friday, Charles Greer stopped at the bank and spoke for a moment with Mr. Pangborn. Later, Pangborn took Boles aside.

"Mister Greer has asked for twelve thousand tomorrow. He thinks there is less risk in sending the payroll up every two weeks from now on. Have it ready when he calls."

In his room, Boles lay on his bed, staring at the ceiling. His mind turned it over and over, like a jewel lying on his palm. $12,000! A golden foundation for his dreams. A chance to gain back at one stroke everything he had lost.

It meant a risk. The shipment would be carefully guarded. But other stagecoaches had been protected by sharp-shooting gunmen with rifles, and their guns had not come off their knees. If he were cool, if he kept his head, it would be no harder than any of the others.

Sunday morning he secured his shotgun and walked to the foothills, keeping to the creek bottoms and the side roads. He had settled on the same place where he had made his first robbery, but, when he reached the hairpin turn, he changed his mind. Let the guard build his courage up to this turn and experience the let-down of passing it safely. Then, a mile farther on. . . .

Lying there in the manzanita, it was hot. The suffocating odors of sage began to bother him. He wore the old linen duster over his coat; the flour sack mask was ready. He started on a poem, his last. He could not keep a wistful note out of it.

Here I lay me down to sleep,
To wait the coming morrow.
Perhaps success, perhaps defeat,
And everlasting sorrow.

Now he heard the horses. He dropped the pencil into his pocket and stood up. His boots moved on the earth, getting set. He saw the stagecoach make the turn. Straight up the middle of the sun-shot road it came. Boles stepped out of the brush.

The guard had his gun across his lap. There was no time for him to raise it, or for the driver to swerve the horses. Boles's weight was on the double-tree, dragging the leaders down; his shotgun covered the pair on the box.

Why had he worried? It could not have been smoother.

Only when he walked around to receive the Wells Fargo box did he realize that the guard was John Price. And Price now had the gun in his hands and the muzzle was swinging upon him.

Boles snapped: "Drop it! I'll kill you both!"

Price shook his head. He smiled pityingly. "No, you won't, mister. That gun is as empty as the cashbox. They're both plants. The gun has fooled a lot of guards, and the twelve thousand dollars fooled you. You might as well get in the coach, old-timer. You're going back with us."

John Price sat across from him. "I'm sorry about it," he

said. "I really am. I can see where any man might do something like this, under the right circumstances. You never did like banking, did you?"

Boles looked out the window. "How did you know the gun wasn't loaded?"

"The kid who found the money told us the nipples were so rusty he didn't think there had been caps on them for years. We'd have had you last week, except for him. He kept the money in the barn for a couple of days after he found it, trying to get up nerve to keep it. By the time he told his father, you'd had time to go to the cave, find the money gone, and get out."

The dust was thick. Boles blew his nose. "I suppose," he said, "it was that remark I made to Greer a year ago."

Price nodded. "You seemed to know so much about Black Bart that he had Wells Fargo put a man on you. That was me, of course. I will say that I never followed a cleverer one. I could have proved the Martins of Petaluma didn't exist, of course, but that wouldn't have proved where you spent your week-ends. It would only have proved where you didn't. But there were some things like the poetry, and all the robberies being on week-ends, that made me sure. The last clue was the handkerchief you lost last week. I traced it by the laundry mark, but it was so far back in the brush you could have lost it hunting, months ago. So I had to set a trap. That was the twelve thousand dollars."

Somehow Boles could not feel too mistreated. He had known it was not a game of marbles when he started. But there was one thorn that hurt.

"Jenny Rogers was a plant, too, I suppose," he said.

Price colored a little. "Jenny didn't know anything about it. I've been trying for a year to convince her that she wouldn't have to take in laundry if she married me. Well, last week I did it! We're getting married next month."

119

After a moment, Boles's tired face relaxed. He said: "I'm glad, John. She's a fine girl. You'll both be happy." And he was surprised to find that he actually meant it. . . .

Charles E. Boles was sentenced to San Quentin in 1883, for a period of two years. The strange part of the trial, about which the public knew nothing for years, was that Wells Fargo settled on him a lifelong pension of $125 a month, to begin the day he got out of prison. It was not, John Price told him, a philanthropic move. Wells Fargo was in business to make money, and they couldn't while someone was robbing their stages every week. They thought $125 a month might, after all, be the most practical means of keeping Black Bart in retirement.

Hell in Dakota

The shock of 'Eighty-Six was still over the Dakotas: the cow towns were shabby and wistful; the ranches were stocked with herds nobody wanted to buy. Cowboys who used to cry about the toughness of a cowpuncher's life lay around towns hoping somebody would offer to board them for work. 100 cattle syndicates had failed. 1,000 independent ranchers had gone back to the wall. Two years—and still nickels were harder to come by than dollars had ever been, and cattlemen who had once scorned a plow now furtively ran a few rows of corn for stock feed and planted kitchen gardens "for the missus".

Sam Randall went back to the wall with the rest of them in Stony County—clear back to the fringe of the badlands— back where cows argued over a blade of grass, and a man's ambition, if it were too voracious, commenced eating on itself and ended by devouring the man. Randall was getting that devoured look. He was lanky and dark-eyed and had knuckles like pipe joints. He had shadows in his cheeks, and deep in his gray eyes were more serious shadows. Randall's convictions one by one were being torn by the vulture's beak of his ambition.

He, too, had had a conviction that he was too good for plowing. But he was plowing the coarse red earth behind his cabin on the late spring day when he reached the end of a furrow and for the first time noticed a blue pencil of smoke rising from his back range. Randall stood with his big hands

121

on the grips of the plow, staring with gray eyes and hard-set mouth. The things some men wouldn't do for a dollar nowadays were hard to name. Cow stealing was coming to be regarded as a shirttail cousin of honest work. The smoke rose from the red wastes of the badlands, where not many of Sam's cattle roamed. The country was overrun by bands of mustangs and the ornerier breeds of outlaw cattle. But it was a nice place to swap brands. Randall turned his plow horse into the corral and rode out with a carbine under his knee.

The good range ran up against a crumbling red bluff and perished. Randall pushed into the erosion-wrecked gully land. He knew the corridors and alleys of the badlands as few men did. This had been his first land, and, now that he had been to the top, he was back with it again. The bank had lopped off all but his homesteaded sections and a grim badlands acreage. Last year, he had had to borrow $400 from the bank, just to keep going.

A recent cow trail drifted in the general direction of the smoke. Randall poked along it. He marked shoe prints among the tracks of a few cows. He was beginning to be sure of what he had only suspected, and now a pulse commenced to throb in him. It was a little startling to think that at this moment a running iron might be conjuring a hybrid brand from the Lazy H his cattle wore.

A faint blatting came to him on the still spring air. His thumb rocked the hammer of his carbine and he went more carefully. A fuzz of burro grass lay on the ground. Blocks, pillars, and minarets of mud made a maze of the area he threaded. At last he came around a rain-gouged peninsula of earth and looked down a long corridor. At the end of it, 100 yards away, he saw two men at a branding fire.

He dismounted. As he started toward them, the flanker jumped back and let a brockle-faced calf lunge up. In this instant he saw the rancher. His high yell sliced the silence. The other man fell back toward the horses. It was a moment or two before Sam realized he had been fired at. Something split the air with a sound like ripping silk. Something exploded against a mud bank behind him, and then the sound of a revolver shot came pouring in a wild cascade of echoes down the cañon.

Randall went down like an infantryman, his carbine taking the shock of his fall. Yonder, both men were in the saddle. They were firing from the backs of their ponies—two men in drab range clothes and dusty Stetsons, two men who were in a hell of a hurry.

Sam jerked a shot away. It was a panic shot, for this was something new and terrifying, this fighting for your life in the same hour you had been plowing the earth. In the next instant the riders were gone.

Sam waited ten minutes. At the end of this time, he caught his horse and rode down to the branding fire. A running iron lay there. After the orgy of echoes, utter silence had flowed back. He moved down a fluted scarlet corridor until he encountered two of his calves huddled in a little pocket. He wasted no time examining them; with a yell, he sent them lunging back up the cañon. He followed, with gooseflesh rippling down his back.

He began to breathe again when he reached the plain. He stopped to look the calves over, finding a Rail T where a Lazy H had been. It was good, craftsman-like work. Sam flanked the calves down again and made an equally thorough job of canceling the blotted brands and re-branding the animals.

But, as he rode on to the cabin, he was worried. No telling how long it had been going on. No telling whether this would end it. There were two reasons why the badlands carried the name, and one was the kind of men who roamed them. Unfortunately many of these men had once been called honest. But their metal had been too soft for the fire and had lost its form. Sam Randall had friends who were getting desperate, and his greatest fear was that someday he might catch one of them crossing his range with a running iron on the saddle.

The round-robin letter from the Dakota mustanger who called himself Mustang Cassiday came last to Randall's ranch, which was tucked back against the forbidding cliffs of the badlands—far from women, grama grass, the town of Tie Siding, and all other things good. Randall had plenty of company back there; Ben Jardine—once the biggest cow man in Stony County—and a lot of others had retreated with him.

Cassiday's letter said:

Mustang Cassiday will be in Tie Siding June 10th, to sign contracts for mustanging no-good broncos off your range. You git forty percent of cannery checks, etc.

Sam shook his head over it. He was hitting thirty, and talking less—but more pungently—all the time. He intended to keep out of arguments over the letter. Sometimes he wondered if he knew what he was talking about himself. He had always worked like a fool, spending carefully, investing with caution. Now he had nothing left but a mortgage and a few leftover convictions, like forgotten papers in a desk. Long ago he had picked out a mistress and a wife: the West was his mistress; the wife was to be Kate Jardine, Ben's daughter. But the West had run off and left him, laughing, and Kate, still clinging to the manner of the well-to-do even if the substance had left her, kept him at arm's length, as she always had.

At dawn on June 9th, curious if not hopeful, Sam left in his big blue carryall, picked up his neighbor, Noah Cardwell, and swung past the Jardine place. The ranch house was shut up. It was still well kept, with yellow paint on it and flowers in the yard.

Sam and Noah camped outside Tie Siding that night. A couple of other men bunked at their fire—ranchers who had nothing to lose and, perhaps, something to gain from a deal like Mustang Cassiday's. Everyone talked with guarded optimism. Maybe they'd make enough to buy a good herd bull, they said. Noah Cardwell figured he had enough mustangs ranging his back country to keep a gang of horse trappers busy a year. They all waited to hear what Sam had to say, but he kept his ideas to himself.

Next morning was hot and brassy, the sun wringing from the earth the last of its spring moisture. It would be hot back in the badlands. In Tie Siding, there were trees, saloons, oases of greenery around windmills. There was a shabby air of festivity about the little railroad town. A lot of men were hoping against hope that they might pick up a few dollars from the horse trapper. The waiting cow crowd hung around the saloons, drinking beer when they wanted whiskey and being sparing with their tobacco because it cost money.

Then, dramatically, there was a yell and a hard-driving sound of hoofs and into the town rode four men on four stout horses running abreast—a dramatic and encouraging sight. The horses scattered dogs and chickens; tethered horses swung their heads. The men laced their ponies to a stop—all but one, a big young fellow with Stetson hanging by the lanyard, whose buckskin went into a pitching exhibition. There was laughter from the other three and some cursing and sparring by the blond rider, and then the horse, shaking its bridle with a rain of lather, came to a stop.

Sam Randall stood staring at the blond bronco-stomper. He could not say why he was reminded of a man at the end of

125

a long, fluted corridor of red earth, holding a running iron in his hands. But when he looked at the man's clean, wedge-like build, a strain of recollection stirred in him. . . .

The men dismounted. One of them—an older man, built like a Percheron, deep-chested and tall, and with a vainglorious Buffalo Bill mustache sweeping dark cheeks—hooked his thumbs over his shell belt and looked about the slim, hungry-eyed crowd. "Which one of you's Ben Jardine?" he asked.

"Jardine's at the bank," said Shank, the saloonkeeper.

"I'm Mustang Cassiday," said the horseman. He began to pull off his gauntlets. His eyes, socketed deep, held glints of amusement. The ranchers were still gaping as if he were Santa Claus. "Who'll tell Jardine I'm here?"

A cowboy loped off to the bank to summon the rancher. Randall was a little puzzled about Cassiday's interest in the once great cowman. Cassiday entered the saloon and called out: "Bartender, set 'em up!" Randall watched Noah and the others rush the rail; he hung back, aware that all this was not helping their bargaining position, should any dickering ensue. Men dying of hunger are in no spot to haggle over the heel of the loaf or a center slice—especially with someone who has bought them drinks.

Beside Cassiday, a warped little rider turned to stare at Sam Randall. This man was red-headed, looking to be about forty, and with a face all bone and hard flesh. He reminded Sam of the kind of man his mother must have had in mind when she warned him against smoking.

"Not drinking, feller?"

Sam stirred. "Why not?" He joined the rest.

In a few minutes, Ben Jardine came lunging into the saloon. Ben was sixty and retained some rags of the grand manner. He had never looked like anything but a farmer to

126

Randall, but had a way of shaking hands that seemed to bestow a favor, of frowning over another man's remark as though pressing out the last of its juice before responding. All the sham was off him today, though. He rushed up to shake Cassiday's hand and those of his companions: Pony Bob Hill, the blond youngster with the buckskin horse; Dick Gormey, the bony-faced one; and a silent Basque named Bandolier, a dour-eyed man as thin as a gallows' shadow.

Why, Randall wondered, had Jardine been singled out as a spokesman for the whole county? There were bigger men than he in Tie Siding. A little of the mustanger's bravado rubbed off on the rancher; a little strut came back to him. He stood at Cassiday's side, laughing too loudly at his jokes, once even paying for a round with money he desperately needed.

Cassiday got down to business. "I reckon you boys know what my deal is. What I want is contracts with every man that's interested in something for nothing. Bronc' checks will be mailed to a blocked account in your own bank. Your cuts come out of it before mine does. Forty percent of the gross, and I've got these rannihans to pay out of my cut."

"What's the cannery pay you for mustangs?" Randall asked.

"Four dollars a head. In K.C."

"I got six for some last year."

Jardine's gaze responded to Randall sternly. Cassiday rolled a cigar between his hands, his eyes staring hostilely. "They're paying four this year. I've got a friend in a cannery."

"That sounds fair enough to me," said Jardine heartily.

Cassiday lighted the cigar and dropped the match in the sawdust. He took a long, satisfying pull. "You ought to run around three-fifty, four hundred apiece."

Noah Cardwell exclaimed, "Jesus Nelly!"

"How do you work?" Randall asked.

Cassiday's eyes handled him carefully, sensing an obstacle. "I generally start at one end of a territory and work to the other. Send out a herd when I've got one. It's a funny thing . . . the ones with the poorest range gen'ally come out ahead. The bronc's drift back there to the brakes. . . . Where's your ranch, brother?"

"Back in the brakes."

Cassiday let a smile touch his mouth, a secret sort of smile just for Randall. "I could almos' gar'ntee you five hundred dollars."

Ben Jardine struck the bar with his fist. "I don't know about the rest of you, but I'm all for it."

Others began declaring themselves, but Noah Cardwell hesitated, glancing at Sam for confirmation. His hesitation caught several others, who waited for Sam to speak his mind. Sam finished his whiskey and set the glass down.

"I reckon it ain't for me," he said.

Dick Gorney, Bandolier, and Pony Bob Hill stared at him as though he could be crowded into line by the mere force of their displeasure. But the big, mustached bronco trapper who ramrodded them said pleasantly: "That's too bad. I like a whole range when I trap, so's there ain't any trouble about boundaries. What's wrong with my deal?"

"Couple of things. Too much money, for one."

Jardine's displeasure burst loose. "Sam, for God's sake! This is the best thing that's happened to us in years."

"How do you know it's the best? You pick up a little every year on canners, don't you? Do you want that to end? For that price, Cassiday's going to have to trap them all. Sure, they're a headache. They breed no-good foals on our mares and eat too much grass. But those things are offset by what we make on them. Look on them as a crop. You don't cut down all your trees because you're getting a good price for your apples, do you?"

Noah scratched his head. Old Moss Belden grunted as though something important had been said. Cassiday came in quickly. "Look what you can do with that four hundred! Herd stock! Shoes for the kids and some dress material for the old woman. Eatin' tobacco till you choke on it." He slapped a gold piece on the bar and straightened. "I've offered you men a good thing. You've got five minutes to make up your minds, or Mustang Cassiday rides out of Tie Siding to some place where fellers like to make a dollar for nothing."

He went outside, his men following. So it was Sam Randall against the crowd, again. But Sam was not in a contentious frame of mind. When Jardine put the full weight of his anger into a curse, Sam only shook his head. "I could be wrong," he said. "But I'll do my own mustanging."

"Are you *for* anything, or just against everything?" Jardine demanded.

"I'm just a man afraid of trying anything fancy. I've seen the worst and know I can sweat it out till things improve."

He walked from the saloon. From across the street at his wagon, he watched the others drift out and engage in conversation with Cassiday. Then they all walked toward the bank. All but Noah. He came across to Sam.

"Damn you and your preachments! I ain't got much savvy of my own, but I think I know it when I hear it. I shore could have used that three-fifty, Sam. . . ."

Sam laughed. "Maybe you and I'll be ahead yet. Maybe by fall we'll be the only ones who haven't been rustled blind."

Later, he was loading some credit-bought items into the wagon when Kate Jardine came from a store. Randall had an odd impression about Kate—that hard times had tempered her, rid her of most of the foolishness of the days when she had had women to make her gowns and hats and every young buck in town was proposing to her, but that her pride would not quite let her admit she was glad to be plain folks.

She gave him her hand. "So good to see you, Sam! Aren't you going along with the others?"

"Made other arrangements," Sam said. Looking at her, he thought that she was like springtime in gingham; poverty had forced her to some incredible things, but she did some incredible things in the acceptance of them. She was thoroughbred-built, light and clean-limbed, with fresh skin and dark hair.

She studied Sam. "I take it you don't think Cassiday is a step in the right direction."

"It's anybody's guess."

"But you guess not."

"I guess there's something wrong with slaughtering all the mustangs in a county in one season. And I don't trust that gang much farther than I could kick a steer."

Kate hesitated. "Father investigated Cassiday last winter, after he wrote. He trusts him enough that he's going to lease our place to him for a year. Father and I are moving back to town."

Sam stared.

"Why not?" Kate insisted. "Cassiday needs a holding ground, and he'll pay well. We'll be ahead, any way you look at it."

Anger stirred in Sam. "You know what you'll have left, don't you? Dirt and rock and lawsuits! He'll move in three times the number of steers the land can support, fatten them, and move them off after the land goes to hell."

"He's a horse trapper, Sam, not a feeder. And things can't be much worse."

"What'll your father do?"

"I don't know. He's had some talks with Will Hoggatt."

In Randall's mind, Jardine slipped a peg. Backroom deals with Banker Hoggatt. . . .

Kate read his displeasure. "It's a poor argument, Sam, that only tears the other fellow's to pieces."

"Maybe I'm a chronic ag'in'er," he said ironically. "What I need, maybe, is a wife with better sense than I've got. I'll have a long way to go to find one, though, now that the girl I had in mind is moving back to town."

She laughed. "If you played your cards right, you could move in, too." She went on toward the bank.

Randall waited for the two o'clock mail train before leaving. It was well that he did, for there was a letter for him. It was from Bill Tofte, an old rodeo sidekick. The last Sam had heard, Tofte had been working in a packing house in Kansas City. He read the letter once, and then again. The second time, a cymbal crashed in his head, and he was on his feet. This was—well, it could be!—the first shaft of light through the storm clouds.

Prices have been creeping up every day for the last month, Tofte wrote. **I'm betting they keep on. I and a fellow here bought a feed lot a while back. Got all kinds of feed, but need steers. No cash. I picked up two good shorthorn bulls a year ago at a sacrifice. Now, if you can send me 500 steers on credit, Sam, I'll ship these bulls as down payment and pay the rest when I sell. Telegraph me if you will do it.**

He found Noah in the saloon and read him the letter. "Pardner, this is it! Beef's started up!"

"It's went up before."

"It hasn't gone up thirty days straight before."

Noah flicked a fly out of the foam of his beer. "It'll clean us out if Tofte's rigging you. But another year and I'll be cleaned out anyhow. Shore, I'll buy a bull! When you want the steers?"

"We can have the cars in a week. We'll start cutting on your place tomorrow."

Outside, Randall tasted the afternoon air. It had the old flavor again. The breeze whispered through the sage beyond the town buildings and whirled the sheet-metal blades of the windmills.

He walked up to the bank. The news was too good to keep. He went up the outside stairway to Lawyer McMurtrie's office, strode down the hall, and stopped outside an open door through which tobacco smoke and conversation came generously. He glanced in. There was an air of consummation about the scene.

McMurtrie, big and florid, leaned back in his swivel chair. Men stood about smoking and chewing, and Cassiday was yarning. When Cassiday saw Randall, he got up from the window where he sat and said humorlessly: "Fellers, here's the sexton come to pass out cards ag'in. Anybody like to be fitted for a shroud?"

Sam Randall smiled and moved into the doorway. He said to big Ben Jardine: "You wanted to know what I was for. I've just found out. I'm for going out on a limb right to the last twig, on the strength of a rise in beef. Bill Tofte writes that beef's gone up every day for a month. Noah and I are sending him five hundred steers, on the cuff. That doesn't need to influence you fellows. But before you do anything your common sense tells you is foolish, why don't you try to hang on till fall?"

"Anything foolish about picking up cannery checks for nothing?" Cassiday demanded.

Randall considered a moment, and, because he was ready

to risk Cassiday's displeasure to get across to the others what he felt, he said: "That side of it's all to the good. But if steers are going to be worth something again, it would be foolish to take the chance of losing many."

Pony Bob Hill, the blond, buckskin-shirted youngster, suddenly came toward him. Hill had the eye of a bad bronco, reckless and headlong. "Want to lay that on the line?" he snapped.

Mustang Cassiday said: "Now, hold it, Bob!"

"I can't say it much plainer," Randall told the bronco stomper.

Hill smashed at his jaw with a long, reaching jab. It caught Sam on the ear and half turned him, driving him back to the wall. Hill lunged in.

Something joyous awoke in Sam Randall. Violence was a cleansing fire for a man who had scrounged and figured too long. He had been counted a scrapper himself, once, and, if he were no longer quite so fast or so reckless, he was stronger and wiser. He permitted Hill to smash two blows to his shoulders, but after that his right came out in a neat uppercut that stretched the mustanger onto his toes. Sam cuffed him heavily in the face with the back of his hand. Pony Bob stumbled back, came up against the desk, and rocked forward again.

The youngster was big-boned and hard. His arms were long and the fists at the end of them had an explosive power. All he lacked was caution. He drove one to Sam's belly by sheer force of crowding, and Sam felt it clear to his liver. It shook him. Hill saw the pallor in the rancher's face and assumed that it was time for the kill. He grunted as his right shoulder rolled and the long haymaker went out. But Randall was not there to receive it. Randall tilted his head, the fist passed him, and Pony Bob Hill came up against him.

Sam Randall gave the mustanger two short blows to the belly, his shoulders behind them. As Hill fell aside, Sam rushed him. Hill's head cracked back. A short but vicious overhand punch smashed into his chin. Hill groaned in his throat and put his hands out for support. Randall let him go to his knees and then slump onto his belly—not out, but paralyzed.

Ben Jardine sounded like a revival preacher exhorting a sinner. "By George, I used to think you had judgment, Randall, if nothing else. Now I see you've lost even that. If you'd turned up a deal like this yourself, you'd crow like a cock. But because they came unannounced, because you couldn't be their tinhorn prophet, you think they're cattle thieves and schemers!"

Randall's iron lay between Noah Cardwell's, on the north, and Jardine's on the south. The railroad crossed Jardine's ranch near his southern boundary, twelve miles from the Lazy H. Several ranchers had gone in together on a loading chute and pens a few years back. There had been no discussion of trespass rights, but Randall thought about this point several times during the beef roundup. Either Jardine or Cassiday could raise a howl over his taking a herd across the Bradded L.

The cars were supposed to be on hand by the 23rd of June. By the 21st, Noah and Sam had built their herds and trailed them along toward the railroad. Noah, who would accompany the herd to Kansas City as train rep, had a telescope bag of city clothes along with him. They bedded the day herd snugly that night between two grassy buttes. Randall heard moaning across the prairie the distant notes of a freight. Their stock cars were waiting on Jardine's siding.

They pointed the steers south again and got them winding

slowly through the draws and buttes toward the railroad, following the shore of the badlands. Out there, Mustang Cassiday's gang would be doing their work. Noah and Sam came down through a long, twisting coulée, both men riding drag with bandannas over their noses and mouths. Suddenly the stinging *crack* of a rifle reached them and Randall could almost feel the blunting of the point of the herd. A tremor came down the herd. Steers began to pile into the rumps of animals stalling ahead of them.

Sam put his pony up a shelving bank and scrambled to the top. Two more shots split the hot noonday. 100 yards ahead, two riders sat their horses at the edge of the coulée and poured slow fire from their saddle guns into the shallow cañon. Randall recognized the warped frame of Dick Gormey and the lank, dark form of the Basque, Bandolier. Something went off in his head like a gunshot. He found the stock of his carbine and swung down. He took a moment to settle his boots in the earth, aligned the sights on the shoulder of Gormey's horse, and took up trigger slack in a single, slow squeeze. The gun set him back with its hard, slamming recoil.

Gormey was on the ground, wriggling from under his fallen pony. The Basque pivoted to face Randall, and Sam stood there with a new shell under the firing pin and the Henry at his shoulder. Bandolier let his gun slip back into the boot. He brought his hands shoulder high and waited while Sam started toward them, afoot.

Gormey was standing over his horse, raging tightly. The pony lay shuddering, raising its head spasmodically from the ground and letting it fall. Gormey could not put his anger into words. He kept saying—"You damned . . . you goddamned . . ."—until Randall reached out and slapped him across the cheek bone with the barrel of the carbine. The gun sight slashed Gormey's cheek, bringing a slow worm of blood from it.

Sam said: "It's too bad you weren't the one wearing the saddle, Gormey."

Gormey wiped the blood from his face and stared at his hand. "You crossed a boundary five miles back, cowboy!"

Noah Cardwell had ridden up, his face the color of ash, his eyes all pupil. "Anybody tell you this was a county cattle trail, Gormey?"

"What makes a trail public . . . you wanting to use it?"

"Four of us have been using this trail for years. If Jardine forgot to tell you, you know now."

Bandolier spoke out of that frozen brown face of his, his accent a curious hybrid French. "Caz'day say, nobody cross we don' deal with."

"Is that what he says? I say Cassiday owes me for five steers and a day's work to round up the cattle you've spilled all over hell's half acre."

Gormey's was a face for hating. His eyes were yellow agates. He said: "I picked you for a troublemaker the first day I laid eyes on you, Randall. Maybe you know how to raise cattle. I don't know and I don't give a damn. But you've got no license to try to crowd everybody else into your mold. You as good as told us to keep off your range. It's a square shake, ain't it, if Mustang tells you the same? Take your damned cows on across . . . but don't bring no more."

Randall said: "I'll bring another herd in the fall, maybe before then. And I'll have Ben Jardine tied to the back of the lead steer, if I have to. I'll collect from Cassiday for those cows."

They spent most of the following day teasing their cattle out of a hundred pockets where they had taken refuge. Finally they came onto the flats where the steel rails of the Milwaukee

& St. Paul skidded by, hot and fluid under the sun. Noah was already half dressed in his town clothes for the trip in the caboose.

They rounded Armory Butte. The pens and chute were before them. But there was no line of empty cattle cars. Only a little covey of blackbirds in the corral and the chute. . . .

Noah's voice had an edge. "Thought you said the cars was waiting!"

"I heard them drop them two days ago. I know every bleat that Milwaukee teakettle makes."

Randall rode down to the pens. There was manure aplenty in the pens. His first thought was that Cassiday had beaten him down here with a herd of mustangs and purloined his cars. But the sign spoke of steers, not horses.

Sam rode back, puzzled. "All I know is we've got to set it out here till we get more men. I'll ride up to town."

The freight agent in Tie Siding said: "Reckon I'll get flimsies on it sooner or later, Sam, since you ordered at this office. But there was twenty cars! I seen them pass."

"Order twenty more. And have that hogger blow ten long blasts when he brings them. We'll have to range the herd farther out." On afterthought, he added: "Maybe you can talk him into giving me the high sign every time he leaves any cars at our siding. I'd like to get a line on who borrowed mine."

It was ten days before they got the next string of empties.

A few days later, they got delivery on the bulls. Sam specified delivery in town; he wanted Tie Siding to see what a real shorthorn bull looked like. He and Noah curried and watered them at the station before driving them out. They let the bulls amble up the main street—grand, short-legged animals with breadth of loin and richness of coat. Ranchers turned to stare at them and to ask questions. Old Moss Belden wanted to know how much the bulls weighed.

"About twenty-five percent more than what you're used to," Sam said. "And they eat the same amount of grass."

Moss cleared his throat, his eyes hungry. "Can we talk about service for my cows sometime?"

Sam smiled. "Any time. All I want is the pick of the litter."

Someone called his name. He saw Kate on the walk, a parasol over her shoulder to cut the heat of the July sun. Sam let Noah take both bulls. Kate gave him her hand; she looked cool and fresh in a green summer dress that brought out the rich tones of her skin. Randall tried to be casual with her, but he failed. All he could think was: *Without a wagon, the finest ranch in the world would be a goat pasture.* And she was still the woman for him.

"Are those the bulls that are going to revolutionize Dakota ranching?" she asked.

"They're going to be the great-granddaddies of the best cattle in Dakota. What do you hear from the mustang country?"

"I suppose they're keeping busy." He found a trace of worry in her eyes. Suddenly she said: "Sam, I stopped you because I wanted to explain something. You knew Dad's been investing in . . . in notes and trust deeds?"

Something in Randall slowed down. He took a long, clear look ahead. He said: "He's been investing in *my* note at the bank . . . is that what you wanted to explain?"

"He was angry when he bought it, Sam! At first he said he was just going to use it to make you squirm. The bank said you'd missed a payment and that they were carrying you as long as you could pay interest. But then . . . oh, we've all been foolish! You've laughed at everything anyone else thought would make a few dollars. And we've said you wouldn't know a good thing if you saw it."

Sam asked dryly: "When am I supposed to squirm?"

"He's used all the money he got for the lease to buy up notes, for interest," Kate said. "Now he can't make payments on some of his own obligations because some of the ones he bought have been slow. He'd counted on people paying on time, but no one has, and . . . Sam," she said earnestly, "if they won't carry him, if he has to close anyone out, don't make it be you!"

Emotion surged darkly into Randall. A lot of answers came into his head, but he checked them. He said shortly: "That's Ben's decision, not mine. Talk to him about it."

Now there was urgency and focus, where there had been relief and pride. He had thought Jardine above knife-in-the-back tactics. But Jardine was, after all, a scared and desperate man. He wired Bill Tofte to get the rest of that payment through the first moment he could.

In the meantime, Randall was too busy to worry. He proceeded as if he intended to stay in business. He and Noah contrived a well rig and sank wells at several spots. They bought junk and fashioned windmills. They pampered those bulls like children.

Now and then the far, lingering cry of a locomotive would reach the ranch house at the foot of Fort Butte, and Sam would look up and begin to count. But it was never the prolonged signal that meant cattle cars had been kicked onto the siding. Either Cassiday was not shipping out many broncos, or Sam's eardrums were thickening.

On a blazing August day, Jardine rode out. Randall was setting out salt lick. The rancher wore better clothes than he had worn the last time Sam had seen him. But his sideburns wanted trimming and his jaws were salty with day-old beard. He looked like a man who had been sitting up late with a worry.

139

Randall let Jardine start it, giving him no help with his tongue or with his eyes.

"Sam, I've got to talk to you."

"I thought *I* was the one who was supposed to ask you for a talk."

"I'm not trying to crowd anyone. But. . . ."

"So you let yourself be suckered into taking too many notes off the bank's hands." Randall grinned.

Jardine frowned. "Kate told me how it would look to buy up notes, but. . . . Well, I'm making it as easy on everyone as possible. All I want is the money to keep out of trouble myself. If you can pay the interest on yours, I'll carry you on the rest till fall." Then he cleared his throat. "I thought I might be getting some of these checks by now. I guess Cassiday's having slow going."

Sam knew that the seed of doubt he had planted months ago had sprouted. "Tell you what, Ben. Why don't we ride over to his camp and see how many bronc's he's rounded up?"

Jardine seized on it. "That's an idea! He ought to be some place around Horsehead Coulée."

Sam saddled his Appaloosa traveler. They cut across the upper corner of Jardine's land into the badlands. The gouged mud hills were hot and dry. A man needed to know the water holes before he entered them. A heavy sickness of decay invaded the air. They came upon the carcasses of four horses, lying bloated on the sand, their legs thrusting grotesquely from the swollen barrels. The two men held bandannas over their noses as they passed.

Sam said: "I thought the idea was to capture them and let the canneries do the slaughtering."

They discovered a well-marked path pointing northeast. In about a half hour, the crowded draw opened into a shallow with a huddle of salt cedars fringing a spring. A dozen mustangs were penned in a corral. Another corral was empty, holding only a cold branding fire with irons criss-crossed. The mustangers' camp was by the spring; it consisted of a couple of canvas lean-tos, a scatter of gear, and a talus of tin cans beyond the cook fire. The mustangers were out, their saddles gone. Randall and Jardine sat down to smoke.

About an hour before sundown, two riders came in sight. They were Pony Bob Hill and Mustang Cassiday. Cassiday reined in when he saw them; his hand fell to the stock of his saddle gun. He said something to Hill and came on at a rack.

Badlands suns had roasted his hands and face a mahogany brown and had bleached his mustache until it was the color of new rope. He gave them each a hard handshake and squatted on his heels. There was some howdying and socializing, then the bronco trapper said: "Figgered to see you out here directly, Jardine. It's plumb scandalous the way I've let you down."

"I was beginning to look for some of those cannery checks."

"Well, keep right on lookin', because they'll be on the way. This is a rip slaver of a trappin' range! A backdoor to every trap! But we're getting them curried out of the brakes, and I look for a good roundup yet."

"You sent out a pretty good herd last month, I hear," Sam remarked.

Hill's drawling words came to him. "Where'd you hear that?"

"Somebody got twenty stock cars I'd spoken for. I figured it must be you."

Cassiday laughed. "Jardine, this feller ought to be a storyteller. Ever think that it might be somebody south of here?"

"No."

For an instant they regarded each other measuringly. Cassiday retained his hard grin, but his eyes were cautious. Then Sam heard Jardine say tartly: "Cassiday, I want to see some action or it's all off. I could use the land myself. I can't see why you needed the range anyhow."

"You can't pen horses in a hole like this for long. And I thought I might take in a few feeders if things looked right. But with beef going up, it ain't a time to buy."

"All right. But I'm prepared to pay back the unused portion of your lease money next month unless you can show me some action. And I'll make my beef roundup as usual."

"If you want to see some action," Cassiday drawled, "just try to put me off the land before my lease expires. I won't be crowded by any note-buying cowman that's got himself in a corner."

Jardine looked startled. His next emotion, Randall knew, would be anger. He moved to block it. Jardine was not equipped for trouble. Sam got up. "He's got you, Ben. I told you to think about it before you signed. Now you'll have to stay with it." He walked to his pony. Jardine came along.

During the next few days, Randall began to see gangs of cowpunchers on roundup for Jardine, for Moss Belden, and for Noah Cardwell, swinging along in a tawniness of dust. Out on the flats, the roundup was quick and thorough, but where the land crumpled against the red bluffs of the badlands, cattle hid in a thousand blind pockets where rope and iron had to pry them loose. Then the reports began to come out of the cañons. Belden was off 200! Jardine ran 400 short!

He and Noah finished their work one hot evening. The tally was on the nose. But Randall sat long over the supper table, thinking of a dozen small, scared men wondering what to do next. They would have the normal reaction of the wronged. Rifles would come out and cleaning rods begin to

142

flash. Then they would think: *How can we prove that Cassiday did it? What if we lynch him and the cattle come back? Suppose they were just scared into the brakes by the mustanging?*

So they would put the rifles away and try to figure where they could pare here and trim there to get by. A little help from the bank, a lot of help from the Lord. . . . Something pried into Randall's consciousness. The hot night air vibrated to a freight signal. Across Jardine's range the westbound was hammering, early lamps swinging in the caboose, the big diamond stack belching clouds of sparks. But something was out of key. Randall suddenly had it. The siding blast had stretched five, six, seven . . . ten!

Stock cars! And no herds on the trail that Sam knew of! He thought of saddling and riding down tonight. But nothing would be doing until the eastbound came through tomorrow morning.

It was still murky when Sam heard horses chopping briskly into the yard. In the gloom of the cabin, he pulled on pants and boots. Seven horsemen were waiting for him. Ben Jardine sat his horse in the center of the crowd, cradling a Winchester in his hands. The ruddy dawn was on his pouched, gray face. He shouted over the trample of horses: "A wise one, Sam . . . but maybe not wise enough!"

Sam said: "So I got your cattle now!"

Moss Belden cracked: "There ought to be a reason why a man that's only shipping a hundred head orders thirty cars!"

Sam's gaze found Noah, his hands lashed to the horn of his saddle. A profane screech came from Noah's throat. "We lead the damned nags to water, Sam, but will they drink? No! They lay for us. They've got it figgered now, where we ordered thirty cars to lead out their damned strays!"

Jardine was pulling a paper from an envelope. "That's not the part that took the figgering. The figgering came when we tried to see where you could use that many cars, after sending most of your stuff early. Here's the order you left at the station the other night. The agent says you shoved it under the door after he'd closed."

"Do you know my handwriting?" Sam asked.

"Not that I recollect. But the agent. . . ."

"Jardine," Sam said, "I don't know why I dirty my hands on you. If you want to follow us to the railroad and watch us lead your cattle, come along. But don't open your mouth again or I'll close it for good."

The eastbound was due around mid-morning. They had hardly entered Jardine's range when Sam Randall heard it shunting in. The freight was an hour ahead of schedule. Randall did not believe he needed for vindication the sight of Cassiday's outfit loading cattle into the cars. But the thing between him and Mustang Cassiday had gone beyond the theoretical and entered the personal. It was cow stealing brought to its ultimate efficiency. Clean out a range with the owner's blessing! Load them into cars like church-going cattlemen and ride the hell on out! Pick up the packer's check in K.C. and hit Texas next time!

Ahead, dancing in heat waves, rose Armory Butte. Faintly Randall heard a whistle, a crash of couplings. Then he rounded the butte and saw the railroad, the chutes and pens, before him. The last dozen steers were being herded up a chute into a car. Mustang Cassiday stood behind Gormey and the Basque, prodding steers up the slatted incline with sharpened sticks. In the other pen, Pony Bob Hill was leading the last of four saddled horses into the final car of the string. The rust-red caboose sat alone on the main line, ready to be picked up after the locomotive had pulled the cattle cars from the siding.

Jardine snorted like a horse. "Kate was right. She said it couldn't be you. But that order, Sam. . . ." He had the Winchester in his hands, and bitterly rubbed the slick walnut stock. "The Bible's got it all down plain . . . 'which have eyes and see not.' Or maybe it's the blind leading the blind. But this blind man's got one more place to lead the rest, and that's right down yonder."

He waited for the rest to come up. Moss Belden scratched his moth-eaten chin beard. "They don't look much like mustangs, do they?" he said.

"No, but Cassiday's going to ride them to hell's hottest coke heap if he raises a hand to us!" Jardine rode his horse down the slope.

Sam's notion was to keep the caboose between them and the pens, so that they might come close without being seen. When they were still 300 yards from the tracks, Pony Bob Hill shouted. A gun cracked, and a slug pocked the ground ahead of them.

Now it was a race for the caboose—Cassiday, Gormey, and Bandolier deserting the steers to run for the shelter of the car. They fired as they came, panicky shots designed to slow men unused to being fired at. Sam slipped out of the saddle. They could not beat the mustangers to the car, but perhaps they could keep them from entering it. Some of the others saw what he was doing and reined up just ahead of him. Sam had the rear platform of the caboose under his sights, trying to hold his breathing as the browned gun barrel wavered. He heard the hard, jangling pound of boots, then a splintering of glass. He kept waiting for the form of Mustang Cassiday to lunge up on the platform.

The first time he knew he had been wrong was when a rifle crashed at a window of the car. He felt a gritty shower of pebbles and heard the blasting concussion of the copper-jacketed slug against the ground. Cassiday had broken a window on the offside and climbed into the caboose.

Another gun opened in the cupola. Suddenly Jardine's men were forgetting about attack and thinking of defense. The prairie was flat and inhospitable, the hot ground sprinkled with tumbleweed and purplish-gray sage. Sam hunched in a wallow half the depth of a horse trough. Moss Belden, Noah, and the others crawled through the brush trying to find shelter, while Cassiday shouted at his men and kept a stinging fire lashing the brush.

Randall, pulling a bead on the blond head of Pony Bob Hill at the top of the cupola, caught a flash of movement at his left. A shock poured through him as he saw that Ben Jardine was still riding, bearing past the car on some wild-eyed mission only he understood.

Pony Bob rose higher on the hidden ladder and swung his rifle after Jardine. The gun flashed, but in the same instant Sam let his shot go. Jardine's horse stumbled and fell. Jardine rolled and came up, and finally staggered onto the tracks. Hill fell back, clutched a moment at a hand hold, and dropped from sight.

Splinters began to feather the edges of the windows, but the hidden mustangers moved about, taking a shot here, lying low, taking their next shot from another point. Belden, huddled near Sam, gasped and came up on his hands and knees. For an instant the dark face of Mustang Cassiday was at a window; the recoil of the shot set him back. But Moss Belden was out of this and any future fights. The bullet had entered his shoulder and traveled down through his body to tear out his side.

Sam was sickened. He pumped off three shots with no design behind them. When he stopped to reload, he saw Ben Jardine crawling down the tracks toward the caboose. He was

146

dragging a couple of tumbleweeds. Randall expected to see him collapse with a hatful of slugs in him, then he realized that Ben was shielded from the caboose, unless someone crawled up to take Hill's place.

A long interval of staccato bursts and echoing lags brought the sweat out on the cattlemen. Cassiday was a man as rich in guts as he was poor in ethics. Cooped up in a flimsy wooden box, he was coming close to making an advantage of a bad spot.

There was a flare under the caboose; a light veil of smoke drifted away on the breeze. Jardine had crawled under the car and set fire to the brush. He was reaching out to snatch tufts of sage from the right of way and pile them onto the greasy red flames. Then he pulled his Colt and emptied the cylinder into the floorboards over his head.

The men in the caboose showed briefly behind the windows. Randall commenced systematically chopping at the sill of a window. Presently a few wisps of smoke drifted through the shattered windows. The drifting fumes thickened and became yellowish ropes. Ben Jardine backed up the tracks away from the caboose.

Sam loaded and waited. This was the last branding, the final tally of the roundup Mustang Cassiday had started last spring. The question was whether he would let the law do the job, or face it here. Sam Randall, who understood outlaw psychology, knew the decision Cassiday would make.

For a while the smoke thickened. Sam wondered how the men inside were able to endure it. Then, suddenly, he recalled the window on the other side of the car. He lunged to his feet and ran toward the caboose.

It was his second wrong guess.

Bandolier, the Basque, stepped quickly onto the platform. He snapped his rifle to his shoulder. Sam sprawled. Bandolier's shot came, a shattering roar. The bullet gouged Sam's boot and drove pain through his leg like a running iron. He steadied himself; the outlaw was big and bluff and disdainful above him. Sam pulled the trigger.

Bandolier took a backward step and collided with Dick Gormey. Gormey flung him off. Bandolier fell headlong down the steps. Gormey leaped across him and began to sprint for the horse car. Up the tracks, Ben Jardine took a snap shot that brought Gormey down.

So now it was Mustang Cassiday. He came onto the platform with a Colt in each hand, jumped down the steps, and walked up the slope into the sage spiked with hot rifle barrels. He was grinning. He called: "Mud in your eyes, boys!" Raising both guns, he fired two shots that were a gesture more than a threat. Then he jerked, took another stride forward, and sagged onto the sand. The sun was high and hot; he lay without a shadow on the earth. The bawling of the cattle was steady.

Sam Randall rode the night passenger train into Tie Siding. Moss Belden had his seat, too, but it was the last ride for him. A few months ago, some men would have said that Belden was the lucky one; he had got out of an intolerable situation with respect and a certain amount of glory. Tonight, he got a lot more sympathy than he might have last spring.

At last, men knew that they had been through the worst the cow country could throw at them. They had come through a trifle threadbare, but they fancied they could see the sun behind the horizon. They were ready to quit dreaming and go back to work.

Sam Randall, limping up the street toward the Jardine house, was just beginning to dream—to dream of a ranch near town, and a cattle herd to look at, and a girl who would make the struggle still ahead of him seem worthwhile.

Hurry Call for Hangin' Gus

I

Sheriff Whipple watched the man across the table eat his steak, each bite a quarter pound of rare beef that made the stout man's florid jowls bulge with the effort of rendering it digestible. He wondered how this man could eat at all, with a job ahead of him that would take most men's appetites for a month.

Whipple felt that some apology was due. He said: "I guess you're wondering why I dragged you all the way up from Three Rivers to hang this man, Marshal. Well, I don't rightly know myself. I've hung a few in my time. Not that I enjoyed it. But this case is different."

"Bunch of lily-livered lawmen in this county," Gus Hobbs grunted.

Whipple stirred his coffee, frowning. "If I was sure he's guilty," he said, "I could go it all right."

"Been tried and convicted, ain't he?" the marshal put in sharply.

"Eleven to one the first ballot," Sheriff Whipple said.

"All right. He hangs. Why'd you bring me up here if you didn't want him stretched?"

Whipple looked at him, finding a paradox in this short, overfed man with the merry blue eyes and overhanging black brows. Marshal Gus Hobbs—Hangin' Hobbs—looked like the sort of man you could josh with and kill a bottle with and count on for a heart as big as his hat, but he had shown nothing but cold-blooded, impersonal efficiency since he had arrived on the stage an hour ago. There were conflicting stories about Hangin' Hobbs, but Sheriff Whipple guessed the one was right that said he would hang anybody in New Mexico for $25 and traveling expenses, when the proper executioner lacked stomach for the job.

"He's been tried and sentenced and he hangs tomorrow at dawn," Whipple admitted. "But to my dying day I'll swear Tom Kane didn't kill Abe Maguffin."

"Twelve other men thought different," Hobbs said. "What's his story? Make it short. I've got to go over and measure him up if I'm going to get a scaffold built by tonight."

"It ain't much of a story," the sheriff admitted. "Kane had trouble with Abe Maguffin over some Taylor land. Maguffin done most of his ranching over a whiskey bottle, and his cattle strayed all over the county. Tom Kane had saved his 'puncher's salary for five years and finally bought a little iron on Cuchillo River, with a Taylor grazing lease. It's only as big as a nickel, and, of course, he's running every cow he possibly can on it. So when he had to keep moving Abe Maguffin's critters off his winter feed, he gets on the butt and one day they have a fist fight in the street. I always understood that straightened things out. But last month Abe was shot in the head in his cabin and they found the heel of Tom's boot jammed in the rocks above the cabin. Tom couldn't explain it."

Hangin' Gus Hobbs pried at his teeth with a silver toothpick. They were big and square and very white against the robust coloring of his face. He had a way of not speaking, while he sucked his teeth and sized up a man, that was disconcerting. It suddenly seemed to go under Whipple's hide like a sliver.

"Oh, hell," the sheriff said, standing. "Let's get it over with. Finish that carcass and come on."

Hobbs paid for his dinner and accompanied him down the street to the one-story adobe jail. Saguaro City was a quiet little town, half Mexican and half white, and the border influence was everywhere. All the buildings were of one story except the Mountain House Hotel; some were whitewashed or painted pink or blue, but the majority were the dusty brown of the earth.

Cottonwood *vigas* protruded from the walls where eaves would have been in wooden dwellings, and Hobbs thought that in a pinch a man could be hung very neatly from one of these rafter poles. He liked the town, with its chinaberry trees and the river wandering past the back yards of the buildings on the west side of the street, and the red mountains humping up against the blue ranges farther back.

There were only three cells in the jail, tiny mud-walled cubicles with a single, barred window in each and a stout oaken door with a grilled window. Whipple unlocked one.

"Tom," he said, "this is Gus Hobbs, from Three Rivers. He . . . I got him to. . . ." Whipple broke off, cleared his throat. "Go on in," he said.

Hangin' Hobbs sat on the cot and studied the young fellow leaning one elbow on the windowsill. Tom Kane was in his early thirties, perhaps, a big man hardened by work. His lips were full, with a lift at the corners—whistling lips, Hobbs thought. His nose had been broken at some time, spoiling the symmetry of his face, but his eyes were pleasant and serious.

Tom Kane finally tired of his stare. He said: "Well?"

"Six-two," Gus Hobbs said. "Weight one eighty. Right?"

"Close enough. Why?"

The hangman grunted as he got to his feet. He squeezed Kane's bicep and struck him on the chest, and then he pinched the hard flesh of his flat stomach. *"Pshaw,"* he said, "take an inch-and-a-half rope. And an eight-foot drop instead of a six."

Kane suddenly pulled away from him, a shadow of fear in his eyes. "You damned ghoul!" he said. "Get out of here before I really do kill somebody."

Hangin' Hobbs appeared hurt. "Why, son," he said, "I'm only doing my job. How can I be sure the rope don't break or that the drop is far enough to . . . er . . . break your neck, if I don't check everything?"

Tom Kane's fists knotted hard. He said: "Get out of here!"

Gus Hobbs smiled. The coldness left his face and his brown eyes were warm and sympathetic. He said quietly: "Got troubles, ain't you, son? Tell me about 'em." To look at his expression of kindly concern a man might have thought he had come to Saguaro City on a mission of mercy, rather than to hang a man.

It caused Tom Kane to turn to the window and stare out, not hard now, but bitter and desperate. "Damn a town that'll hang a good man and let a coyote run loose!" he said.

"Who's the coyote?" Hobbs asked.

Tom Kane was watching someone across the street. He said: "Come over here, Marshal."

Gus Hobbs looked at the man he pointed out. He had just dismounted before an office at the end of the mercantile building, a thin man with a white Stetson and a spruce-looking brown suit. He lit a cigar and went into the office. The gilt lettering on the window said: **Cuchillo Valley Properties.**

"That's the coyote," said Tom Kane. "George Peeples. Everything but the pointed ears. He killed Abe Maguffin. Or had him killed."

"Is that guesswork?" the marshal asked.

"It's the kind of guesswork that tells you where there's smoke, there's fire. George Peeples owns Saguaro City and Cuchillo Valley. Lock, stock, and barrel. Abe Maguffin wouldn't pay his lease rent and neither would I. So he killed Abe and framed me. Nobody else, much, has had the guts to stand up to him. I was at Abe's cabin the night he was killed. I'd ridden over to see if he wanted anything from town. Me and him had been hitting it off pretty good since our tussle. I saw Abe through the door, dead. Somebody shot at me and I fired back once, and then took off, not knowing what I was up against. When they caught me in town later, that empty shell, and my broken heel, fixed me up fine."

"Who's this George Peeples?" the marshal asked. "A loan shark?"

"No. A range pirate, you might call him. You ever heard of the Treaty of Guadalupe Hidalgo?"

"Ended the Mexican War, didn't it?"

Kane sat down and built a cigarette. "Yes. Get a holt on yourself, now, Marshal, because you're going to think you're hearing the daddy of all windies. According to that treaty, the U.S. gover'ment agreed to honor all former land grants in the land we took over from Mexico. All right. So for forty years everything goes along fine. Then one day this fellow, Peeples, rides in and announces that he owns half the county, because his uncle had died in Mexico and willed him everything he owned under the Vizcaino Grant!"

"Ambitious feller," the marshal grunted. "Could he prove it?"

Kane threw the cigarette out the window, partially smoked. "That's the funny part of it. It's all listed in proper order in the deed book down at the courthouse. It's a forgery . . . got to be. But he's been getting rent money from everybody in this section for a year. Everybody but Abe and

153

me . . . and look what happens to us!"

Hobbs walked across the floor a couple of times, pulling at his lower lip. "Young fella," he said, "I kinda like you. I'd hate to be the death of a man that has the craw to stand up for his rights. Now, if you want to trust me, I'll see if I can't put that rope around the right neck."

Tom Kane smiled. "This don't fit in with your rep, Marshal."

The hanging marshal said, smiling: "I'm going to tell you something in confidence, Kane. I never hung a man in my life except a couple of confessed murderers. And that time I got sick. But it's got around that I like hangin' jobs, so whenever a lawman runs into a case like yours, he sends for me, because he don't want the death of a maybe innocent man on his head. And you know what I usually find? That the man ain't no more guilty than you. I ain't had to hang one of 'em yet."

Kane grinned. "I hate to be the one that spoils your record. But you're slated to hang me in about fourteen hours."

"Can't be done," Hangin' Hobbs said. "I said I'd need inch-and-a-half manila for this job. I checked at the mercantile before lunch, and they don't carry bigger'n an inch. That means a delay of two days while my special rope is brought up from Three Rivers by stage." He studied the cowboy a moment. "There's a girl, too, ain't there?" he said.

Kane looked away. "Yes, but she don't count. Her name's Kerry Hayden. She's too busy with other men to worry about me. Men that ain't starving on a two-bit spread."

"Hasn't she come to see you?"

"Once. I told Whipple I didn't want to see her. It would just be pity she gave me, and I don't need much of that. She never had time for me before, and it's kind of late to start now."

Gus Hobbs said sternly: "When a man gets to talking like that, it's time he sunk his teeth into a couple of pounds of beefsteak. I'll send one over from the café."

II

George Peeples's office amounted to no more than a safe, three chairs, a table, and a counter. There was a big map of the Arizona Territory on the wall, with a section shaded in red that represented Peeples's holdings under the Vizcaino Grant. A number of red and blue pins were stuck into it. Peeples was marking figures in a ledger when Marshal Hobbs entered. He said to a second man behind the counter: "Change Reilly's pin, Ed. He's finally paid up."

The man called Ed was a heavy-featured, thick-chested man of middle height, with black hair parted in an elaborate bartender's curl. He changed a pin from red to blue. He saw Hobbs when he left the map, and he said: "Customer, George."

George Peeples came to the front, a slender, dark man with narrow features and eyes of a yellow-brindle color. Hobbs took him in slowly—diamond horseshoe stickpin, fine silk shirt, tailored suit, massaged and talcumed jowls. He had a twenty-four carat smile with which he favored the marshal.

He said: "Something for you, friend?"

Hobbs introduced himself. "I always like to know something about the men I'm hanging," he told Peeples. "Just thought I'd get your idea about the case."

Peeples shrugged and took a gold cigar case from the pocket of his flowered brocade vest. He offered the marshal one, selected a Havana himself, and carefully moistened it with his tongue. "Well, sir," he said, "if I've seen one case like this, I've seen a dozen. Man gets on the peck at his neighbor. Neighbor don't take the hint and keeps on annoying him. Man loses his head and puts a bullet into him. It started with Cain and Abel." Peeples lighted the cigar.

156

"That's the way I look at it," said Hangin' Hobbs. "Open and shut. By the way . . . who found the boy's boot heel up there?"

"You came to the right place to ask that one." Peeples smiled. "Take a bow, Ed. Ed Shand, here, had ridden up to collect from old Maguffin that night and he came across the body."

Shand said: "I could see where he'd laid on his belly on the slope above the cabin, waitin' for a shot. After he done it, he got up quick and lit a shuck up the hill. Caught his heel between two big rocks as he was climbin' and tore it off. I come along about an hour later and clean stumbled over the body as I went in."

Hobbs said: "Why'd you stumble? Wasn't the lamp burning?"

Shand glanced quickly at his employer, and George Peeples gave him a steady stare out of those pale, yellowish eyes. Shand said, scratching his ear: "Why, no, I don't recollect that it was."

"Then I wonder," the fat marshal remarked, "how the boy saw to shoot him?"

"Must've got him just about sunset," Peeples offered.

"Funny Maguffin didn't see him on the slope, then."

Peeples's mouth looked small and tight. "Didn't happen to look out, I suppose."

"I may ask you to take me up there later, Shand," Hangin' Hobbs said.

Ed Shand looked troubled. He shoved his hands in his pockets. "All right."

Peeples put in testily: "Ain't it just a little late to be doing detective work, Marshal? After all, the man hangs tomorrow morning."

"Afraid not," said Gus Hobbs. "I'm sending to Three

Rivers for my special inch-and-a-half rope. That sets the party over till Friday."

Hangin' Hobbs was on the point of turning in at the Mountain House Hotel, when a girl who was standing near the entrance came toward him. "Marshal Hobbs?" she inquired.

Hobbs was not one to advertise the fact that he would rather save a man than hang him; it tended to restrict his movements and even, at times, endanger his life. He gave the girl a crisp glance and said without warmth: "Hangin' Gus Hobbs, ma'am, yes. And busy."

"I'm Kerry Hayden," the girl said. She was not much over twenty, he thought, a girl with the piquant Gælic combination of dark hair and blue eyes, and she had a clean-limbed, girlish figure.

Hobbs said: "I'm pleased to know you, ma'am. If you have a message for young Kane, Sheriff Whipple will be glad to take it."

Kerry Hayden said: "My message is for you, Marshal. Will you sit in the plaza for a few minutes with me?"

The marshal looked at his big silver watch. "Five minutes," he said shortly. "I've got to get a scaffold built, and considerable odds and ends cleaned up."

They sat on a bench by the bandstand in the dusty little plaza. There was a family of Mexican farm people from the lower valley eating a picnic lunch nearby, but they were too far off to hear anything that was said.

Kerry said: "Tom is very bitter toward me, isn't he?"

"As bitter as a man can be when he's crazy about a woman."

The girl's eyes searched his face. "Do you think he loves me, Marshal . . . after all this?"

158

"Afraid he does, Miss Hayden. A shame he's wasting it thataway."

"He isn't wasting it. I've been in love with Tom Kane for years. The reason I've held him off was for his own good. Tom was a 'puncher for Mort Reilly when we fell in love. He couldn't support a wife on forty dollars a month, so he saved all his salary till he could buy a ranch. He got enough for a down payment on the Anchor iron. He thought we should marry then, but I knew his expenses were just beginning. He's barely been able to hold on this last year . . . and what would it have been like with a wife and maybe babies? And now, when I've tried to explain it to him, he won't even see me."

"I'll pass it on to young Kane," Hobbs said. "Is that all you had to say to me?"

Kerry looked around quickly. "No." She had something tied up in a handkerchief, and she untied this and showed the marshal a twisted piece of gray lead. "Marshal," she said, "I dug this out of the wall of Abe Maguffin's cabin. There was blood splattered on the plank around it. It must have been the bullet that killed him. What caliber would you say it was?"

"Forty-One."

Kerry said: "That's it! And how many cowmen in this country carry a Derringer? Tom, for instance, doesn't own one."

"You're a smart young woman," said the marshal. "But this slug isn't going to do us any good here. If I officially dig it out of the wall, with a witness, I reckon the boy might get off. Now, then, you get back to Maguffin's cabin and put the bullet back where you found it. I'm riding out later with Ed Shand."

Kerry Hayden leaned forward and kissed him, and she said to the blushing marshal: "You aren't half as hard as you want us to think, Gus Hobbs. I'll bet you never hung a man in your life."

"I got a deppity to do all that kind of work over my way," Hobbs admitted. "But there's something about that Peeples gent's neck that arouses my professional interest. I may decide to cut my hangin' teeth on him before this is over."

When Marshal Hobbs returned to the hotel, Pike Grandin, the proprietor, had a message for him. Grandin was a big, friendly man who wore run-over boots, baggy trousers, and a plaid vest. He liked to talk, and, when he told a story, his face grew red with amusement and the sound of his laughter was a large and impressive thing.

Grandin brought a gunny sack from under the counter. "George Peeples sent this," he said. "Funny. Feels like a rope inside. He said to tell you he bought it off the livery stable."

Hangin' Gus Hobbs looked at the stout inch-an-a-half manila rope, and suddenly it was as though he had been going by a clock that had run down, and someone had reminded him of the correct time. He had been acting as though he had two days in which to unscramble this affair, and now he knew he had exactly thirteen hours.

"A cold-blooded man," he murmured. "And a smart one."

"George?" Grandin said. "Yes, he's nobody's fool. A man with less brains would have tried to dispossess some of the big ranchers around here and got himself into a peck of trouble. Old George just sets down and says . . . 'Keep your ranches, boys, but remember I can drop the axe any time I want. To keep me happy you can all just pay me two dollars an acre per year for your land.' Even us merchants pony up. I pay twenty bucks a month on the hotel, and I don't take in a hundred."

"Where can a man see this grant of his?" Hobbs asked.

"I can fix that for you," said Pike Grandin. "I'm county recorder as well as hotel man. Had to take the job a couple of years ago when the voters drafted me. Of course, the salary didn't hurt my feelings, either." Grandin laughed and took a key from the cash drawer. "We'll go down now and have a look."

The county records were kept in a small room in the back of the courthouse. There were three big volumes of maps and some faded sectional maps on the wall. Grandin, humming, thumbed through a ponderous leather tome until he located a yellowed sheet of foolscap with fine black printing.

"This is just a copy, you understand," he pointed out. "The original is in a bank somewhere. This one was printed up at the command of the old Mexican governor, in Eighteen Thirty-Nine. There's his signature. We've had experts go over it, and danged if it ain't legitimate! All these years it's been laying here like a powder keg, and now he's touched 'er off. Claims it was willed to him by some uncle who married a Mexican girl thirty years ago."

Hangin' Hobbs inspected the document, held the sheet of paper to the light, and rubbed his fingers over the printing. "Looks like the real thing," he said.

"No doubt about it," Grandin said. "Well, I reckon we can be glad he didn't get federal help and take over the whole kit and caboodle."

Grandin put the book back in a cupboard. As he snapped the padlock shut, the marshal noted the large diamond on the middle finger of his right hand, and it occurred to him that it was a large stone for a poor man. He said: "I take it you haven't always been a tavernkeeper?"

Grandin smiled. "The ring? Yes, sir, that's all that remains of the old Pike Grandin. Time was I could have bought out this town. Owned half of Kings County, Texas. Hard times whipped me. I hocked everything I had left but this ring to build the hotel."

He had his hand extended for Hobbs to examine the diamond, when the sound of a shot came into the room like a slammed door. Hobbs was hardly sure it was a shot. Then he saw the men running down the street toward the jail, and he said unhurriedly: "Excuse me, Grandin. I got a feeling I'm bein' paged."

Jake Parker, Sheriff Whipple's deputy, was at the door to keep the curious out when Marshal Hobbs reached the jail. He was a lanky, grim-lipped man with a face like a funeral. When he saw Hobbs's badge, he let him inside. Sheriff Whipple lay on the desk. The doctor was trying to stanch the flow of blood from a wound in the sheriff's side. Whipple was very pale, but he looked up at Gus Hobbs as though he knew him.

"Mighty tough, Sheriff," the marshal murmured. "Did Kane do it?"

"I don't know," Whipple said. "I was shot from the back as I stood out in front. It laid me out cold for a while."

Deputy Parker said: "Yo're damn' right he did it. Cell's empty, ain't it?"

Doc Estes indicated a bloody lead slug in a wash basin. "He had a Derringer," Estes said. "That's a Forty-One slug I took out of him."

Hangin' Gus Hobbs went out and stood on the boardwalk, smoking a cigarette and trying to sort his thoughts. He was thinking that a man could hide a belly gun in his boot. He was wondering how grave this trouble between Tom Kane and Abe Maguffin had been. It was in his mind that, if Kane were really guilty, he would not consider it of any help to him to have the case investigated further, and he might take his chance and get out.

162

It perplexed and troubled Gus Hobbs. He considered himself a good judge of men, and he didn't think he had mistaken young Kane. Yet the sheriff was shot, and Kane was gone.

Hangin' Hobbs went over to the restaurant and ordered the biggest steak in the house. There was solace in the good red meat, the same solace many men found in whiskey. It soothed him but did not addle his brains.

After he ate, he went over to George Peeples's place. Ed Shand was there alone. The marshal said: "Get your hat, Shand. We're riding out to Abe Maguffin's."

Shand looked at the clock. "George is out," he said. "I've got to be around till five."

"By five o'clock," Hobbs said, "you'll be halfway to Maguffin's."

Shand looked at his badge and did not argue.

III

Where the sandy shallows of Chloride Creek joined the Cuchillo, Abe Maguffin had built his little adobe shack in a motte of black oak on the ridge. The hill went up steeply behind the cabin, embossed with gray outcroppings of stone and a jungle of manzanita and buckbrush. They left the ponies in the corral and climbed up the gravelly slope in the somber twilight.

Shand led into a thicket. He showed the marshal how tall grass under the red fingers of manzanita had been beaten down, and how a man could put a bullet through the window of the adobe from there.

"Here's where he lost his heel," he said.

The rock behind the thicket had been split by some movement of the earth, so that a man might catch his boot heel in the slot if he were not watching his step. Near the top, bits of black leather clung to the rough granite. Hobbs gave them only a glance, and then went down the slope to the cabin. It was almost dark. He struck a match before entering and held it above his head, standing in the doorway. The cabin was empty, soundless; he went inside, and lighted a lamp.

Shand pointed at a formless brown blotch on the floor. "Yonder's where he lay."

Marshal Hobbs went to the window through which the shot was supposed to have come. He sighted across to the spot Shand had indicated, and then scanned the wall for the bullet hole. When he finally located it, down near the floor, he was far out of range of the window. Gus Hobbs pried the bullet out. He sighted across the blood spots from that point and said: "Abe Maguffin was shot through that door. A Forty-One short slug killed him. That means either a

Derringer or a light carbine. Shand, let's go look at your saddle gun."

Shand was standing by the door, his face wiped clean of expression, his hands hanging. His fingers clenched, and then slowly opened. He said without moving: "We don't need to look, Marshal. It's a Forty-One."

"See where that puts you, don't you?" Hobbs said.

"I been seein' ever since Maguffin was murdered. I never done it, Marshal. But it was done with my gun. The night he died somebody borrowed my rifle."

"Who?"

"I don't know. It was gone from the boot in the morning and the next night it was back again. But I can tell you some gents to ask about it. . . ."

Hangin' Hobbs suddenly threw the lamp at the stone fireplace, and his yell went through the brief flare of light before darkness came: "Down! Somebody outside!"

He heard the *wham* of lead hitting the wall. He heard two quick shots from the night. Ed Shand cried out, staggered to the center of the room, and collapsed there. Hobbs threw himself flat and fired back at the gun flashes.

Up in the buckbrush, a horse nickered. Hobbs crawled to the window and watched the brush for movement. The darkness was almost complete. He heard gravel *crunch,* and poured two shots into the thicket. The shots were not answered, but somewhere across the ridge stirrup leathers creaked and a horse moved down the trail.

The marshal, still cautious, reloaded and crawled to where Ed Shand lay. Shand was not dead, but he was unconscious and breathing in a sort of strangling snore. Hobbs did what he could for the man. He found the wound in his back and plugged the hole with a torn handkerchief. He dared not try to move him.

When he was sure the bushwhacker had gone, he unsaddled Shand's pony and left it in the corral. At a reaching lope, he rode back to Saguaro City.

Time was melting like a wax candle, and nothing the marshal could do would slow it down by the second. He had until morning to stop an avalanche that was gathering momentum every hour—unless Tom Kane made good his escape. But the town was small, and after the shooting of Sheriff Whipple the boy would have few friends.

It was eight-thirty when he reached town, and he was ravenous after the ride. He told Doc Estes about Shand, and then had a foundering meal, based on a T-bone and mashed potatoes and tapering off with apple pie and coffee. Weariness assailed him. He allowed himself a half hour to rest in his room, then he wanted to see that Vizcaino Grant again.

When he went into the Mountain House, Pike Grandin was playing solitaire on the counter. Grandin said: "Well, what'd you find out?"

"I found out who killed Abe Maguffin," Hobbs told him.

Grandin said: "No! You mean you don't think Tom Kane done it?"

"Did I say that?" Marshal Hobbs smiled. He went up to his room, and, entering, groped for the lamp.

Tom Kane's voice said: "No light, Marshal. I'm not taking any chances."

The hangin' marshal saw him as a long black shadow, standing by the bed. He took off his hat and mopped his forehead, and he sat on the bed. "Young fella," he said, "you ain't made it any easier for me to get you out of this scrape. If you shot Whipple, you're a hydrophobia skunk. If you didn't, and were fool enough to choose that time to duck out, you're just a damned fool. Which is it?"

"Just a fool," Kane said disgustedly. "I was jobbed. Some-body dropped a note in the cell. It said for me to be ready to light a shuck when I heard a shot. The cell door would be un-locked. It said there would be a horse out in front . . . and it was signed by you. Well, the door was unlocked . . . I heard it bein' unlocked just before the shot, but the man didn't show himself. I reckon he slipped in while Whipple was down to eat, and, o' course, Deppity Parker is down to the saloon most of the time. But when I came out, there is Whipple on his face on the walk, and, instead of a horse out in front, there's a dozen men legging it toward the jail." Kane licked a cigarette nervously. "What was I going to do . . . stay there and hang for two killings? I got out."

"Whipple won't die," the marshal said. "But this has put you in a bad light, even with your friends. Fortunately I know now who killed Maguffin."

Kane said: "Who did it, Marshal? Who killed Abe?"

"Shand. He gave me a cock-and-bull story tonight about somebody stealing his gun. But no thief would bother to bring it back, even if Shand was stupid enough to leave a good rifle hangin' in a saddle shed. This thing is bigger than a sixty-a-month gun hand, though. Somebody paid for Maguffin's death, and I've got to be sure who . . . and why. That little gal of yours put me onto Shand killing Maguffin. She's a smart filly, Tom. You could do worse than to let yourself be talked into marrying her someday."

Kane said skeptically: "You reckon she'd have me?"

"I reckon she's just waiting to be asked, now that you've got yourself a start. But that'll keep. I'm going over to the courthouse, now, and do some head scratchin' over that Vizcaino Grant."

Tom Kane put on his pinch-crowned Stetson and went to the door. "I get the gun hand's itch, sitting around doing nothing," he said. "I'll go out the back way and meet you at the courthouse."

"You got a gun?"

Kane shook his head. "I won't need one."

"All right," the hangin' marshal said. "Be at the top of the steps, back in the shadows."

Gus Hobbs, sighing, watched him leave. What he had to do was painful, but it was for the boy's own good. Hobbs went across to the jail and said to Jake Parker, the cadaver-eyed deputy: "I've found young Kane."

Parker dragged handcuffs from the desk drawer. He took a scatter-gun from the rack. He was all cold steel and vengeance. "Where is he?" he asked.

"Down at the courthouse. He's unarmed. He didn't kill Maguffin and he didn't shoot Whipple. But I want him jailed for his own protection, and, if I hear of his getting plugged or lynched, I'll put a slug right between your eyes."

Hobbs didn't raise his voice, and his red face was good-natured, but the deputy knew he meant exactly what he said. "I'll swaddle him in cotton if you say so," he said, smiling. "Around election time it'll be nice to be able to say we never lost a man."

As he went out, Hangin' Hobbs called after him: "I'll want a scaffold built before mornin'. A good stout one."

"Me and Whip always just used the loadin' boom down at the hay barn," Jake Parker said.

Hobbs grunted: "What kind of a hangman you think I am? I ain't tossin' hay bales . . . I'm performin' last rites for killers, in a dignified, twenty-five-dollar manner. But bein' it's short notice . . . the hay barn it is."

He was across the street from the county courthouse when Parker captured Tom Kane. He heard Kane's surprised curse, and then he heard his own name garnished with vituperation. But the thin-faced lawman defended him.

"Hobble your tongue, Tom," he said. "This is strictly a formality. You ain't got a better friend than Marshal Hangin' Gus Hobbs. We're just doin' this to keep you off the streets after curfew."

"An' what if this hunch of his don't pan out?" Kane complained. "Then I hang as per schedule?"

After they left, Hobbs went over to the courthouse and, as quietly as possible, punched a hole in a lower pane. He pressed back against the wall, listening. There were some small noises about town, but no sound of questioning voices, or of approaching feet. Hobbs reached inside, undid the catch, and raised the window. He hauled his bulk through the opening. He was on the point of lowering the window when a gray shape lunged at him through the gloom.

Hangin' Hobbs had never let his eating overlard him with fat he could not handle. He was a stout man, but his short legs were well-sinewed and his wind was good. He could chop through a four-inch oak sapling with two strokes of one arm. He was able to slide away from the gun barrel that chopped down, and the window sash took the blow. Hobbs caught the man's arm and twisted it, and his assailant gave one short, sharp cry and dropped the gun. Hobbs pumped a short blow to his jaw, and the man grunted and went to his knees. The marshal let him fall on his face.

He lowered the window, drew the shade, and lighted a lamp. He had not seen the man before. He was elderly, a baldish man wearing a green eyeshade. Black sleeve protectors came up to his elbows, and his hands were smudged with black. He wore a white mustache, similarly soiled.

It was no surprise to discover that the cupboard in which Pike Grandin had locked the deed book had been rifled. On the desk lay the Vizcaino Grant.

The man on the floor began to stir. Hobbs lugged him to a chair and sat on the desk while he came around. When he saw Hobbs and recognized him, he began to plead.

"I'm no killer, Marshal! I . . . I was just. . . ."

"Nobody said you was. You're Banta, the printer, ain't you?"

"Yes, sir. How'd you know?"

"You got your trade in black ink all over you. Sorry I hung that one on you, neighbor. You didn't give me much choice."

Banta's hands worked at the oak arms of the chair. His eyes were china blue and full of terror, and his voice was uncertain. "I guess you wondered why I was here," he said. "Well, sir, I do all the county printin' and I found out I'd let a pied line slip into a deed. So I come down to get it and do the job over."

Hangin' Hobbs sighed. "Do we have to go through all this?" he asked. "I'm tired and sleepy, and I don't feel like grillin' you all night. I was planning to look you up, but you've saved me the trouble."

"I . . . I don't savvy, mister."

"The deed . . . the Vizcaino Grant," Hobbs said. "It's a phony, ain't it?"

"Why, I wouldn't know, Marshal." Banta attempted a laugh. "That was printed just a little before my time."

"You mean you wish it was. It's printed on paper with an American watermark, and the typeface is as modern as tomorrow's newspaper."

The printer slumped. "All right," he said. "They promised to kill me if I talked. But I might as well get shot as hung. This is how it was, Marshal. . . ."

Gus Hobbs heard him out. As he listened, the case fell apart like a Chinese puzzle when it is shaken. Some odds and ends of information he had picked up, but had been unable to fit into the rest, now assumed their proper positions.

Gus Hobbs said: "Now, you've played it smart. You won't get shot. Go back to your shop and lock yourself in, and set down with a shotgun until I come for you in the morning. I'm going to hang this cold-blooded gazabo a mile high, and sell shots at his carcass."

Banta crawled out the window and hurried away. Marshal Hobbs folded the grant and stowed it under his shirt. He turned then, and saw Jake Parker standing in the doorway. He was caught so cold that he could not move even when the deputy sheriff walked toward him. A second man, chunky and red-headed, stepped in from the dark hallway.

Gus Hobbs felt the .45 prod his belly, and stared into Parker's fish-eyed countenance. "Yep," he said, "I figured you was in it, Jake. Who else could have got the keys to unlock Tom Kane's cell? And who else would Whipple let get the drop on him in his own jail?"

"I got to hand it to you," Parker said. "You're one of the smartest lawmen that ever botched things up in Saguaro City."

Hobbs scratched his head. "This reminds me of the time I cleaned out a rattlesnake's nest on my uncle's ranch," he said. "I threw a stick of dynamite in the cave to kill 'em, and then began to drag out the dead 'uns. By damn, I thought I never would get through haulin' out snakes! Well, it's just the same here. I've dragged out three snakes, now, and I ain't to the big bull snake yet. But I'll keep on trying."

The redhead drawled: "You're all done tryin', Marshal. Let's go over to the hotel and have a drink on your speedy departure."

Parker kept a gun in Marshal Hobbs's side as they went by deserted back streets to the rear entrance of the hotel. Parker drew the shade in the room and lighted the wall lamp, and sat the prisoner down in the only chair. He said: "Got the bug juice, Lud?"

Lud took a pint of whiskey from his pocket, poured half of it on Hobbs's clothes, and gave the rest to the marshal. "Drink 'er down, pardner," he said.

Hobbs shook his head. "Never touch it."

"You do this time," Jake Parker told him. "When you finish that, we may be able to rustle up some more. By hangin' time, you're going to be so sorry-eyed drunk you couldn't hang a picture."

Both of them laughed, Lud slapping his fat thigh.

"I suppose," Hangin' Hobbs said, "you know I can hang your boss, anyway, when I get loose. You're only helping to take an innocent man's life."

Parker shook his head. "You ain't going to hang anybody. We'll take care of Banta if he tries to open his mouth. Shand's already out of it. He'd crawled off in the brush to die by the time Estes got there. You can't hang a man on a hunch." He made a motion with the gun. "Drink up, hangman."

Gus Hobbs had done some tippling in his younger days. He drank an inch of the whiskey, making a great show of having his throat burned by the spirits, but it hardly warmed his blood. He took an hour to kill the bottle. When he was done, Parker went downstairs and brought four more bottles.

The deputy was sleeping. He'd pulled off his boots and lay down on the bed, leaving the guarding of Marshal Hobbs to Lud. Hangin' Hobbs's mind went back and forth over the situation, and it looked dismal from every angle. He had gone into it under the assumption that he was bucking only one man; instead of that, he could name only one, offhand, that he was not bucking. And that man, Tom Kane, would hang as surely as the sun came up.

About five o'clock Jake Parker awoke. He washed his face in cold water and rubbed it vigorously with a towel. He glanced at the marshal, who by now had four whiskey bottles at his feet, a breath like a distillery, and a limber-jawed look. Parker smiled.

"He'll do," he said to Lud. "I'll get things lined up. I'll make a show of having to pinch hit for Hobbs. After you see that things are getting under way, bring him down. One look at him and the crowd will do the rest. Hobbs won't do any talking in Saguaro City."

Hangin' Hobbs shook his finger at the deputy. "Now, lissen 'ere! Lemme tell yuh something, Deppity! Nobody'sh gonna make a fool out o' me. . . ."

Parker slapped him on the back. "Take it easy, old-timer. I'll see that you get a one-way ticket back to Three Rivers tonight. Maybe you'll stick to your own corral after this job!"

Hobbs began to study the redhead after Parker departed. He had spilled a lot of whiskey on his clothes, but very little down his throat, and his head was as clear as quartz. Lud was dead for sleep, and quite a bit of the whiskey had found its way to his stomach. He sat there on the bed, heavy-lidded, a revolver in his lap.

About six o'clock they heard the sounds of a crowd collecting before the feed barn. A wagon was rolled into place under the hay boom. Hangin' Hobbs picked up one of the bottles and tilted it.

He said disappointedly: "Dry's a bone."

Lud grinned. "You got the makin's of a first-class soak, hangman." He went to the window and looked out. That was his last conscious act for some time. A pint whiskey bottle shot across the room with a low whistling sound and caught him at the base of the skull. He went down like a shot beef.

Marshal Hobbs left the hotel hurriedly. Time was almost up.

Jake Parker was trying to throw a rope over the loading boom when the marshal reached the street. Tom Kane stood with his head lowered, a hood covering his face, at the tailgate of the wagon. Pike Grandin and three others stood at the tongue, ready to pull it out from under him. The crowd was small and silent. Saguaro City was now convinced of Kane's guilt, and there would be few who didn't relish his death.

Hobbs stopped at Banta's print shop and brought the frightened old man out of his fortress. He was wearing two revolvers and carried an 8-gauge shotgun. They skirted the crowd and approached from the rear of the wagon. Parker raised his arms for attention.

"According to the verdict of the jury, this man, Thomas Kane, has been sentenced to die by hanging this Fourteenth day o' June," he announced. "In the absence of Sheriff Whipple and a certain Marshal Hobbs, from Three Rivers, I'm forced to substitute. Kane, you got anything to say?"

Kane's voice was muffled by the black hood. "Yes. If there's such a thing as ghosts, quite a few *hombres* in this town are going to get haunted for the next few years."

Parker placed the rope about his neck. Hangin' Hobbs climbed to the wagon, pulling Banta up behind him. Hobbs said: "Just a minute, Parker."

Parker jumped. When he saw the marshal, he shouted: "There's the drunken apology for a lawman! I don't reckon we need any o' his talk."

Hobbs said: "I reckon you're gonna get it. Banta, say your piece."

Banta was terrified by the eyes of the crowd and by the presence of unseen guns. His voice hardly carried to the listeners.

"I don't know about Tom Kane, folks," he said. "I just know about this George Peeples set-up. They got me to print up that old Vizcaino Grant six months before Peeples came to town. I thought it was a joke, and, when I found out different, they threatened to kill me if I opened up. Peeples don't own anything in this county but his clothes, so far as I know."

Hobbs kept his eyes on George Peeples, sitting rigidly on the hitching rack. "Something else that might interest you," he said, "is that Ed Shand killed Abe Maguffin. I took a Forty-One slug out of the wall of Maguffin's cabin, and he admitted it come from his carbine. Shand tried to pass the buck, telling me that somebody else borrowed the gun. But what he really meant was that a certain *hombre* paid him to do the killing. Isn't that right, Shand?"

The crowd murmured at the name, and Jake Parker started. But the marshal had seen the blood-spattered ghost just inside the alley next to Peeples's place, and he knew why Shand had dragged himself, dying, back to town. Shand had a job to do.

Ed Shand stepped onto the boardwalk. His shirt was stuck to his belly with blood, and he looked as though he had crawled all the way back to town. He said hoarsely: "That's right, Marshal. I got interrupted when I tried to tell you who hired me before. This time I'm not being stopped. The man that I drop is the one that paid me to kill Maguffin . . . and paid Parker to shoot Whipple!"

Pike Grandin's gun roared. He had slipped away from his post at the wagon tongue to the walk. Shand staggered, fell against the building. But he brought the carbine up to his shoulder and fired, and Pike Grandin, hotel man and dreamer of empire, stumbled forward two steps and clutched at the air, and fell underneath the wagon.

Hangin' Hobbs turned to match Jake Parker's gun play.

175

His old .44 bellowed. Parker went to his knees, clutching his arm. His lips were back from his teeth, like those of a wounded animal, scared but still defiant.

"Finish it, lawman!" he challenged harshly.

Hobbs ignored him. Parker would live to hang—by Sheriff Whipple's rope. He was looking for George Peeples, but he could not shoot at him for the mob that swarmed over the hotel man's dummy. Peeples would swing, too, if he wasn't trampled to death.

The marshal untied Tom Kane. Kane was the color of a croaker's belly, but he was grinning. He helped Hangin' Hobbs carry Parker to a cell, and afterward he said: "You were right, Marshal, but here's one thing I don't understand. . . . Who was the kingpin, Peeples or Grandin?"

"Grandin," the marshal told him. "He'd had a lot of money once, and it ain't easy to come down from that to running a two-bit hotel. So he cooked up this yarn about the Vizcaino Grant. But he was smart enough to cover his tracks with a dummy, in case it ever broke. Probably he and Peeples split the take. Lord knows there was enough for both."

Kane rubbed his neck, where the rough touch of the manila still lingered. "You saved the day for me and Saguaro City," he said, "I don't know how to thank you, Marshal."

"That's easy," Hobbs said. "You can buy me a T-bone and we'll call it square. And you can do me another favor by getting the preacher to tie the knot for you and Kerry *pronto*. It'll hold you just as tight as one o' mine, and it'll be a whole lot easier on the neck!"

I'll Take the High Road

Ginny was drying her hair on the porch when Clark rode in. It was late afternoon of a day in May. Over the mountains soaring from the pasture the sun distilled an amber light that was just right for the leaves, for the grass, and for Ginny's hair. It was like twenty-four-carat gold, with sequins in the highlights. She heard his spurs on the walk, and called to him.

"Did you catch him, Clark?"

Clark grunted. "We'll catch that horse when he's ready to be caught." Wearily he let himself into a porch chair. Cocking his feet on the rail, he squinted at the light streaming through the fine mesh of her hair. "Blondes," he reflected, "are nice to come home to."

"But not nice enough to stay home with," Ginny said.

"Well, you see, horses are nice, too." Clark had been gone four days on this wild-horse chase. He deserved the worst, but instead of tears and recriminations he anticipated fried chicken with biscuits and gravy.

Ginny's eyes sparkled. They were blue; close up, they were the blue-gray of pine smoke. "So you wasted four days on that horse, and he's still his own man."

"We got so close to him this time that I could see the burrs in his tail. By George, that's a horse!"

"I'll bet! Fourteen years old, string-halted, and he drags his chin unless he's standing on a ridge trying to impress you gullible cowpunchers. It takes good blood to make good stallions. That's what you said when we bought Red instead of the station wagon."

Clark smiled complacently. It was nice to know she was teasing. They both knew he wasted too much time on wild-horse chases and rodeos, yet she pretended to believe they were part of the business. Hunting and fishing weren't, of course, and neither was spending a couple of days a month with old Billy Hazard, up among the glaciers. Clark's philosophy was to give tomorrow its due, but not to sell today short, either. But Ginny never rode him for his derelictions. Theirs was a comfortable relationship that assumed devotion rather than demanded it.

After three years of marriage, they knew each other pretty well. They talked of making a fortune in Quarter horses and white-face cattle, but they knew they wouldn't. It didn't bother Clark, and he didn't think it bothered Ginny.

A car rumbled across the plank bridge. Dud Winter's pickup swung into the yard. Dud flashed an envelope. "Telegram, Clark! Picked it up in town."

He lumbered up the steps and leaned his substantial hindquarters against the railing while Clark opened the wire. Dud's big, simple face was avariciously inquisitive.

"Huh?" Clark said.

"Who's coming?" Ginny asked.

"Somebody named Lee Cushman. Wonder who he is?"

Ginny brightened and began tying a handkerchief about her hair. "Why, don't you remember? He was at the Salinas rodeo last year. He tried to buy Red. I think he said he was a horse trainer for the movies." She caught the iron look of warning suddenly rising in Clark's eyes. "Or something," she added.

"Don't think you ever mentioned him to me," Dud said.

About Dud Winter, Billy Hazard had once remarked:

"Dud ain't got the sense to pour whiskey out of a boot, but he can smell a horse sale two counties off."

Clark laughed offhandedly. "You know those movie people! Lots of talk but nothing behind it. I think he runs a boarding stable near Hollywood."

Dud's round blue eyes turned to Ginny. "I thought you said he trained bronc's?"

"I was just guessing."

"What do you suppose he wants?"

Clark put the wire in his pocket. "He's wasting his time if he still thinks he can buy Red. Four hundred, he offered."

"When's he coming?" Dud asked. He ran a horse ranch just east of Clark's, and it was no trouble at all to drop over any old time.

"Saturday." The wire said Thursday. It said: **Have opportunity for you to supply colts to movie trade. Your price.**

Dud drove away with a pleased and thoughtful expression.

Lee Cushman drove up on Thursday. He was a likable man in his early forties, deeply tanned and with tightly waved gray hair and a mustache three hairs wide. He dressed casually in wrinkled slacks, a field jacket, and scuffed boots.

After lunch they went out to the corral. All the horses had been curried to the fine sheen of oiled silk. Cushman could not keep his hands off them. They were highly bred and responsive, and he was a Quarter-horse man, one of the fraternity that held a pony capable of roping cows on weekdays and beating Olhaverry in the quarter mile on Sunday was a lot of horse.

After Clark let him ride Morocco, a half-trained bay, he regarded it respectfully. "That's the finest Technicolor stud I've seen in years!"

179

"What's the difference between a Technicolor stud and any other?" Clark laughed.

"About two hundred dollars. It used to be color was just something to wrap a horse up in. Consequently there's people raising buckskins, blue roans, and grays everywhere, but try to find somebody you can count on for bays and chestnuts!"

"You can count on me," Clark said. He hardly knew whether to take Cushman seriously or not. "There hasn't been a cold color in this line for generations. It just happened, but we can try to keep it that way, if it matters."

Cushman wanted to try the horses out. They rode five miles up Spanish Creek. It was a spectacular country of breath-taking extremes. Behind and below them were the flat gray desert and the burnt-sienna hills hiding the smoking ugliness of Death Valley. Before them the Sierras presented towering façades of granite, lofty rims where the snows never melted.

Clark was pleased to observe Cushman responding to it. Yet there was a drop of the motion-picture producer in Cushman's enjoyment.

"You ought to run dudes here, Clark," he said seriously.

Clark shuddered. "I've always avoided anything that required special feeding."

They rode on up to Jawbone Lake, a splinter of emerald caught in giant boulders. Clark had a stone corral here. From the branch of a twisted oak hung branding irons and scraps of harness. Lee Cushman said again: "With a spot like this, it's a crime not to capitalize on it!"

Clark let it lie. In a windy dusk, they rode back to the ranch.

It was cool enough that night for a fire. With one of Ginny's fine meals under his belt and a drink in his hand,

Cushman relaxed. The big living room was as informal as a bunkhouse. The floor was of rubbed tile; the tawny adobe walls pointed up the bright Mexican rugs. The house was Ginny's hobby—one of those hobbies women have before the children come and after they leave.

Cushman got down to business. He was training eight or ten horses a year. He could use all the Steeldusts Clark could raise. Anything that did not come up, he could sell as a saddle mount.

"You see, I'm tired of following up leads. I hear about a horse in Arizona, but by the time I get there he's just being loaded into a trailer. And maybe he's got thoroughbred blood in him, anyway, and a gunshot would send him into hysterics. I'll pay you twenty-five percent more than you'll get anywhere else, just to know the horses will be right and ready. How about it?"

Clark glanced at Ginny, and, if she did not speak, the small tight smile on her lips talked a plain language. *If the money means more to you than your mountains, go ahead.*

He got up and poured Cushman another drink. He was rather surprised to discover that he was excited. Not over the money, but over the idea of going into horses big, of having a show ranch. He saw it in redwood: **The Travis Quarter-Horse Ranch.** And, of course the material things were pleasant to contemplate, too, the fine trappings of prosperity. But it would mean the end of wild-horse chases for a while.

"Well . . . ," he said finally, and then hesitated. "Well, how about it, Ginny?"

"You're the businessman," Ginny said. She wasn't helping any.

Clark drained his glass and spun the ice in the bottom of it, and set the glass down and pressed it against the coaster an instant. "I guess we'll try it."

"Fine!" Cushman smiled, but didn't get excited. He spoke to Ginny. "I have been trying to interest Clark in taking some paying guests, Missus Travis. Somebody's always asking me about a ranch where they don't dress for dinner or go on tours. They wouldn't want anything but good food and horses. I'd say you have the perfect set-up. And if you charged less than twenty dollars a day, they'd feel cheated."

Ginny laid a finger on her cheek. "It sounds wonderful. I suppose I could fix up the storerooms and partition the bunk-house."

Clark looked startled. "Sure that's what you want to do, hon?"

"Why not? You tend to your horses, and I'll tend to my dudes."

After Cushman went to his room, Clark said: "You aren't sore about the deal with Cushman, are you?"

Ginny sat on the rug before the fireplace. "No. A little worried, I guess. Because if this is another of your enthusiasms, Clark, it will be the most expensive one you've had."

He didn't like the word "enthusiasms". It made him think of an elderly playboy cavorting through his love affairs. He was nearly thirty, a little old for whimsies. "It's no enthusiasm," he said shortly. "It's time we got an angle, and I think this is it."

His last thought that night, an irrelevant thought called up by a subconscious calendar in his mind, was: *I'll have to get some leaders soaking for the opening next week.* It was a pleasant thought to go to sleep on, but a small, stern-lipped objection showed on its face just as he fell asleep. *You won't have time for the opening. You have those ponies to get ready. . . .*

As Cushman was leaving the next morning, Dud Winter rode in on his palomino. Clark noticed that the big Quarter horse, Dutch, had been curried until it gleamed like greased gold. Cushman turned from the car to stare at it.

Dud, grinning fatly, dismounted. "Just thought I'd stop by, Clark, in case you wanted anything from town."

"Pretty long ride," Clark said, "when you could have taken the pick-up."

Cushman hadn't even seen Dud, yet. He walked around the great golden horse. "Got any more of these?" he asked Dud.

"You kinda favor palominos?" Dud asked coyly.

"Haven't, up to now." Cushman rubbed his chin. "Might be something in it, though. That's a good-looking stud."

Dud turned the stirrup and remounted. "Glad to help you any time I can. Be seeing you, Clark. Glad to've met you, Mister Cushman."

Cushman drove off, and a few minutes later Clark noticed Dud swing his horse east and start for home. "I hope that crock head breaks a leg," he told Ginny. "If it rained pennies over here, Dud would be on hand with a piggy bank."

It was hard to tell whether this was an end or a beginning. It was the end of loafing and inviting one's soul. It was the beginning of working with horses, instead of what Clark used to call "fooling with bronc's." He attended endless horse auctions, for there was no magic that would give him more colts without buying more mares.

At the same time, Ginny seemed possessed of an urge to turn Spanish Fork into a trading post. She brought in carloads of rugs, hides, and furniture. She hung ollas from the beams of the porch. Window boxes appeared, and all the walks were traced with whitewashed stones. Clark began to suspect she was taking advantage of a situation.

One day Billy Hazard came rambling in on his red mule. Clark, working with a horse in the corral, saw him stop short and peer at the ranch house. In a city, he would have checked the address. Billy scratched his head and sat uncertainly on the mule.

Clark went out. "What drove you out?" he asked. "Fire?"

Billy had been born in the hills, offspring, so the legend ran, of a glacier and a mountain goat. His features were narrow, flat, and brown, and he wore an Army campaign hat that made him look like William S. Hart. Billy lived on a Spanish-American War pension. He could have made good money guiding sportsmen, but he contended a hunting dog wasn't made to run with poodles. He had a fine Thoreau-like philosophy that was like whiskey to Clark's soul.

"What the hell's going on around here?" Billy demanded.

Clark hedged. "Oh, Ginny's getting ready for guests. A woman gets lonesome, you know, out like this."

"Lonesome!" Billy looked around. The trees were still there. The creek was talking its usual good sense, for whomever wanted to listen. The mountains hadn't moved away.

"For company," Clark said.

"Oh!" Billy accepted it without trying to understand. Women were said to be necessary, but God help the man who tried to understand them. He glanced into the corral. "What are you trying to do . . . corner the horse market?"

"I've made a deal with a fellow to take all the horses I can raise. Pretty good money in it."

Billy looked concerned. "You hard up, Clark? I've got a bit put by."

Clark wished he had rehearsed this scene. "We're doing all right, Billy, but I've got to think about the future. I've got to save for the children, when they come along, and . . . well, a lot of things."

Billy peered at him, and finally dismissed the whole matter by spitting in the dust. His eyes freshened. "Better saddle up, Clark. I've got old Silvertip spotted. He's got his mares in Ice-house Cañon. We'll shore put a halter on him this time."

A cool, clean breeze entered Clark's mind, scattering the hundred vague worries of the past weeks. It brought the green fragrance of the pines. It rang with the silver music of a stallion's call.

Sternly the worries reassembled. "Billy, I'm going to have to skip it this time. I've got three horses to get ready before next week. Some folks are coming, and they'll want to ride. Besides," he said, "what would we have if we did catch him? A cold-blooded, wall-eyed outlaw."

"Then why have we been chasing him all over Inyo County?" Billy demanded.

"For the same reason we hunted that lost gold mine last summer . . . an enthusiasm."

Billy scratched the mule's neck. Finally he swung around. "Come on up after you turn this nuthouse back into a ranch."

It was unreasonable, and Clark frowned after him. But that night, when the darkness flowed down from Billy Hazard's mountains, he had a tingle as he thought of Billy, setting his trap to catch the stallion.

On the 3rd of July, Cushman arrived with two guests, a good-looking young fellow dressed like Roy Rogers, and a sultry-eyed brunette. The Roy Rogers character was an upcoming Western actor named Barry Carter. The girl, Lois Lane, also played in Westerns, although there was nothing homespun about her in a belted tan skirt and a diaphanous blouse that she filled marvelously. She had dark, earthy-red lips and an undeceived look in her eyes.

Clark installed them in their rooms and saddled the horses. It seemed that every time he rounded a corner he fell over Barry and Lois, embracing. Not passionately, although with extreme determination, as if they were practicing. They never seemed embarrassed by him.

In the afternoon, they went out for a ride. Ginny stayed to attend to dinner. As Lois started to mount, Clark said quietly: "Look out, Miss Lane. You're going up backward."

Lois discovered she had the wrong foot in the stirrup. She laughed. "They always give me a ladder . . . in my pictures."

Cushman wanted to show Barry Jawbone Lake as a possible location. They were a couple of miles below it when Lois pointed at a cliff west of the trail. "Isn't that a cave over there?"

"It's called Painted Cave," Clark told her. "There're some Indian pictographs in it."

Lois insisted that they look for Indian pots. Cushman shook his head. "You and Clark go on. I want Barry to see this other spot."

It was an hour over a rough trail to the cave. Once they were there, Lois showed only mild interest in pots. They sat in the shade to smoke. She was a pleasant companion, but somehow the subject was always some oblique aspect of sex. They got around to the old question of why men had excelled in every field of endeavor.

"The only place we've beaten you," she deplored, "is in having babies!"

"You girls have done pretty well in acting," Clark said.

Lois laughed lightly and touched his hand. "Mister Travis, you're gal-lant!"

She had, he thought, the most personal eyes he had ever looked into. An instinct from his bachelor days caused him to glance at her hand. No rings. All the old mechanism began to whirr, with surprising smoothness. He found himself thinking: *Why not?* A little ashamed, he remembered he'd relinquished his amateur standing. He changed the subject to horses.

186

It was nearly dark when the two reached the ranch house. The others' horses were already in the corral. As he entered the back door, Clark tried to whistle away a little ghost of guilt. He was not reassured to see a heap of overdone biscuits in the sink. The Indian woman was putting a fresh pan into the oven, and Ginny, at the sink, was starting to make a fresh pot of coffee.

"You two didn't need to rush," she told him. "I can always warm things over and make more biscuits."

"She wanted to see Painted Cave." Clark grinned.

Ginny trilled a little laugh. "Remember the time you brought me up here before we were married? I had to see it, too . . . after you dragged me there by the hair."

"Now, look . . . ," Clark began.

Ginny brushed past him. "Later," she said.

In their room that night, she demanded to see his handkerchief. She studied it on both sides. "No lipstick," she decided. "So maybe you have changed your habits. Just the same, I think you can see how it looks to other people to be sneaking off with lady guests."

"I told you it was her idea!" Clark protested. "The others could have gone along if they'd wanted to. Good Lord, if you're going to walk up the walls every time I saddle a lady's horse. . . ."

She kicked off her shoes. "It's not that I'm jealous, Clark."

Clark said: "Ha!"

Her chin went up. "It's just that any woman that's married to a . . . a playboy doesn't know where he'll stop playing." She saw the effect of it in his face, and said quickly: "Clark, don't be silly. You know what I meant. You aren't a *playboy*, any more than Billy Hazard is. But you're certainly a nonconformist. I only meant. . . ."

"Forget it."

"I won't forget it! I've got a right to make myself clear." She sounded something more than earnest. There was a small shadow of fright in her eyes.

He went into the bathroom and showered. When he returned, the light was out. He got in bed carefully, but in a moment he heard her say: "I wish every horse on the place would get the epizootic. And that goes for the dudes, too!"

Cushman and his dudes left, new bunches came up, and Clark sent his first batch of horses down to become Triggers or Silvers or merely dusty animals in a sheriff's posse. Whatever they became, they brought the money in. Clark looked at the figures in his passbook and wondered what had become of the thrill he was to feel.

It was July, now, and high in the 1,000 lakes wedged in crevices of the mountains the fish were gliding shadows. Clark decided he had to have a week off. The night before he was to leave, a mare dropped a premature foal. He lost it, saved the mare, and wondered where he could find another colt to take the dead one's place.

Then Dud stopped by in his pick-up. He and Dutch were on their way to Salinas. "Ain't missing the big 'un, are you, Clark? They say ol' Bob Crosby may be there."

"Wish I could. Pretty busy right now." Clark tried to sound as if he were too busy getting rich, but what he felt was the ache of a boy kept in after school the day of the game.

Good old Dud did not fail to stop on his way back. Yes sir, it had been the hottest thing yet! He and Dutch walked off with $200 roping money, and there was a new record set in the team tying.

Clark noticed a new horse in the double trailer. "Buy yourself a plug?"

Dud smiled, a little embarrassedly. "Little ol' mare. Cost

too much, but I'll get the money back. I . . . uh . . . Cushman was there, Clark. He's going to take a colt now and then."

Clark laid down the bridle he had been repairing. "Look! Is this my market or yours?"

"Cushman says there's room for both of us."

Clark snapped: "Stop kidding yourself. Your tongue's been hanging out ever since you saw that Hollywood address. This thing may last ten years, and it may end tomorrow. The movie public is deciding that . . . not Cushman. While it does last, it's my baby."

Dud's light blue eyes toughened. "You got a patent on selling horses?"

"I'm appealing to your sense of sportsmanship. You know what I've got sunk in this outfit. And you know that every horse you sell him is one I won't."

Dud glanced at the trailer. "I've got two thousand dollars in that mare, Clark."

"Why, you damned fool!"

Suddenly Clark saw the whole thing. Lee Cushman was the only man who would walk out of this mess with a profit. Unconsciously or otherwise, he had pitted them against each other. All that could come out of the situation was price cutting. That was one step further than Clark would go to make a dollar.

In Dud's face, some inkling of it began to dawn. "If I hadn't bought that mare. . . . You see, I had to borrow money to get her."

They sat on the running board. Clark said: "How much sporting blood have you got, Dud? Willing to stake Dutch against Red in a match race?"

"That's pretty steep." Dud rubbed his neck.

"If we keep competing with each other," Clark reminded him, "we're both going to lose more than just a stallion. We'll be giving horses away, and working like fools to do it."

Even Dud could see that. He took a deep breath and began to nod. "OK, Clark. OK."

They decided on the Labor Day rodeo at Bishop for the match. Clark did not tell Ginny about it. Quietly he set out to get Red in shape.

Cushman brought up some dudes for Labor Day weekend. On Sunday they all drove down to Bishop. Clark took Red along in the trailer. The town was an hour away, a cool vista of trees along a creek, with the desert for a doormat and the mountains for a back yard. The day was hot, but under the trees at the fairground the broken shade was cool.

Cushman found Clark unloading the stallion. He frowned. "You're not going to rope with *him!*"

"Going to race him."

"What's the idea? If anything happens to Red, our deal's off."

The stallion stepped off the ramp, and Clark held him by the cheek strap. "As a matter of fact," he said, "I'm racing Dud's palomino."

Cushman began to comprehend. "Clark, you're not sore about my arrangement with Dud?"

"I'm not singing carols about it. You've put us in competition with each other. Since neither of us can make a living cutting prices, we're settling it this way. Winner takes both studs."

Cushman was still standing there when he led the horse away. . . .

A few minutes later Ginny hurried over to where he was walking the horse. Cushman had told her about the race. Clark had done a lot of wild things in their married life, but nothing had upset her the way this did. He pointed out to her the same things he had told Dud, but his logic did not reassure her.

"If you lose Red," she told him, "you may never find another horse like him. Clark, you've worked so hard!"

"But I don't intend to lose him, Ginny."

He led the horse through the trees and worked him until the kinks were out. The race was set for two o'clock. He heard the loudspeakers announcing the results of the first round of bronco stomping. With a cold, nervous vacancy in him, he rode back toward the track.

The barrier had been moved to the end of the chute, the tail on the oval track that provided a quarter-mile straightaway. Dud was behind the barrier on his palomino. He said— "H'are you, boy?"—with forced gaiety.

By now, Clark thought, he must realize he had been maneuvered into a wrong race. Dutch was too light in the hindquarters for a winning start, unless he was running out of his class and Red was away off.

The track was a clean set of lines converging near the trees. Above them the mountains beckoned, lean and blue and ribbed with granite. This time of day the fish lay, deep and lazy, where only the trout flies of such giants as Billy Hazard could rouse them. The wildflowers would be a light on the ground. In the morning, now, there might be a glint of frost in the air.

The starter was waiting. It seemed to Clark that the bay was excessively nervous. Clark dismounted, loosened the cinch a bit, and then realized it was not the horse that had the jitters, but himself. He remounted and brought Red up to the barrier. As the stands quieted, the timers looked at their watches. Then, automatically, Clark and Dud raised their whips. The barrier banged open.

There was a surge that pulled Clark back against the

cantle, and then the horse was in long and easy stride down the track. You could ride all your life, Clark thought, but riding one like Red was forever a thrill. For a while you were freed from the slow prison of gravity, riding a breeze as strong and as sweet as a prairie wind.

Dud was right there beside him, lying along the neck of his horse, quirting fiercely and pleading. He and Clark were of a weight, but Dud's was mostly in the seat of his pants. He could distribute himself any way he wanted; the load remained that of a sack of wheat. Gradually he began to slip out of Clark's view, until it was no longer Dud beside him, but the head of his mount.

They were streaking past the bleachers now, breasting an almost tangible roar. *They're yelling for you,* Clark thought. *You lucky stiff! You're winning the best palomino in Inyo County. Ten years, and you'll own the finest Steeldust herd in California, plus a bank roll, a paunch, and a face that turns purple every time you lift a bale of hay.*

He glanced back at Dud. There were tears in Dud's eyes and his big clock face was a strangled red as he tried desperately to ride the whip to victory. And somehow the golden horse was beginning to close it up. The stands saw it and came to their feet with a shout. Dud began to quirt like a madman.

But Clark let Red reach, stretching along the horse's neck and giving him the whip, and the thin shadow line of the wire lay across the track just ahead. When they streaked across it, there was a bare six inches of dark-red muzzle between the palomino and the finish.

Clark and Ginny sat on the tailgate of the trailer, drinking beer from cans beaded with cold. Ginny's eyes were still moist.

"Oh, Clark, I'm so happy! It was a beautiful race."

Clark looked at her. She had something of the enameled brilliancy of a party girl, flinging roses riotously, but not fooling anyone.

"You are, are you?" he said. "You look like the face on the mortuary floor. If you really wanted Red to lose, why didn't you say so?"

There were tears in her eyes, then, and she said gently: "Oh, darling, I did want him to win . . . but I wanted us to win, too, and I guess we couldn't do both, could we?"

Clark squeezed the beer can and felt the cold sting of it in his hand. "I suppose not," he said. "You know, we used to have a lot of fun up there, didn't we?"

Ginny sighed. "We'll never get over it."

"Well, is there any reason why we shouldn't have fun again?" Clark demanded.

"None that I can think of."

Clark finished his beer and jumped off the trailer. "I'll be back," he said. She watched him until he disappeared into the crowd.

Just before sundown they drove out of town with the empty trailer booming along behind them. "Dud like to broke down." Clark chuckled. "He thought I was doing him a favor. He pays me a thousand apiece for the horses, and twenty-five percent of his net from Cushman for two years."

Ginny laughed. "That was mean. But he'll probably make a fortune out of them, at that."

"Serve him right if he does."

She sat close to him as they drove through the warm, rocky hills. "When do you think you'll be back?"

"About a week. And I'll have a rope around that

193

broomtail's neck this time!" He added: "Why don't you have some friends up?"

"Maybe I will. We do have plenty of room now, don't we?"

"Plenty." Room to kiss your wife. Room to dream. As they turned up the road toward the mountain, Clark began to whistle.

Death Valley Silver

I

All afternoon Jim Bayliss kept thinking: *I ought to get out of this while I can.* But at sundown he was still in the room over the saloon, waiting for a man to stop across the street, light a cigar with three matches, and walk on up the street. It was supposed to occur precisely at nine o'clock, and it would signify: *All set. Horses ready.*

Yesterday, when the dodger was posted in the express office, Bayliss knew he had to move along. But the picture looked like something in a wax works, the description meant nothing, and Bayliss was going by the name of Avery. But there was always that chance. . . .

Because he stopped to read what they said about him, he had felt obliged to look at some of the other dodgers hanging, fly-specked, on the wall, to avoid suspicion. This was how he happened to notice the mustached quartet crowded onto a single poster alongside his own. There was one face he couldn't forget: a bluff Irish face that resembled those of bartenders he had seen pulling beer pumps behind many a bar. This was Charlie Hoffmeyer, **age 46, height six feet, weight 180, dangerous,** and the gang bore his name. Jim had heard of Hoffmeyer.

He went from the express office to a restaurant, and damned if he didn't see that same face at a table next to his! Only the mustache was gone and there was a fancy beard that ran from his sideburns to his chin and back up the other side.

But the deep, dark eyes were the same, and they were looking straight at Jim and saying: *We meet again, lad.* . . . Charlie Hoffmeyer apparently read the dodgers, too, and with a keener eye than most.

Hoffmeyer was alone. He paused with a chunk of rare beef held reflectively on the tines of his fork and smiled. "Didn't I know you in Red Bluff, friend?"

"Blamed if you didn't!" Jim said. He went over to his table.

They made nonsensical talk for a while, then Hoffmeyer asked: "Going to be around long, Avery?"

"Not very."

"I was wondering if you wouldn't want to get into a thing with me and some friends of mine. Prospecting. Death Valley."

"Man, this is July!" Jim Bayliss said. He would not forget Death Valley in July very soon.

"Not many people over there this time of year, I guess," Hoffmeyer said. "Nice and quiet."

Jim got it. What he didn't know, however, was whether he was being invited down a dark alley to have his head knocked in, or whether it was legitimate. Hoffmeyer was too smart to gamble on a stranger. On the other hand, he had been forced to feel Jim out, after discovering that Bayliss recognized him.

Jim looked him over. Hoffmeyer was a hearty, florid man with black hair going gray at the temples. His fingers were thick and capable and his arms looked as if they could squeeze a bear to death. He had contemplative eyes and easy-smiling lips; if there were one thing he did not look, it was dangerous. Any minute, you expected him to hand you a cigar, tell you a joke, and try to sell you something.

Hoffmeyer, conscious of the appraisal, remarked sardonically: "Do I pass?"

Bayliss grinned. "A-one. But you don't want to go over there this time of year, mister. After Stovepipe Wells, anything can happen."

Hoffmeyer's glance was reflective. "Know the valley, Jim?"

"Nobody knows it. I can guess better than most, though. Rousted around the valley most of one summer, in the troopers."

A light kindled in Charlie Hoffmeyer's eyes. He hesitated an instant and then it came out. "Jim, the saints have a hand in this! Look here!" He hunched over his plate and his large, broken-nailed paw cuddled his coffee cup. "I've got a map, son. If I could just use it, there ain't no doubt that I'd pay expenses. Not a mine. Better than a mine! But I'd rather be pore and alive than countin' gold as I died. If I had a man to go along that knew the water holes. . . ."

The door opened; Hoffmeyer glanced up. Jim saw his eyes cool like heated iron plunged into the tempering bucket; they cooled and the life went out of them and the warm blue they had been was a dirty gray.

"No," Hoffmeyer said. "I don't want another winter in that range. Not this Injun. I frostbit three toes on my left foot."

"That right?" Jim said. He was wondering whether the man was insane when he saw the stranger who had just entered the café.

He was a short, stolid-looking man with crisp gray hair, a gray mustache, and an expression of harassment. The lines in his face were part of his disposition. He was a man who slept with his worries. He looked the place over, and swung onto a seat at the counter.

"Wells Fargo detective," Hoffmeyer muttered. He said it in the act of raising his coffee mug. He was as cool as a cigar store Indian in February. He finished his meal, sharpened a match for a toothpick, and asked Jim if he'd have anything more.

They went out.

"Those damn' Wells Fargo men will run the pants off you, ever you get on the wrong side of them," Hoffmeyer said. "That's Dutch Willard. Just a four-bit express detective, but as dangerous as any of them if he spots you. They don't make so much money but what that bounty looks good to them."

They sauntered along the rutted street. Sawbuck was a desultory little cow town on the west side of Nevada. Miners outfitted here for runs into Death Valley and the Amargosa, but at this season there was nothing much doing in the grubstaking line.

It was pretty quiet. But suddenly it wasn't quiet enough for either of them. Hoffmeyer walked with the slightly stiff gait of a man who did much riding. His gaze was on the boots measuredly thudding along on the boardwalk.

They reached the end of the street. Dusk was beginning to rouge the sky, bringing into sharper focus the broken desert hills. Hoffmeyer sat down at the edge of the walk and began to fill a pipe.

"Don't know your plans at all, Jim, but I'm going to make a guess. The dodger says desertion and manslaughter. They wrap both them words up in rope. You're young, though, haven't been on the trail long, and maybe you figure you can square them. But it takes money. Got any?"

"Not what you'd call money." Bayliss was moved by the outlaw's tacit sympathy to speak warmly. "Damn them, Charlie, I can't crab about the manslaughter charge. But when they start talking desertion, I get sore. Sure, I was in the cavalry at Fort Independence . . . I left before my hitch was up. But I bought out. I didn't desert."

Hoffmeyer's smile was quiet. "Don't let it steam up your spectacles, Jim. If a man on the dodge eats his beef rare, they says he's a cannibal. The point is you can't go back broke. Now, where I and the boys are going, there's plenty of money, if you call a quarter share of eighty thousand dollars plenty."

"And you want me to guide you into the valley. When?"

"Tomorrow night." He squinted at the wet stem of his pipe, adding almost sheepishly: "I suppose it's like all the rest of these buried-treasure stories, only I had it from a pardner of mine that had checked on it. He was going after it himself, but . . . he waited too long. It's not a mine. It's an Army paymaster's wagon that was lost in 'Sixty-Four, during the Paiute trouble. He had a feeling they were going to get him, and he drew me a map."

To Jim Bayliss, $20,000 sounded good. He wasn't on the dodge because he liked it. He'd had a wild boyhood and had wound up at seventeen in the cavalry. Eighteen months of fighting Paiutes and establishing water holes in Death Valley convinced him the Army was not his trade. He bought out and tackled cowpunching, finally drifting over to Nevada City, in the Sierras, to work in the hard-rock mines. Mining drew his needle strongly. He would still have been there, but for the fight. . . .

Sam Huling was a Cousin Jack who thought nobody could set a charge but himself. If anybody else did set a charge in California, it ought to be another Cornishman. There were thousands of them in the Lode, and nobody denied that they were the best hard-rock miners in the world. But Huling's way of needling him finally got under Jim's hide. It wound up in a fight.

How was Jim Bayliss to know that Sam Huling had a bad heart? The Cornishman died in the first wild minute of fist swinging. He had approximately 15,000 friends in the towns of Nevada City and Grass Valley who came to Jim's cabin armed with everything from tempers to dynamite. Jim was already gone, knowing how long he would have lasted against the Cousin Jacks. It wasn't a too-serious thing, and the law might have forgotten it, except that the Sons of St. George raised $5,000 for the arrest and conviction. . . .

He saw clearly enough that an alliance with an outlaw like Charlie Hoffmeyer might damn him forever. On the other hand, no one needed to know he and Hoffmeyer had ever met. There was supposed to be honor among thieves, a code with its roots in self-protection, the best soil in the world for honor to grow in.

Jim Bayliss thought all these things, and in the end he said: "All right, Charlie. Share and share alike?"

Hoffmeyer said levelly: "Right."

Jim said: "Light a cigar in front of the Bullfrog Café when you're ready."

II

Now it was dark in the street, and there was time for a few more pipefuls, in the smoke of which he might find wisdom. He owed Charlie Hoffmeyer nothing. He had only to remain in the room after the outlaw lighted his cigar, and Hoffmeyer would drift away and Bayliss would never see him again.

He started as a match flared in the gloom of the cow-town street, directly across from him. It blinked out. A second match was lighted, but it required a third to get the cigar burning. It was Hoffmeyer, but he was two hours ahead of schedule.

There had been a hitch of some kind. Yet it could not have been too great a hitch, or Hoffmeyer would not have been there at all. Jim hesitated, a throbbing and an emptiness in him. Then he leaned forward to knock out his pipe on the window ledge. He arose, picked up his telescope bag, and went out.

Hoffmeyer fell in beside him. They proceeded unhurriedly toward the stable where Jim's horse was boarded.

"You're ahead of time," Jim said.

"Seen Dutch Willard poking around this afternoon. I'm gettin' edgy."

Two men were on duty at the stable. A lantern hung inside the doorway. One of the men, a tall and frowsy old-timer smelling of liquor, came forward with a long-jointed gait. Hoffmeyer stayed outside. His horse was racked here and he untied it.

"I'm Joe Avery," Bayliss said. "Will you get the bill on my horse?"

The stableman went into the office. He found Jim's name

on the ledger, and then began poking about among dusty pigeonholes.

"I'll find a pencil and figger it up."

"You don't need a pencil to figure seven times a dollar, do you?"

"No, but you'll want a receipt."

"The hell with it. All I want is a horse."

"Sorry, mister. Them's my orders."

During the interval it took to fill out a receipt, Jim heard Hoffmeyer clear his throat. After this there was an exasperated hunt for the horse, up one line of stalls and down another, until Jim himself took the lantern and found it.

And still Jim's exasperation was not flavored with suspicion. Not until he had saddled the horse and led it to the door, and the stableman, following, watched him mount and head toward the other horseman waiting at the edge of the road.

"Have a good trip, boys!" It was practically a shout, an unsteady cry in the cracked register reserved for old men of alcoholic habits.

Jim glanced around. He heard a rustle inside the stable and saw at the door the other man who had kept in the shadows. An explosion of nerves occurred in Jim's head. Rigid on the saddle, he said: "Thanks, dad." He rode on to meet Hoffmeyer.

But this was not a bad dream he could make vanish by turning his back on it. The man in the shadows was walking into the road with a shotgun in his hands. "All right, boys," he said. "I mean you, too, Charlie!" It was Dutch Willard.

Jim turned his eyes to Hoffmeyer, a dark shape slouched in the saddle. It was not apparent that he had heard, nor that he had moved, but flame lashed from the vicinity of his saddle horn, and the blast of the revolver caused Jim's horse to wheel and begin to buck.

There was a second explosion that momentarily illuminated the roadway, a flash and a vast roll of sound that packed a physical jolt. Pellets of buckshot tore through Jim's coat and ripped at his back. The pain made him gasp and clutch at the horse's mane. For a while he was fighting the pony and trying to keep from being thrown, and, when he curbed it, he was across the boardwalk and in a vacant lot next door to the stable.

He heard Hoffmeyer call. "All right, kid?"

"All right."

"Let's go!" Hoffmeyer wheeled his pony and struck hurriedly eastward across lots.

Jim looked back. The old man had vanished, but in the street lay the body of the Wells Fargo agent. A silent cry rose through Jim Bayliss, a cry that was the eulogy of all the things that might have been. He had made his choice and now there was no changing it. It was sealed with the blood of a murdered man.

An hour later, Hoffmeyer led Jim into a rocky draw somewhere south of town. Past a twisted smoke tree, they entered a camp. Pack animals stood ready and two men rose silently from the ground. The taller one said: "You've been runnin'."

"Willard was waiting at the stable," Hoffmeyer grunted. "Jim, these are my pardners. The long drink is Comanche Harris. The little jigger's got no title, but some shore bad habits. We call him Wino."

They shook hands and mounted, and five minutes later were moving rapidly southward, with their backs on Sawbuck. They rode until noon the next day, and made camp in the broken shade of a mesquite thicket. With the animals unsaddled, Hoffmeyer relaxed on the sand. "Wino, let's have some music."

Wino was an undersized, dissolute character with the humor of a clown. He wore dark woolen pants, an undershirt, and a black Stetson with the brim pinned up on one side, dragoon fashion. In one of his canvas water bags he carried muscatel; this was his staple drink, water being carried for emergencies.

He sang a bawdy ballad of an amorous miner, playing a verse on a Jew's harp and singing alternate verses. Then they all slept a couple of hours. In the middle of the afternoon they hit the trail once more. They traveled this way for two days. On the second evening they reached a sunburned village on the apron of the badlands, called Kingbolt. They drew up outside of town.

"Jim better go in first," Comanche declared. "Don't reckon anybody's been here ahead of us, but no use taking chances."

As he left, Wino said: "Bring me back a couple jugs of muscatel, will you, Jim? I'm plumb dehydrated."

"I'll bring you a fifth," Jim said. "After we hit the desert, you can do the same job with a gun that you can with wine, only quicker."

Jim found the town too sleepy and hot to be concerned with anything beyond the necessity to keep in the shade. He went back and got the others. They bought supplies and carefully extracted from the storekeeper information on the water holes between there and Amargosa. Jim made a point of marking these oases on a map, under the storekeeper's eye, because he intended to travel halfway around the compass from Amargosa.

They camped at midnight in the Grapevine Mountains. At dawn, Comanche awoke them by banging on a skillet. "Let's eat and git, boys."

Around them the mud hills were soft with shades of tan

and rose and purple. Close inspection turned up a few grim-looking shrubs and hammered-down grasses, paper-bag bush, Mormon tea, cigarette brush. In contrast to what lay under Daylight Pass, this was a mountain meadow.

Jim rejected Comanche's suggestion that they push on. "We'll rest here today and drink all the water we can hold. The only time to leave is after dark."

Comanche gave him a flat, hostile glance. He was a lank brown man with sardonic eyes. "Rest won't do us any good when we're hanging from a tree."

"We've lost them by now," Jim said. "I travel by night or not at all. Death Valley's only a name to you. I've seen it."

They spent the day under the eaves of the ridge. The temperature pushed 110°, but in the dry atmosphere of the desert mountains it was not excessive. With leisure, Jim sank into morosity. He nursed an orphan hope that the stableman had been too dim-sighted to furnish a description of him. Otherwise, Jim Bayliss would now be listed as the latest acolyte of the Hoffmeyer gang, and their crimes would be his.

At dusk they broke camp and shoved on through Daylight Pass. There was good water here, and a sulphurous breeze. Below them, the long wastes were a dark mirror of the sky.

They traversed Hell Gate sometime after midnight. Now they began to feel the arid suction of the desert air, thirsting for every drop of water in a man's body. They camped that day at Stovepipe Wells, raising a shelter of tarpaulins on poles Jim had cut from mesquite trees.

He inspected the burros. There was the beginning of sores on the back of one. "What's this critter packing?" he asked Hoffmeyer. "Horseshoes? He's overloaded."

Wino sidled in as they began to unpack the *aparejos*. Jim felt the smooth skin of a glass jug and pulled it out. Wino began to explain in his foolish, grinning fashion, and Jim dug deeper and found three more gallon jugs of muscatel. He picked one of them up and heaved it against a rock, and Wino squalled as the wine vaporized on the hot stone.

Jim grabbed him by the shirt. "I said no liquor! You fool, it's poison in this heat!"

Wino's lips slipped back from his teeth and he pulled his gun as Jim raised a second jug. Jim halted with the wine at shoulder height. "No, sir!" Wino panted.

Charlie Hoffmeyer said: "Drop it, Wino."

Wino did not look around. He dropped the Colt in the sand. Hoffmeyer said to Jim: "Set it down, Jim. We'll give him today to sop up what he wants. If it kills him, there's plenty of rocks to mark the spot with. What's left tonight, gets left."

Jim hesitated. Then he put the jug down. It was a brutal gospel Hoffmeyer preached, but it had its logic. The loss of Wino would be no loss at all.

They breakfasted and saw the valley's colors gasp out in smoky haze. The danger and the aloneness began to bear down upon them. A caved-in spring, an injured horse, could mean death. They had challenged in combat the great, smoking valley with the bitter names: Chloride, Funeral, Badwater, Skull.

They slept a little. They smoked. Wino drank. Toward dusk, Jim filled the water bags and left them to soak in the spring. At dark, Wino sadly shambled over to the rocks guarding the spring with his jugs of muscatel. A few moments later they heard the bottles breaking.

They crawled by moonlight across a desolation of baked mud, wrinkled like the face of an old squaw. They stopped at eight the next morning at a spring guarded by twisted creosotes. Jim inspected the seep and turned wearily to Hoffmeyer. "This is why I like to carry water instead of wine.

This one's gone dead."

So they spooned the water out to themselves when their throats were screaming for it. They were flushed and tired, with salt rime on their skin and shirts. Jim gave the horses and burros enough to keep them going. The next spring was Paiute Well, never a good one. If it, too, had dried up, it would be a tough scrape to the next.

They set out at sundown. Now, when they wanted speed most, the animals were slowing up. They were footsore with traversing a salt bed, gaunted by the heat radiating from the ground that, like an assayer's furnace, never cooled. Jim stopped the cavalcade just before sunup, dismounted, and walked stiffly into the tangle of brush hiding Paiute Well. He went slowly to his knees and turned the sand with his fingers. Dry. Dry as dust. Dry as bones on the desert's face.

He went back. "We'll camp here," he told Hoffmeyer.

"Water?" the outlaw demanded.

"No. Sand."

Hoffmeyer stared at him. In his face, the fears that had followed them all the way had now caught up. They were down to their reserve water bags. Jim was doling out jerked beef when he heard Hoffmeyer begin to roar like a bull.

He went back. Charlie had Wino down on the ground and was pounding his face with his fist. There was a strong perfume of wine in the air. On the sand nearby lay a spilled water bag.

Jim dragged him off. He fought Hoffmeyer for his gun and threw it aside. "I'll give him his wine!" Hoffmeyer shouted. "So help me, God, he'll drink every drop of it before I kill him!"

III

Jim calmed Hoffmeyer by slugging him. He carefully dumped most of the wine out of the water bags, saving a little with which to dilute the remaining water. They rested that day in the worst heat they had encountered so far, in a punishing glare from the salt beds that pursued a man whichever way he turned his face.

It was necessary to walk the horses occasionally that night, and this slowed them still more. They had to keep an eye on Wino, who was suffering from one more thirst than the rest of them, and began to show it.

In the bright moonlight, Jim discovered a saddle in the Panamint Range, at his left. Sunup revealed a slot-like cañon tailing out into the valley. Charlie Hoffmeyer, gloomy and gaunt, studied the mauve-and-gray hills a moment, and then let out a yell. "That's it, Jim! He told me about it so many times I'd know it anywhere! There's four mule skeletons just inside the wash and the wagon's supposed to be near them. And there's water!"

They rode into the narrow cañon with the sun scorching their faces. As they hastened up the twisting, red-walled cut, Hoffmeyer turned to show a face wild with excitement. "There's the mules!"

Right from the start, Jim had hardly been able to believe the tale, but with the sight of the four mule skeletons he began to catch Hoffmeyer's fever. He spurred his horse on and was right behind him when he pulled his horse around on the trail and sat staring ahead. There was a wagon, all right, a ruined Army ambulance with the canvas top in rags. There were crates and kegs in it, but somehow they did not look like the sort that double eagles would travel in.

They dismounted and went at the boxes with shovels. Jim's first crate contained shoes, dried and twisted like rashers of bacon. Hoffmeyer exposed a box filled with twigs and stones, the offerings of pack rats that had removed the beans it had once contained. Wino drew dusty cans of saleratus, and Comanche's prize was a crate of bandoliers.

On the map, the spot was named Bitter Spring Wash. Water was indicated farther up. Under a sun that sifted its dazzling incandescence upon them, they shoved on to a small, tilted basin. A cliff formed the eastern wall and ruddy hills ringed the valley. A spring near the cliff was crowded with indigo bush and desert fir.

They drank the water of this spring that tasted like something out of a rusty can. Their kneeling at it was a species of worship. It was nearly sundown before anyone spoke. They were too busy drinking and being gloomy.

"Well, Jim," Hoffmeyer said, "Big Charlie didn't bring you much luck. What's next?"

Jim shrugged. "If it had been anybody but a Wells Fargo detective. . . . Every express office in California will be watching for you, and maybe me. We stay here. That's the answer."

Wino shuddered. "Sooner blow my brains out. Water that tastes like the cistern the cow fell in. No likker. Nothing to eat but sagebrush."

Jim looked around across the basin filling with dusk, at the mountains timbered thinly at their crests. "You sound like a dude," he said. "Look at the ground by the spring. There's the answer to what we'll eat. Bighorn sheep, rabbits, quail. Chuckawallas for dessert. We'll get a chunk of sandstone and filter the water. This is the Garden of Eden, boys."

They spent a week at the spring, playing poker and trying not to think of what they would do when their tobacco gave out. Comanche, in whose narrow breast whirled a neurotic dynamo, began to behave like a caged animal. Hoffmeyer watched him a while one evening and said: "We've got to dig a cave. I'm tired of moving every fifteen minutes to keep out of the sun. Might as well start tonight."

Jim knew the cave was merely a prophylactic measure, but he approved it. They had one pickaxe and three shovels, and they made a good start on the cave that night. Then they stretched out under the tarps to sleep. The heat woke Bayliss, and he lay there for a long time gazing broodingly at the pile of loose rock and endeavoring to persuade himself that he did not actually need a smoke until after breakfast.

The hell with it, he decided; he'd enjoy the tobacco while it lasted. The tobacco woke him up. It made him aware that the pile of rock was of a strange color, a fact that had been scratching at the door of his consciousness. He picked up a piece of gaudy blue-green stone. There was a bright thread in it; he tested it with his fingernail.

He heard Hoffmeyer growl: "What've you got, Jim?"

He turned. A pulse in his head was trying to break loose. "I don't know," he said. "I don't know whether it's anything or not. But if it's what I think it is, that paymaster's wagon we lost was just peanuts. This is mineral, Charlie. Silver!"

Hoffmeyer bounded from the shelter. He picked up chunks of ore in both hands and looked at it, pounded it with the pick, and studied the filament of silver. "By God, Jim!" he said.

He strode over and gave Wino a kick. "Get outta there, old boozer! We got digging to do!"

Under the shade of the canvasses, they dug until noon. They followed the ledge as far as they could in this primitive fashion. Jim knew ores, and with every shovel full of rock they moved he grew more enthusiastic.

"We've got to assay this stuff! There's a ghost town about fifteen miles from here, up in the north Panamints. Maybe there's chemicals left in the assay office."

Jim and Comanche packed out with two burros. They found the crumbling remains of an old gold camp called Garnet on the second day. Many of the stone buildings had fallen, but the old mine office was in repair. There was an anvil in the midst of a pile of slag and broken glass, where metal had been pounded free of glass during the refining process. On a table sat saucers filled with powdered ore. There were still acids in the bottles.

Jim found charcoal outside and stoked the brick furnace in the center of the room. He processed the ore as best he could. At the end, he had a small button of silvery metal. He worked up through the acids and found it to consist largely of silver and copper.

"How's she look?" Comanche demanded.

Jim swished the acid remaining in the beaker. "I'm no assayer, but if this runs less than a thousand to the ton, I've never seen ore before!"

Hoffmeyer was less enthusiastic over Jim's report than it seemed he should have been.

"Know what we've got here, boys?" he said gloomily. "A million dollars in Confederate money. How're we gonna work this ledge with three shovels and a couple of pocket knives? We'd look nice tramping into a Land Office to register it, wouldn't we?"

The idea was not entirely new to Jim. He regarded Hoffmeyer thoughtfully. "How far do you trust me?" he asked him.

"How far have I got to?"

Jim shrugged. "Trusting anybody is a gamble. But I'll gamble, if you will. I'll gamble that Dutch Willard didn't recognize me from my dodger that night. Even if he did, he wouldn't know me with three months' beard on my face. Suppose we stay here till fall. When it's cool, I'll go over to Independence and register under an alias. I'll raise some money to work the claim. After that, we just count the mill checks as they come in."

Comanche snorted. "So where do the rest of us live after the rush starts . . . in the bottom of a well?"

"What's the matter with Garnet?"

They didn't look pleased, but Hoffmeyer, at least, looked thoughtful. They were not men given to trust, and this called for a sublime faith that Bayliss would not sell them down the river. Comanche said: "No dice." Wino shook his head, his small, pottery-brown eyes sour with distrust. Perhaps it was this opposition, arousing a stubborn streak in Charlie Hoffmeyer, that cast the balance the other way.

"Don't talk like a couple of box heads. Jim's called the shots this far, and I reckon he can do it the rest of the way. Sure, Jim, we'll trust you. But we've got memories a thousand miles long for anybody that ever sells us out. Your deal."

The town of Independence lay forty-five miles northwest, across a stark range of mountains and a couple saline sinks. About the town was the grimness of the desert, but from its back yard the Sierras soared blue-black to the sky. 100 streams tumbled down the palisades to the desert, the kind of streams men had died babbling of only a few miles away, icy rills of snow water that creased and flashed in the harsh sunlight.

On a cool day in late November, Jim Bayliss made camp in a loop of Pine River. He rode a gaunt and hungry horse and led two pack burros. It was about noon. Jim picketed the animals, slung two heavy sacks of ore into a willow thicket, and stripped off his clothes to bathe. The water knocked the breath out of him, made his joints ache, and turned his skin red. He climbed out, dried with an extra shirt, and dressed.

Now he felt clean, even if he looked as dirty as ever. On the dodger, it said **hair, light brown.** The untrimmed beard he wore was as yellow as new straw. He had lost twenty pounds in the valley; there were ruts about his mouth and eyes that aged him, and the bleached eyebrows deepened the mahogany tones of his skin. He was a wide-shouldered rack of a man on which weight could be hung, but he was now nothing but muscle and bone and dehydrated layers of thirsty flesh.

He walked the half mile into town. A dozen borax and mining outfits had their headquarters in Independence. It seldom hit 115° here, and desert men thought of it as a summer resort. The wide main street paralleled the foothills and was sentried by tall cottonwoods and poplars. Jim's first appointment was with a T-bone steak. He washed it down with two bottles of beer, and trimmed off the edges of his plans. First, to register the claim. Second, to get some money. Last, to have the ore assayed.

At the Land Office, he registered the two claims he was entitled to as discoverer of the vein. He had expected the land agent to be curious about his strike; he found the man bored with a process he had apparently gone through every day for years.

Then there was the matter of raising a few thousand dollars. Jim had this worked out, too. There was a bank on a corner shaded by a giant elm, a narrow, two-story building of brick. Inside, it was hardly wider than a hall, a high room with a section on the right railed off by panels surmounted by windows. There was a single wicket. Behind the soapy glass, clerks were ruining their eyesight over ledgers and letterpress volumes.

Jim presented himself at the wicket. A teller with rabbity features glanced at him and automatically threw off the lock on a brass scale. He waited disinterestedly for the dust, until Jim shook his head.

"Who do I see about a loan?"

"Mister McGaffery."

Jim looked about and saw the name on a door at the rear. He walked back and laid his knuckles manfully on the panel of the door. Someone made an unintelligible sound. He went inside.

This room held a double-doored safe, two cases of ore specimens, maps on the walls, a calendar of the year 1878, some office furniture, a spittoon—and Banker McGaffery. A lamp on an extension arm flowed its light over a littered desk and one side of the face of the sallow, long-faced man in his fifties. He wore a trimmed gray mustache and his mouth was a gather of taut skin, like a barely noticeable scar. With a single word, he made the most impersonal sound in the world. "Yes?"

"I want to borrow some money," Jim Bayliss said.

McGaffery's hand removed his spectacles; with thumb and forefinger he massaged his eyes. His weariness did not seem to involve his eyes exclusively; the point was made that he was continually badgered by men wanting money.

"What do you want the money for?" he asked.

"To develop a mine."

McGaffery's St. Bernard eyes winced. "Oh, my," he said.

"I need about five thousand dollars. Not less than four."

McGaffery was beginning to be amused. "I see. Did you want to put up any security?"

Jim placed his hand on the back of a chair. "If you aren't too busy, I'd like to sit down and have a smoke with you while we talk about it."

"As a matter of fact," McGaffery told him, "I am busy. If you want to tell me briefly just what you've got in mind. . . ."

"All right," Jim said. "I've got hold of something that looks like a bonanza. I won't sell it outright, but I haven't got money to work it myself. That's why I want to borrow."

"Got the assayer's report?"

"That's the point. The claim is registered, but I haven't had an assay made because I don't want to start a run. Since I haven't got any security, I'm offering you the chance to get out there and file the first claim next to mine. Because after the assay is made, you'll be out in the cold. There's a lot of men that'll walk, crawl, or run to beat you there."

"They won't have to"—McGaffery smiled—"because I'm not going any place. What is this, another Death Valley gold mine?"

"No. It's a deposit of pheasant's eggs on top of Mount Whitney. You ought to know better than to ask a question like that. You damn' well ought to know better!"

McGaffery froze. "Then I'm afraid I can't help you. If you knew how many of you fellows are in here every week. . . ."

"It must be tough," Jim said. He went to the door, and the banker said off-handedly: "You might give me your name, in case I change my mind."

"Toll," Jim said. "James Toll."

He had a drink on this. There was one other bank in town, but he had no reason to believe he would make out differently there. He had a thought and, going back to camp, selected a specimen of ore that he put in the pocket of his coat. He went to the other bank and tackled the manager.

He left the bank five minutes later with a determination to keep any money he ever made in a tin can. It was growing dark. A cool wind came down from the mountains, where early snow had already dusted the peaks. He walked slowly along with his head down and his hands in his pockets. He heard someone say: "Here you are, old-timer!"

A silver dollar arced toward him. He caught it, and looked up at a young woman in a full skirt and blouse, with a velvet pelisse over her shoulders. Because of the dusk, what he noticed chiefly about her were the more obvious phenomena, such as her height, which was below average, and her figure, which was above. The gown nipped in at the waist, emphasizing her slimness and the womanly roundness of her hips, and the blouse was demure, but not too demure.

Jim looked at the dollar and then back up at her, and by this time she had discovered that he was neither of the age nor of the condition to go with the beard and clothes he wore. Her fingers touched her cheek.

"Oh! I'm sorry! I thought you were. . . ."

Bayliss flipped the dollar with his thumb. "Well, how do you know I'm not?"

"It was so dark, and with those whiskers on your face. . . ." She laughed. "If you'll give my dollar back, I'll save it for somebody else."

Jim dropped it in his pocket. "This is going to be my good luck piece. If I can just find another four thousand, nine hundred and ninety-nine like it, I'll be passing out dollars myself before long. Thanks, lady, and, if I ever shave this muff off, I'll send it to you."

When he started on, she turned after him. "Just a minute!" She caught up with him; the light of a restaurant fully revealed her features. They were extremely pleasant; to a man just in from four months on the desert, they brought an ache for a softer way of life he had forgotten. Brown was her color, although the sun had bleached the ends of her curls; the tone of her skin was sun-warmed.

"What did you mean, if you could find some more money,

you'd have dollars to give away? Were you joking?"

Jim put on an inner brake and looked the road over. Speaking to men on the street wasn't part of her business, that was for sure. But there was another kind of woman, a notch higher, who liked adventures of an amorous sort. He had heard it said that having a girl of this kind was better than being married, for she brought all kinds of delights as a dowry, and didn't hound a man for a home and children. When the metal wore thin, the chain broke, without anyone's feelings being hurt. But the girl didn't appear to be this kind, either. She must, he decided, simply be young and ignorant.

"No," he said, "I wasn't joking. I'm not hard up for dollars, but I'm hard up for thousands of dollars." He lowered his voice and said in mock confidence: "I've got a silver-dollar mine! All I need is money for wagons to freight them out. They come all wrapped in rolls of twenty."

Her face underwent a stiffening. Her elbows pulled in against her sides. "I see. I didn't mean to be curious. But I have some money to invest and I thought perhaps . . . I'm sorry," she said, and was turning to hurry off.

This time it was Jim Bayliss who did the running after.

IV

There was a restaurant called the Mount Whitney Café. It had a lofty ceiling and red-and-white gingham tablecloths, iron-legged tables and chairs, and homey odors of frying meat and onions. It was pretty close to the dinner hour.

She said her name was Katherine Lawrence. "You can call me Kitty." In the way of young people, they used an initial unpleasantness as a springboard to friendship. Kitty confided that she owned the Panamint Borax Works. "Dad died last year. I've got a good manager, but I try to keep up with what's going on."

"And you really want to invest some money?"

With her fingers linked under her chin, she nodded briskly. "Borax has been good this year, but I figure I ought to be doing something spectacular with my money."

When she talked about money, there was a kind of holy light on her face. It occurred to Jim that, if nothing worse, she might be a nut on the subject of speculation. Almost dubiously, he placed the ore specimen on the cloth. The fizzing gas lamps overhead made a strong white light in which the ore burned like blue-green fire. He watched her examine it. When she set it down, he placed it under the canister set, where it was still visible as a sales point, but not too obvious to other diners.

With a tine of his fork, he wrote on the cloth: **$1,000 to the ton**.

"No!" Kitty said.

"It hasn't been assayed, but I ran a crude test myself. I'd say at least that."

"How can I get into it?" Her eyes had caught the shine of the mineral itself.

"By advancing me five thousand dollars. I'll pay the regular interest rate and give you three days' head start on the others before I have the stuff assayed. You can stake out your claim next to mine."

"Why can't we be partners? I'll stake out my claim, we'll pool them, bring in the best equipment, and start production on a big scale! Why, Jim, it'll be bigger than the Comstock!"

Her enthusiasm was catching fire so vigorously that Jim tried to close the damper. "I ought to warn you that McGaffery and Hannaker both turned me down."

She sniffed, glancing across the room, and Jim turned to see McGaffery eating with another man. "Mister McGaffery is what you might call conservative. If there were only one horse in a race, he'd want odds. Jim, I don't mind saying you've excited me very much. You can have the money the first thing in the morning."

Jim grinned. "You don't think it might be a good idea to have a geologist look the ledge over first, just to be sure I didn't buy this from an assayer?"

Kitty spoke defiantly, her fine hair tossing. "If you'd known Lucky Lawrence, you'd know me better, Jim. My father left me two things. A borax outfit and a proverb . . . 'Never let your luck get cold.' If you win on double zero, back it again."

"I'm glad I look like the double zero to you, Kitty. I just looked like an ordinary zero to McGaffery."

Their steaks came, but Kitty was almost too excited to eat. Jim kept glancing across the table at her. The dress she wore was light green.

It was a paradoxical thing that, the more entranced he became with Kitty Lawrence, the darker grew a facet of his mind. He saw mirrored the lank, bitter features of Comanche, the clownish, dissolute face of Wino, and Charlie

Hoffmeyer's undeceived eyes. Hoffmeyer's expression said: *A nice kid, Jim, but not our type. If you took her seriously, she'd slow you down. And if you didn't, you'd break her heart. I'll introduce you to a little sweetheart in El Paso sometime. Couple of nights with her and you'll forget all about the Kitty Lawrences.*

They finished dinner. "We really ought to incorporate!" Kitty exclaimed. "We'll capitalize for fifty thousand dollars, to start. I'll put up the money and you can pay me back out of the first six months' profits."

Jim chuckled. "Kitty, I'd say you did need a good manager. Or a guardian. Let's talk about hundreds, not thousands."

"If you're betting pennies, you win pennies. I'm going to talk to my lawyer in the morning. Come and see me at the National Exchange tomorrow at noon."

Jim helped her with her chair. At this moment McGaffery and his companion approached. The banker's sallow face was unusually animated as he paid his respects to Kitty.

"Are you boycotting me?" he asked. "Never see you any more. Got money that's trying to be loaned, too. You can't make money without branching out, Kitty. Why don't we have a talk someday?"

Kitty said: "That's the nice part about being solvent . . . the only robbers you have to worry about carry guns."

McGaffery laughed loudly and slapped his leg. He introduced his companion, who Jim had just discovered. "This is Mister Willard, with Wells Fargo. Dutch Willard, to his friends."

They shook hands, while the big, yellow-bearded young fellow behind Kitty had the impression that his insides had turned to sawdust. Willard had dropped some weight, but he was essentially the same man who had stepped from the livery stable that night with a shotgun in his hands, a square-headed, sour-visaged man with the crisp hair of a terrier and a mouth for chewing cigars.

"Pleased," he said to Kitty. Then his glance went to Jim.

McGaffery looked at him, too. "Why, it's young Toll," he said. "Didn't know you, James. Shake hands with Mister Willard."

Kitty said coolly: "So many men have yellow beards that you wouldn't remember him, would you? Good night, Jim. Remember, now, I saw you first!"

The amazing thing was that Willard gave no sign of remembering Jim. That he was alive was understandable. He moved to a chair on a stiff leg that told Jim where Hoffmeyer's bullet had gone that night. But he had finished with Jim. He was looking over the wine list.

McGaffery said: "Mind if we join you, Jim?"

"I'll be going back to camp directly. Have a drink with you, though."

McGaffery picked up the piece of ore. "One of your samples, Jim? Don't look half bad."

This, then, was the magnet that had drawn him. This, and Kitty's presence with him. He was afraid to back a sure thing, but it pained him to see anyone else do it.

"Jim," he said, "I've been thinking. I don't generally go for these mining deals, but if you'll co-operate with me, I'll send a geologist out and we'll look that ledge over."

"You're too late. I'm already committed to Miss Lawrence."

"On paper?" McGaffery's fist clenched on the ore and his voice was like a screech through a stone wall.

"Just as good as on paper. I've accepted the offer she made me."

"Whatever she's offered you, if that ore runs a thousand to

the ton, I'll go her a couple better! You can't trust her, Jim. She's hare-brained. She's got no more business sense than a chuckawalla."

"She's also a friend of mine," Jim remarked. He took his hat from the extra chair and put his hand out for the specimen.

McGaffery was perspiring. "Jim, I can do things for you that Kitty Lawrence never could. We'll develop it from the bottom up . . . install a company store and build shacks to rent. My God, the possibilities! If you'll come over to my office for a while, Jim. . . ."

"No, thanks. That's a good idea about a company store, though. I'll see you around, boys."

It might have been funny, except for a small voice whispering: *He must have known you.* . . . Jim started for camp. Behind him, the sounds and lights of Independence became absorbed by the immense emptiness of the desert. The black sky was frosted with stars, and only by the absence of stars was the gigantic bulk of the mountains believable.

A horned owl made its cry, and the wind whispered in the willows; the river sucked along its eroded banks. These were the only sounds as Jim approached his camp. But there was an odor. It was the rank brown taste of a cigar.

Jim stood beside his bedroll, his hand touching the walnut butt of his gun. As he waited, a shadow slipped from the willow thicket a few feet away. In that intense darkness Jim failed to see the man until he was on top of him. He stepped back, tugging his gun free, but something cracked him alongside the ear, and he was going down with a shattering pain in the side of his face.

From this swarming dizziness, he emerged to terror. The shadow was still there, a bent shape with arm upraised. The barrel chopped again, biting into the muscles of his forearm, and there was paralysis in his nerves that caused him to drop his Colt.

Jim rolled away, his left hand groping for anything to defend himself. He heard the willows crash. He saw that he was alone again. When he found the gun, his injured arm was unable to raise it. He shifted the gun to his left hand. His thumb rocked the hammer. Through the tangle of willows, the sound of snapping branches was easy to follow. Jim fired and heard the bullet slam through the brush. A gun crashed twice within the thicket. There was no sound of tearing branches, no high ricochet of a bullet caroming from the ground; this was a small fact and one he was not in a mood to frown over, but later it acquired a significance.

Again Jim fired into the thicket, but this time there was no answering fire, and a moment later he heard a stutter of hoof beats, a splash in the creek, and then the smooth, fast tempo of a horse loping across the sand.

V

Jim spent an hour following tracks the next morning. The gunman had come from town and departed into the desert. He had ridden three miles north, toward Bishop, then cut west into the Coso Hills. The amazing thing was that he had taken nothing. His guess was that McGaffery had sent the man to try to find a map.

But his relief was blasted suddenly by the conviction that he had criminally bungled his whole plan. He had left a trail a yard wide and a foot deep. The registry! It had been the one precaution he could not fail to take. But because of it, his whole arch of reasoning had crashed. He had based it on the belief that the first man he talked to would buy. McGaffery hadn't, but now that he was crying to get into the deal, he had merely to step over to the Land Office and find out where Jim Toll had located!

Jim slung the ore sacks on one of the burros and rode to town. He left the sacks at the assayer's and hurried to the National Exchange.

He found Kitty in the dining room. In that room, filled chiefly with middle-aged cattlemen and borax miners and their middle-aged wives, she stood out like a nugget in a gravel wash. In Jim's head, a moving finger of logic wrote: *You'd better sign up with McGaffery. You won't be falling in love with him.*

He sat down; Kitty looked at him and shook her head. "I lose five dollars. I bet my lawyer you'd see the barber today before you saw me. Are you going to wear that thing forever?"

"Only till the second coming," Jim said. He looked about for McGaffery. He was both relieved and disturbed at not seeing him. "Can you ride?" he asked her.

"Of course," Kitty said. "About two blocks. Why?"

"Because unless you trust me to stake out a claim for you, you're starting a fifty-mile ride this morning. The cat's out of the bag. I left the ore to be assayed."

Kitty laid down her fork. "But you said you'd give me three days to put up my monuments! Jim Toll, if you've sold out to McGaffery. . . ."

"I sold out to him last night, without knowing it. He put the pressure on me to let him into it. I turned him down, but what I forgot was that he could get into the Land Office this morning and find out where I located! That means he's either on the way, or he's waiting for the assay report before he leaves."

She looked at him. "Am I beaten out then, Jim?"

Jim made a mark on the cloth with his fingernail. "I'll get you some kind of a claim, even if the best ones are taken. In the meantime, start rounding up men and equipment, just in case we're in business."

On the loose boardwalk outside the restaurant there was a *tom-tomming* like 100 war drums in a rising cadence. A man dashed past, two more sprinted by, a dozen went running down the walk. One man paused to thrust his head inside.

"Grab yer picks, boys! Brown's just assayed twelve-hundred-dollar rock! Man named Toll, Bitter Springs Wash!"

They looked at each other, while every man in the room who could get on his feet did so. Waiters departed, ripping off their aprons. A dozen women were left with double orders and the check.

"That's it!" Jim said. "The only break we get is that I know a short cut or two. Send that stuff when you get it, Kitty. I kind of figure to be the first there, after all."

Kitty reached up and got a small fistful of beard in each

hand as he rose. She pulled his face down. "For luck, Jim!" she said. "Don't ever mistreat your luck." In all that golden tangle of beard, her lips found his.

Jim had left his horse at the assay office, so there was a run of four blocks through a street thronged with horses and men. The assay office was the loneliest spot in town. The hitch rack and porch were deserted. Jim had left his horse under a tree in back, but, when he turned in to the lot, he saw no sign of the bay. For a moment he stood there, not receiving the full impact of the discovery. Then he ran around to the back of the building. Jim rattled the door and found it locked. Brown was getting in on the rush, too.

Panic began to rise in him. He ran back to the main street and joined the throng at the livery stable. Horses were going out as fast as the hostlers could throw saddles on them. Jim left town in a yellow-and-brown box buggy pulled by a high-stepping black. He stopped at the harness shop to buy the cheapest saddle in the place. It was a pity to spoil a good livery horse, but he meant to be among the first to reach Bitter Spring Basin.

By noon, the caravan had strung out in a long, frayed pennant of dust. Most of the miners liked the notch between the Coso Hills and the Inyo Range, but some had taken cut-offs. As long as the buggy could travel, Jim figured he was ahead to stay with it. He began to pass other riders as he followed the trail into the pass, those who had ridden their horses too hard and those whose mounts were poor travelers. Now that the road was climbing, it was becoming too rough for the buggy's lean wheels. Jim reluctantly pulled aside and took the black out of the collar. He was surprised to find the idea of a saddle not entirely repellent to the horse. Just before he started on, he noticed a fresh trail leading on a long curve off to the west. This was an odd thing, and worth thinking about, since all the trails to Death Valley lay east.

It was guesswork, but Jim Bayliss was ready to bet that the horse at the other end of those tracks was a bay with a XYZ brand on its shoulder. It meant loss of time to follow it, but there was nothing like a horse you knew for a ride like this. Jim let the black run. The tracks entered a jumble of eroded rocks. He saw fresh signs and suddenly realized how close he was. The rider had not counted on being followed from Independence.

Somewhere nearby a horse whickered. Jim Bayliss dismounted and found a stone to place over the reins. He stood a while with his Colt in his hand, studying. He began to work up through the rocks to a point above the spot where he had heard the horse. He discerned a flash of color. The color was a patch of the rich reddish hide of his horse. The animal stood, head high, behind a large flat rock, sniffing the wind. The man lay atop the rock, watching the trail below. He had a revolver in his hand, gripped by the barrel. It was not murder he had in mind, but it was at least concussion. Jim slowly bent his legs and leaned forward. He launched himself in a short dive. Just before he landed, the horse thief sensed him and turned his head. There was a look of fright in his face, and Jim was almost sorry it had to be done this way, because the man was the rabbit-featured teller from the bank. It was plain that he had no stake in the gamble but the prospect of keeping his job. Jim's weight squeezed the last puff of wind out of his lungs. Jim's fist drove with a flat smack into the point of his chin.

The rest of that day he made extremely good time, with a horse to ride and a horse to lead, changing over when one grew tired. He rode that night when all the men who weren't sure of the trail had to rest. At dawn, he was taking the straight-line trail across Panamint Valley.

The chips were down now. The men who had asked a little too much of their horses were falling back. Jim passed two of them and, as he neared the small gang in the lead, switched to the bay. They heard him coming and looked back. Some kind of discussion went on. As he moved in to pass, three of them veered to block him. Jim cut back and a rider was again in his way. *If that's the way you want it!* he thought. He fired two shots in the sand and the horses began to pitch. By the time they were under control, Jim was through them.

Two other miners, riding hard, were ahead of him as they went into the wash. Jim made no effort to pass. They spilled into the basin and for an instant the others held their ponies in, hunting for monuments or signs of digging. Jim went past them at a lope. He dismounted as they thundered up, and slipped a paper under the monument he had prepared before he left.

"Plenty of room on up the line, boys." He grinned. "This here's already taken."

All that afternoon they came in. Through the night their horses plodded into the small round valley under the cliffs. By sunup, an army of chloriders was encamped in the basin. Every foot of land around the rim was taken and men were putting up monuments in such improbable places as stony hogbacks and deep gullies. They named the town Grubstake, after the Lawrence-Bayliss mine.

There was a week in which Grubstake was a kettle boiling with all the ingredients of violence. Now that the seed of civilization had been sown, the plant had broken through the earth like a weed. First came the merchants with blankets, overalls, shirts, guns, and mining supplies. A man had to be pretty backward not to make money in Grubstake. In fact, it seemed to Jim that the only man who wasn't making anything out of the bonanza was McGaffery. Then a new store building went up at the south end of Main Street, and the sign they nailed up was: **C. A. McGaffery Enterprises.** There was a freight string. There was a loan department.

A gang of carpenters looked Jim up one day. They had wagonloads of lumber and a set of plans for a ten-room home-and-office building. Kitty Lawrence had sent them. It would cost around $10,000. Jim was all for stringing by with a minimum of expense for a while. On the other hand, they were taking out $2,000 a day, and, if it would bring Kitty out any sooner, he was all for it.

On the 15th of the month, he recalled with a jolt that he was to have been in Garnet that day to give Hoffmeyer a report. He made some kind of alibi to his mine boss and took off that evening. It was nine o'clock the next morning when he reached Garnet. The ghost town slept soundly in its shroud of weeds, but, as Jim rode up the main street, a hinge squawked somewhere and from a boarded-up saloon stepped a bearded man with uncombed hair. Charlie Hoffmeyer was not thriving on isolation.

He walked up to Jim, the others following. Jim dismounted and Hoffmeyer snapped: "I thought it was going to be the Fifteenth of each month, bucko."

"I've been busy, Charlie. I missed the day."

Hoffmeyer, spoiling for a fight, went back and heaved the packs from the other horse. The sight of bottles of liquor, the odors of pipe and eating tobacco, eased him a little. Jim gave them the story as they all stood around passing a bottle and having their first smoke in weeks. "We've got a pardner," he finished, "that's going to advance us fifty thousand."

"A pardner!" Hoffmeyer barked. "What happens when we decide to sell and git?"

"We sell. Only she's got an option to make the first offer."

They looked at each other. "She?" Wino grunted.

"That's all this outfit needed."

Hoffmeyer reacted violently. He had Jim by the arm and his fist drew back; violence flared in his eyes. "By God, you've sold me out to a skirt! Where'd you find this girl?"

Jim had a sack of food in his hand; he dropped this and slapped Hoffmeyer in the belly with the back of his hand. When the outlaw grunted, he tagged him with a smash in the face. Hoffmeyer fell back into Wino. He had his hand on the butt of his gun, and Comanche was reaching for his. But Jim's .44 was already lining out. There was a moment of decision. Hoffmeyer stood up.

"Nice bunch of boys," Jim said. "I guide you into the alley on a long shot that doesn't pan out. I risk my neck going into town for you. Now I come back with a fifty-thousand-dollar backer, and you squawk!"

"A woman!" Hoffmeyer said.

"A woman that's a bigger gambler than any of us. I tackled two bankers before I met her. She pays all expenses until we're making a profit. If the ledge peters out, she loses, not us."

"How do you know she won't freeze us out?"

"We're a corporation. She can't." Jim scratched his beard and added: "I'm thinking we were lucky to find anybody. You see, I ran into an old friend of ours in town, Charlie."

Hoffmeyer said: "Yeah?"

"Dutch Willard. He was with a banker named McGaffery. He didn't recognize me. The point is, Charlie, he's alive. That one ain't on your head."

VI

On a day in January, Kitty Lawrence came out with a wagonload of furniture and fixings. In the newly finished office building, Kitty got to work. She took four rooms for herself and the mines drew six. She began to hold what she called *soirées*. Well-to-do miners who had been the chloriders of last year came to eat her food, listen to her play the only piano in town, and wonder when she would marry.

Jim Bayliss stayed away. He already had a sweetheart, and her name was freedom. She was a jealous wench who he kept only by paying continual court—watching the angles.

An important angle developed the day Dutch Willard came to Grubstake. Jim was in his office that morning, checking mill tickets. He heard Clark McGaffery talking to someone outside, and presently McGaffery stuck his long, pallid face in the doorway and said: "Got a few minutes, son?"

"Always got a few minutes for my friends," Jim said.

McGaffery came in. Right behind him came Dutch Willard. McGaffery stood there with one hand on Willard's shoulder. "You remember Dutch, Jim?"

"Sure do," Jim said.

He watched them sit down. Willard lighted a cigar. In that slightly plaintive voice of his, he asked: "Doing pretty good, Toll?"

"We're meeting expenses."

"You couldn't give me a rough idea how much your payroll runs?"

"Six hundred."

"I should think you'd be afraid to bring that much money in."

"We hire a guard."

Willard made the cigar glow. "We've got a tip there's some bad boys hibernating over this way. Charlie Hoffmeyer's gang. If they decide to knock over a payroll wagon, one guard ain't going to stop them."

"Is that a fact?"

"Mac, here, gave me the tip about you," Willard said. "You see, we can't be putting express offices in every little camp that sticks its head above the sand for two weeks. It costs money to get a line of wagons running. But I'll OK you for a branch office if you'll make me a commitment that, if you put in a reducer, you'll send the bullion out by Wells Fargo. Otherwise, we can't be bothered."

Jim wanted to answer, but his brain was in a clasp of paralysis.

Willard frowned. "What's the matter?"

"I . . . it's coming out of the mine into daylight too fast. My eyes can't. . . ." He let it hang. "Sure, I can promise that. And thanks for bringing it up."

Dutch Willard smiled and laid two copies of a contract on the desk. "Sign these and send me one when you get around to it." At the door, he looked back. "Take care of those eyes, mister. In your business, you're apt to need them."

This was at four o'clock. Jim stayed in his office for fifteen minutes, but suddenly he had to get outdoors. He walked up the scrabbled slope to the mines, and he was standing on a grizzly inspecting rock when McLowery, the superintendent, came up at five-thirty. McLowery said: "Clark McGaffery is down at the Chloride Bar. He said to tell you that if you can get down, he's got something to tell you."

McGaffery was smoking before the saloon. The Chloride

232

Bar was quiet, between shifts. They were able to get a pool table. McGaffery racked the balls, but Jim said: "We could talk better in your office."

"I can't take the chance of your being seen there. Willard's onto you, Jim. The name's really Bayliss, isn't it?"

He followed the remark by breaking the balls smartly. He watched a ball drop, and glanced up. Jim did not respond, and McGaffery bent and began to saw the cue across his cocked fingers.

"What are you going to do about it, Jim?"

"What do you think I should do about it?"

"Leave town."

He missed the shot, and Jim circled the table. "What's the rest?"

"Maybe we can work something out around the Grubstake."

"Maybe so."

McGaffery stood close to him. "Jim, I don't care how you look at it . . . you've got to clear out. The only reason Dutch didn't arrest you today was that he hopes you'll give away where Hoffmeyer is hiding. Hoffmeyer is the boy he really wants. You've got till day after tomorrow."

The door swung open. A half dozen miners, chalked with dust, came in with loud talk. McGaffery said quickly: "Here's what you do. Sell me your share of the mines for ten thousand dollars. That's gold, handy to carry in a saddlebag. It will take care of you for a long time."

"What do you do to earn it? Or do you figure you already have?"

"I figure I already have." McGaffery took out his watch and glanced at it. "Got to run."

"How long have I got to decide?"

"Tomorrow morning."

On the way up, Jim stopped at Kitty's. "I've got to talk to you. Can you come outside?"

She looked at him a moment. Then: "I'm glad you've decided to tell me about it, Jim. Why didn't you do it sooner?"

Jim stared. "How did you know about it?"

"I didn't. I only knew that we lost the Jim Bayliss I met in Independence somewhere between here and there. You've been about as cordial to me as you have to McGaffery."

They walked slowly up the wagon road in the crisp night. On the slope of the hill, lanterns bobbed in the darkness. There was all the noise of midday, wagons rattling and occasionally a shot thudding dully in the hillside. Jim said: "Ever heard of a man named Hoffmeyer?"

"I don't think so."

"Wells Fargo wants him for express robberies. The state wants him for murder. Counting myself, there are four men in his gang. Hoffmeyer and I discovered the Grubstake last summer. I'm fronting for the gang."

She stopped to look at him. "Are you joking?"

"If I am, I'm not laughing. Kitty, I'm going to tell you the things the dodgers don't. And then I'm going to get out. And it looks like I'll have to leave you a new partner, named McGaffery."

He brought her up as far as Sawbuck, and the night Willard was shot. Then she said impulsively: "Jim, you've got to go back. You've got the money you need for a lawyer. Why haven't you left before?"

"Because I owe something to Hoffmeyer. I can't walk out on him cold. McGaffery offered me ten thousand. It's the only way I can get anything now."

Kitty protested angrily. "Do you think Willard would ever have let you leave town with that money? It's just a way of giving McGaffery the mine and cutting Willard in for a share of it! If Willard were playing it straight, he'd have arrested you today. But that wouldn't do him any good, and your share of the mine would go to any heirs you left. It's a trap, Jim!"

It gave him a jolt. "Why, the low-grade. . . ."

"And I suppose you think you'd make out better with Hoffmeyer?" Kitty went on. "You'd never ride out of his camp while the odds were three-to-one against you and you had any money on you. You're getting out tonight, Jim. *We're* getting out! We'll get a good lawyer in San Francisco and work out a change of venue. That means they'll have to try you outside of Nevada City because of local prejudice. We'll get you off with a fine for disturbing the peace!"

All the way up to the office he kept thinking: *There's a way. There's some way.* There was a way to take care of Hoffmeyer and evade Willard at the same time. But it wasn't to leave and try to clear himself first, because he'd never find Charlie Hoffmeyer again. Charlie would find him first.

He went in. The clerks had all finished and gone. He had a cot in his office where he slept. He went on into the smaller office and lighted the lamp, feeling the dry cold of the room. Suddenly he started. He stood looking at them for a while, and nobody spoke and nobody smiled.

Finally Hoffmeyer said: "OK, kid. Pull the curtain and sit down."

Hoffmeyer and Wino sat on the cot, Comanche on a chair.

"You damned fools!" Jim said.

"Just worryin' fools," Hoffmeyer said. "Seen somebody snooping around the hills near us the other day. Decided we'd played our luck out in this neck of the woods. Sick of waitin' for the profits to come in, Jim. I want you to sell out."

Jim stared at him a moment. "You do, eh? Do you know Dutch Willard's in town?"

Hoffmeyer said: "Good. I'll see him before I leave."

"He's recognized me. I've got twenty-four hours to get out. And you come busting in asking me to sell out!"

Hoffmeyer's eyes digested it, while Comanche stopped chewing and Wino lost his grin. "Who's giving you twenty-four hours?"

"McGaffery. He wants me to sell to him for ten thousand cash and leave before Willard gets wise. Willard doesn't know he's tipped me off."

"Ten thousand! My dead carcass is worth more than that. What did you tell him?"

"I told him I'd think it over."

Hoffmeyer shrugged. "McGaffery ought to be able to think up a better one than that. He pays you the ten thousand and gets the mines. Willard knocks you over for the ten and the bounty after you leave town. What about the girl? How much do you figger she'd pay for all this?"

"There's six or seven thousand in the safe. It would take a week for her to get more."

"You've been diggin' silver, ain't you?" Wino complained. "Where is it?"

"In the bank."

Comanche stirred. "Charlie," he said.

Hoffmeyer gave his oracle a quick look. He did not speak, and the half-breed said: "You know what I think? Willard hasn't reported this to his office. I think he's bucking the game alone this time, for all it'll pay him. Nobody knows but him and McGaffery."

Hoffmeyer glanced at Jim. "Looks like a job for you, *compadre*."

"If you're talking about my killing McGaffery and Willard, forget it. I've only got one killing against me, and I may be able to square that one."

Hoffmeyer rubbed his heavy thighs with his palms. "All I want from you is some help, Jim. Have that Number One drift shut off for repairs. Get Willard and McGaffery up there and I'll do the rest."

"How am I going to get them up there?"

"You've got something hot and you want to show them. Play it straight, like you don't know Willard's got the drop on you. Bring them down that drift, and I'm telling you they won't make any trouble when they come out again. There's going to be an accident. That's logical, ain't it? The tunnel was closed off, but they went in and you damn' near got killed when you seen what happened and went in after them. You'll have a few scratches to show them even."

"A few scratches, eh?"

"You've got an ace, Jim, the biggest ace in the deck. We need you. After the cut, we'll split up. I ain't sure you're our type. But until then, we're all good buddies."

Jim walked across the room.

"Better close up that drift now, Jim," Hoffmeyer drawled. "We'll move right in. Bring the others up tomorrow."

Jim thought it over, conscious of their silent scrutiny. Then he pulled his mine cap off the hook and took a moment to set the candle. "All right. Give me an hour."

VII

He had Number One closed off and afterward killed an hour in the Chloride Bar.

In the morning he looked up McGaffery in his office. "I'll take the ten thousand," he told him.

McGaffery got up and shut the door. His smile was a mere bending of his bloodless lips. "You're a smart boy, Jim. The way Dutch has been talking, he intends to make you plenty of trouble."

Jim said shortly: "I want the money in a saddlebag, at nine o'clock. Wait for me at the first side drift in Grubstake Number One. It's closed off."

McGaffery's features, the color of old chamois, soured. "Why can't we transact it all right here?"

"Because you're going on through that tunnel with me to the other end. I'll have my horses there. You're going to ride one of them a mile out of town. You'll be my safe conduct, if you get what I mean."

McGaffery frowned a moment longer, and then began to nod. "All right, Jim. Any way you want it."

Jim entered nearly every saloon in town before he found Dutch Willard. He invited him over to a table and ordered a bottle of J. H. Cutter. They drank to each other, but their eyes circled like stray dogs. "I was talking to McGaffery last night," Jim told him.

"That right?"

"Good old Mac. He's been trying to make a map out of me ever since we met. He wants me to think you're a Wells Fargo detective, instead of a traffic agent!"

Willard laughed and moved in his chair so that his coat

hung open and his right hand could rise swiftly to the spring holster under his left armpit. "Who told him that?"

"You did. Hell, I knew it anyway. I recognized you from that night in Sawbuck, and don't say you didn't recognize me."

Dutch Willard did not change expression. Jim sat with both elbows on the table and his whiskey glass held lightly between the thumbs and forefingers of both hands, engaging Willard's eyes.

"I'm talking turkey, Willard. You could get that gun of yours quicker than I could get mine. That's how much I'm on the level. McGaffery wanted to make a deal with me. He says you're going to jump me tomorrow. You haven't done it before because you hope I'll give away where my pardners are."

"That was nice of McGaffery. How much did he want for his tip?"

"Half of the Grubstake mines. What I was wondering," Jim said, "is why he should have them instead of you?"

Willard sat there stiffly a moment longer. Then he relaxed and picked up his drink. He smiled. "You know, that's a thought."

"All I went into this for was a little money to beat that other charge. Mac's going to give me ten thousand. Can you match that?"

"I haven't got five hundred."

"That's what I thought. But I'll dicker with you. You get a quarter. I keep a quarter. You can hold yours under my name if you want and pick up checks at a post office somewhere. Nobody will ever know we made a deal. I hightail it to Frisco tonight and wait for Kitty Lawrence to send me the money for my trial."

Willard frowned. "A quarter," he said, dubiously. He did

not seem aware that he was giving away his hand. *A gamble like this, against ten thousand cash* was what his hesitation said to Jim. He knew now that Kitty had been right, and he felt no compunction about what he was going to do.

"Our geologists say we won't take out less than half a million," he said. "That's a hundred and twenty-five thousand apiece."

Willard made rings on the table with his whiskey glass. "That sounds good."

"You bet it does. But you don't get a paper on it, Dutch, until I know I'm getting away."

Willard waited.

"Meet me at the mine office tonight," Jim said. "From there we go to where I've got my horses. After I'm in the saddle with a couple of rocks between me and you, I'll let you know where the quitclaim is. It won't be hard to find. But you won't find it unless I want you to."

Willard peered a while longer into the amber of his whiskey glass; he must have found his answer there, for he said at last: "What time?"

"Nine-fifteen. On the dot. If you're late, I'll figure it's a double-cross. Come then or not at all."

He let it pass as any other day. There was a sheaf of assayers' reports to go through. There were mill tickets to check and some correspondence. With McLowery, the superintendent, he inspected the face of a ledge in Close Shave Number Four to decide how to take the ore out.

Darkness came with a cold wind bending stiff desert shrubs and snatching at every puff of dust from the mines. When Dutch Willard came up the road from town at nine-fifteen, the wind and the cold had increased, so that the Wells Fargo detective had the collar of his coat turned up and his hands in his pockets. He stopped near the door to make a shield with his hat and shoulder in which to light his cigar. He let two matches go out, and then Jim came from the shadows to hold his hat as a windbreak. Willard got the cigar glowing. He said—"Thanks, mister."—and he put a long, searching look on Jim's face before he dropped the match and turned to look up the hill.

"Nothing to carry?"

"It's all packed. I've got my horses at the other end of one of the tunnels."

They walked up the road, avoiding lights as they made their way to the tunnel near the north end of the string. Jim lighted a lantern. One on each side of the strap-iron tracks, they started down the drift that curved into the hill.

Charlie Hoffmeyer was whispering in his mind: *Bring them down that drift and I'm telling you they won't make any trouble when they come out again.*

There was a scuff of their boots on the rough footwall, a close, unresonant sound. There was the dry, dusty air, warmer than outside. No one spoke for some time, but at length Willard grunted: "Damned stale air, for a double-ender."

Jim chuckled. "Suspicion seems to be your business, Dutch. The other end's got a door."

They passed beneath a timbered raise Jim had condemned. They reached a point only 100 feet from the first side drift. All this time his eyes were on the hanging wall, watching for evidence of recent drilling. He did not find it there, but on the tracks he suddenly discerned an eddy of rock dust. Willard watched him reach up to grope on the upper side of a timber. Jim's fingers found the fuse.

He let his hand drop away and grinned at Willard. "Force of habit. Every time I see dirt on the tracks, I want to know where it came from."

Willard's eyes did not look happy about it. He was suspicious of any deviation from the normal. They went on, and suddenly they were abreast of the drift and Willard was turning to glance into it.

"What's that?" His voice struck a high, alarmed pitch, and he moved back from the drift.

Jim swung the lantern. He saw a patch of green blossom in the gloom. It was a distinctive shade of apple-green, and he remembered the first time he had seen it, in Independence. Kitty, wearing the green linen dress, stood there beside Clark McGaffery, in his dark banker's suit.

"Hello, Jim," she said. "Isn't it nice, all of us meeting this way? Why, it's Mister Willard, too!"

The element of surprise was no longer Jim's, but hers. She clung to McGaffery's arm, dragging him out into the main drift. "I saw Mister McGaffery going up to the mines, and I thought I'd trail along and see where he was going. He hasn't been a bit hospitable about my staying, though."

Jim said dryly: "Get over here, Kitty." It was a voice to knock the cockiness out of her. She stepped across the tracks, holding her skirts up as she did so. Willard and McGaffery stared woodenly at each other.

"What are you doing here?" Willard demanded.

"This is a fine thing!" McGaffery retorted. "A lawman aiding the escape of a criminal! I just learned about this man today, Willard. I want to know why you haven't . . . ?"

Willard's grin was a sour twist of his lips. "I got a hunch you and I'd better hang together, Mac."

Jim gripped Kitty's arm. He thrust her behind him and said: "A good idea, kid, but the wrong time for it. Start walking." He heard her move away a few steps and halt.

"Jim, I won't leave you!"

"Get out!" Jim snapped. When he heard her footsteps

once more, he set the lantern down on the tracks and looked across it at the others. "Let's drag out the carcass, boys. It smells to high heaven, anyway. This looks to me like a three-way double-cross. You were both double-crossing me, so I got in on it, too."

Willard stood thinking about his gun but doing nothing. "You're a long way from civilization to try one like this, Bayliss."

"Not so far. . . . You'd like to take Charlie Hoffmeyer back, too, wouldn't you?"

Willard grunted. "No more deals. I'm playing it straight. Know what that means?"

"It doesn't mean you're taking me," Jim said. "Nobody here is going to put a finger on me, because I figure I'm the straightest man in this mine. That goes for Charlie, too."

Willard stood very stiffly, a grayness in his face, and in that silence the trickling of earth to the floor somewhere down the drift was like an avalanche. Willard said carefully, not letting his head turn: "What about Hoffmeyer?"

There was a crunching of boot heels on coarse earth, and dimly, at the end of the short drift, Jim saw Hoffmeyer advancing. He saw Wino and Comanche rise from the floor to follow him.

McGaffery, unlettered in violence, was the first to break. He ran a few steps and turned back, his Colt in his hand. His gun roared twice. The explosions were a force that pulsed against the eyeballs and deadened the ears. The lantern flame throbbed. Charlie Hoffmeyer, still walking, laughed. Hoffmeyer, whose carbine had blasted short and thunderously into the echoes of the banker's shots.

McGaffery went back to the wall with a hand clutching his shoulder. There was the shrill, unnerving sound of Kitty's scream. Jim's gun was out, but he waited. . . .

Willard turned toward the outlaws, ripping his shoulder gun loose. He stood with his feet set wide and his gun held steadily, but he was facing a trio of guns all talking at once. It was concentrated hell, a Biblical hell that included flame and thunder and the wailing of bullets that had missed their targets.

Jim took his first shot at Comanche. It was not a thrill, but a sickness, to see him falter, to watch the tall outlaw clutch his belly with one hand and lean against a stull. His gun sparkled dully as he brought it up once more. He squeezed the trigger, and Jim heard the bullet slam off the rocks behind him. Strength went out of the half-breed; he slipped loosely to the floor.

There was something savagely deliberate about the meeting again of Dutch Willard and Charlie Hoffmeyer. They were face to face at a distance of thirty feet, and they were taking their time about getting their shots off. Jim's view was of Willard's back and the flat, bearded face of the outlaw. Then he saw the flash of Hoffmeyer's saddle gun, and Willard's solid stance broke. He hunched, and there was pain in that quick, convulsive movement. Hoffmeyer fired again, his face loosening into a grin, and the Wells Fargo man received the second shot high in his body, staggering back a couple of feet.

Then, to Jim's surprise, his gun cracked a final time. It was his last shot, but it was good. He was even with Hoffmeyer for everything. More than even. Hoffmeyer's throat was a red ruin. He was going down. Wino, the likeable sot, lurched up to straddle his body. He held his Colt low and fired again and again into Willard's body until the firing pin had fallen twice on dead shells.

There was a hysterical burst of shots at Jim's left. McGaffery's little nickeled banker's gun was still in his hand.

244

He was too hurt and frightened to know what he was doing; he was merely shooting. He happened to fire all his shots down the side drift, and Wino had the bad luck to be standing where one of them went.

McGaffery watched him sag, and then turned and looked down the bore of Jim's Peacemaker. "Man," he said, "we've got no quarrel with each other."

"You can prove that by dropping your gun."

McGaffery almost threw it from him. "Listen, Jim," he said, "we want to talk this out before we leave here. We can save ourselves a lot of grief."

"How?"

McGaffery stopped a moment to clutch his shoulder, but even in pain his brain could not stop calculating. "Maybe it won't matter to me, anyway," he said. "But it does, Jim . . . I'll tell them you gave Willard the tip on Hoffmeyer and I came along to help. Nobody but Hoffmeyer knows you were ever with him. Something went wrong, we'll say. You and I were just lucky to come through it alive."

"No good," Jim said. "Why would Willard have trusted a wanted man?"

"We'll say he didn't know you were wanted! Nobody will know until you tell them, anyway." McGaffery gave an uncertain laugh. "Why, they'll call us heroes, Jim! Isn't that better than . . . ?"

"It is for you," Jim said. "But I'll take a shot at it, Mac. If there was any money at stake, I'd say to hell with you. Since it's just your reputation, and that isn't worth four-bits, anyway. . . ."

The judge at Marysville, where Jim Bayliss's trial was held, threw the book at the young fellow.

"I'm going to make an example of you as a warning to

other young bucks who think they can start swinging every time they get heated up. If that miner hadn't had a bad heart, you might have killed him anyway. It will cost you twenty-five dollars, a week in jail, and court costs. If it happens again, I'll double it."

"Yes, sir," Jim said. He paid the fine. Then he signaled the brown-haired girl who had come to court with him, and the bailiff let her through the gate. "Your Honor, if you've got time, the young lady and I would like you to marry us before I go."

The propriety of it bothered the judge, but at length he stepped down, found his Bible, and performed the ceremony.

"The record," he said, "will be amended to read . . . 'Defendant shall serve two sentences, one of one week and one of life, the terms to run consecutively.' Case dismissed."

About the Author

Frank Bonham in a career that spanned five decades achieved excellence as a noted author of young adult fiction and detective and mystery fiction, as well as making significant contributions to Western fiction. By 1941 his fiction was already headlining Street and Smith's *Western Story* and by the end of the decade his Western novels were being serialized in *The Saturday Evening Post*. His first Western, *Lost Stage Valley* (1948), was purchased as the basis for the motion picture, *Stage to Tucson* (Columbia, 1951) with Rod Cameron as Grif Holbrook and Sally Eilers as Annie Benson. "I have tried to avoid," Bonham once confessed, "the conventional cowboy story, but I think it was probably a mistake. That is like trying to avoid crime in writing a mystery book. I just happened to be more interested in stagecoaching, mining, railroading. . . ." Yet, notwithstanding, it is precisely the interesting—and by comparison with the majority of Western novels—exotic backgrounds of Bonham's novels that give them an added dimension. He was highly knowledgeable in the technical aspects of transportation and communication in the 19th-Century American West. In introducing these backgrounds into his narratives, especially when combined with his firm grasp of idiomatic Spanish spoken by many of his Mexican characters, his stories and novels are elevated to a higher plane in which the historical sense of the period is always very much in the forefront. This historical aspect of his Western fiction early drew accolades from reviewers so that on

247

one occasion the *Long Beach Press Telegram* predicted that "when the time comes to find an author who can best fill the gap in Western fiction left by Ernest Haycox, it may be that Frank Bonham will serve well." Among his best Western novels are *Snaketrack*, *Night Raid*, *The Feud at Spanish Ford*, and *Last Stage West*. *High Iron* will be his next **Five Star Western**.

About the Editor

Bill Pronzini was born in Petaluma, California. His earliest Western fiction was published under his own name and a variety of pseudonyms in *Zane Grey Western Magazine*. Among his most notable Western novels are *Starvation Camp* (1984) and *Firewind* (1989). He is also the editor of numerous Western story collections, including *Under the Burning Sun: Western Stories* (Five Star Westerns, 1997) by H. A. DeRosso, *Renegade River: Western Stories* (Five Star Westerns, 1998) by Giff Cheshire, and *Tracks in the Sand* by H. A. DeRosso (Five Star Westerns, 2001). His own Western story collection, *All the Long Years* (Five Star Westerns, 2001), was followed by *Burgade's Crossing* (Five Star Westerns, 2003) and *Quincannon's Game* (Five Star Westerns, 2005). His next Five Star Western will be *Coyote and Quarter Moon*.